# On Deadly Tides

# On Deadly Tides

## A PENNY BRANNIGAN MYSTERY

## Elizabeth J. Duncan

CROOKED LANE

NEW YORK

Published in the United States by Crooked Lane Books, an imprint of The Quick Brown Fox & Company LLC.

Crooked Lane Books and its logo are trademarks of The Quick Brown Fox & Company LLC.

Library of Congress Catalog-in-Publication data available upon request.

ISBN (hardcover): 978-1-64385-468-7
ISBN (ebook): 978-1-64385-469-4

Cover design by Scott Zelazny

Printed in the United States.

www.crookedlanebooks.com

Crooked Lane Books
34 West 27th St., 10th Floor
New York, NY 10001

First Edition: November 2020

10 9 8 7 6 5 4 3 2 1

For Dolly, Chris York, Bentley, and Charlotte, with love. Thank you for everything.

# Chapter One

"That's him," said Penny Brannigan, with a subtle tip of her head across the crowded bar of the Beaumaris Arms Hotel. "Bill Ward. He's just over there."

Alwynne Gwilt's eyes followed the direction Penny indicated and came to rest on a short, stocky man, his belly curving out of a beige, fishing-type vest with rows of pockets, worn over a red plaid shirt. Green trousers completed his outdoorsy look.

"He must be awfully hot in all that gear," said Alwynne, fanning herself with a cocktail napkin. "Those look like the same clothes he was wearing when he spoke at our meeting back in early March, and this is the end of July."

"It's like a uniform," Penny responded. "He wears the same get-up in all his publicity shots, too." She gestured at Alwynne's wine glass and held up her own. "I'm ready for another. Do you want a refill?"

Alwynne drained the last of her wine. "Thank you, but no, I don't think I do. This room is so crowded and noisy I'm starting to feel a little uncomfortable. I can barely hear you, and I hate having to shout to have a conversation. It's been a long day, so I'm going upstairs to finish unpacking, and I should ring home and make sure Medwyn's surviving without me. And then I'm going to get into bed and read for a bit." She handed her empty glass to Penny. "I want to try to get a good night's sleep. We've got an early start, and I'd like to be fresh for our early morning painting session." She leaned closer and offered an ear so she could hear Penny's reply.

"Okay," said Penny. "I'm just going to let Bill know that his artists from Llanelen have arrived. Sleep well, and I'll see you at breakfast." The two women turned away from each other. Alwynne headed for the relative quiet of the carpeted corridor that led to the main staircase, and Penny to the dense hubbub of the bar, where people waited two deep to be served.

"Young Llifon not in tonight?" the customer in front of Penny asked the woman serving behind the bar. He pocketed his change, picked up his drink, and prepared to move away.

"No, he's not, the little blighter," she replied. "Rang in sick at the last minute, leaving me to stand in for him, and on a busier than usual night, too. I'm not best pleased, I can tell you." She cast a resigned eye over her waiting customers. "Right. Who's next?"

"Me, I think," said Penny. "A white wine, please." The barmaid appeared to be in her late forties, and though still attractive, she gave the impression that she wasn't paying as much attention to her appearance as she had done a few years ago. Her brown hair, dull, dry, and greying at the roots, had been carelessly styled in a twisted half-up, half-down arrangement, loosely held in place on top of her head with a large plastic hair claw. The glossy red lipstick she'd applied at the start of her shift had faded, and deep, tiny lines etched around her lips gave her away as a long-time smoker.

As she poured Penny's wine, a strained-looking man in a tired suit joined her behind the bar. He appeared to be in his early fifties, with thinning hair and hazel eyes hiding behind glasses that had gone out of style.

"What are you doing in tonight, Sarah?" he asked the woman as she finished pouring Penny's wine and replaced the bottle in the chiller. "Isn't this meant to be your night off?"

"It is. I'm filling in for Llifon. He's only called in sick. Again." She slid the wine glass in Penny's direction without looking at her and accepted Penny's banknote.

"Has he now? How many times is that this month?"

"I'm not sure. Two or three, I think. I'd have to check the attendance records."

"Well, we'd better find out what's going on with him and see if we can offer any support. And if you had plans for this evening and want to get away, just say the word and I'll take over."

"No, it's all right, Martin. I'm here now and I can use the extra hours." The woman handed Penny her change.

"I could take over here for a few minutes to give you a chance to collect the glasses and wipe down tables, if you like. I noticed on my way through that the tables are all full, and the glasses are starting to pile up."

"I know perfectly well how to run a bar service, thank you very much," snapped the woman. "I'm managing just fine, and I'll sort out the glasses the minute I get a chance."

The man seemed about to say something else, but then thought better of it. "Well, if you're sure you don't need my help, I'll leave you to it, then."

Holding her glass of wine in her left hand, Penny shifted along the bar in the direction of the man in the plaid shirt and fishing vest. A couple stepped back just as she reached him, so she was able to squeeze past a woman who had been monopolizing him for several minutes, and extend her hand. He set his drink on the bar, grasped Penny's hand, and held it in a beefy grip. When he released it, she withdrew her fingers and placed her hand behind her back.

A trim, attractive woman in her early fifties, Penny introduced herself and explained, "My friend and I are here from Llanelen for your painting weekend. We're delighted to be joining you, and looking forward to learning lots."

Bill Ward glanced with bleary brown eyes at the name badge pinned to Penny's jacket. Sallow skin hung in loose folds around his neck, underscoring a broad, jowly face. "Glad you could make it, Penny," he said in a surprisingly warm baritone. "Some of your fellow painters are scattered about the room, so be sure to introduce yourself to other members of the group. There are about a dozen of you, all together, so hopefully we'll have lots of lively discussion, and we can all learn from one another."

"It's so crowded in here, I thought surely all these people can't be part of our painting group," said Penny.

"Nah, the rest are just ordinary tourists booked into the hotel. The town's always busy like this during the high season. There's a lot to see and do."

Besides an abundance of antique shops, boutiques, and bustling pubs and cafes, the seaside town of Beaumaris, on the Isle of Anglesey off the north coast of Wales, is home to a medieval castle built in 1295 by King Edward I.

"There was a massive queue for the castle when we arrived this afternoon, and the promenade along the sea front was positively heaving," said Penny. "But really, it's like that all over North Wales every summer now, and getting worse. In Llanelen, where I live . . ." She broke off as his gaze drifted over her shoulder, and his wide-set eyes narrowed slightly. Sensing that her time with him was up, she finished, "Well, I've taken up enough of your time. Just wanted to say hello and let you know we're here."

"I'm glad you did. Enjoy your painting, and I'll see you tomorrow afternoon at the critique session, if not before." As Ward turned his attention to a woman standing just behind Penny, she took a step back.

"Whoa," exclaimed a man's voice behind her. He raised his beer glass above his head and stepped nimbly to one side just in time to prevent her bumping into him.

"Oh, I'm so sorry," Penny said as she turned to face him. Her eyes rested on him for a moment and then flickered away. "It's so crowded in here. I hope I didn't cause you to spill your drink. If I did, please, let me get you another."

"No harm done." His sandy-coloured hair was lightly flecked with grey and his blue eyes crinkled at the corners as he smiled at her. He gestured with his almost empty glass at the crowded bar. "I was going for a refill, but maybe I'll give it a few minutes. It's pretty crowded."

"Probably best if we step away from the bar, then," said Penny. By unspoken agreement, they moved toward the opposite end of the room, and when three women seated near the doorway that led to the hotel lobby stood up to leave, they seized the opportunity and grabbed the table.

While Penny pondered what to do about the three used wine glasses left behind by the previous occupants, the man pushed them to one side of the table, making room for their glasses. When they were seated, he peered at her name tag, as Ward had done a few minutes earlier.

"Brannigan. That's an Irish name. But your accent isn't Irish. It's . . . Canadian, right?"

"Yes, it is."

"Well, hello, Penny. Oh, sorry. I should have introduced myself. I'm Colin Campbell."

"Campbell. That's a Scottish name. But your accent isn't Scottish. Would I be right in thinking it's also . . ."

Colin laughed. "Yes, it is. I'm from Toronto. But I don't get back there very often because my work involves a lot of travel, mainly Europe and Africa, but sometimes Asia as well."

He withdrew a silver business card case from an expensive-looking black leather messenger bag, opened it, and handed her a card. She exclaimed over the photo of a red squirrel, its tiny front paws clutching a leafy twig while it looked at the camera with bright, inquisitive eyes.

"Oh, I love this," she said. "Look at his lovely white chest and the tufty ears." She then read out, "Colin Campbell, wildlife photographer." She gave him a wide smile before tucking it in her handbag and offering him her card, which featured one of her own watercolour paintings.

"Did you paint this?" Colin asked.

"I did. I'm a watercolour artist."

"So is that what brings you here?"

"To North Wales?"

6

He made a little affirming noise that sounded like "Mm-hm."

"No, I live here. Well, not here on Anglesey. I live in Llanelen, a market town on the mainland." She gestured at her business card, which he still held. "That bridge on my card is the seventeenth-century bridge in our town. It's very famous, actually, and we're proud of it. I'm here in Beaumaris with an art group for a weekend of painting. We're here until Monday lunchtime."

"I wondered what was going on. The bar is a lot more crowded than it was last night, and there are people, like you, with name badges."

Penny fingered her name tag. "Tonight's the welcoming drinks party. The sketching and drawing starts in the morning."

"Have you got a place in mind you'd like to paint tomorrow?" Colin asked.

"The lighthouse," Penny replied without hesitation. She tasted her chilled white wine before continuing. "I know painting a lighthouse seems really obvious, but this one is especially picturesque, and I've wanted to paint it for a long time." She set down her glass. "What about you? What brings you here?"

"I'm here taking photographs to illustrate a feature on the island of Anglesey for a nature magazine."

"Oh, you're here for the puffins, then," said Penny.

Campbell grinned. "That's right. Tomorrow, in fact. There's quite a colony of them, and with their colourful beaks, puffins photograph beautifully if you can get close enough to them. But there are lots of other interesting birds and wildlife, too.

Red kites, cormorants, and choughs—and seals. And there might even be bottlenose dolphins if I'm lucky."

"The red squirrel on your business card is adorable. Do you do a lot of your work here in the U.K.?"

"Quite a bit, although lately I've been spending a fair bit of time in Africa. But I do love photographing British wildlife, especially in Scotland and the islands. I'm freelance, so my assignments can take me anywhere in the world. Unfortunately, I've just finished a project documenting some of the wildlife that will probably be lost due to the climate crisis, and believe me, there's a lot of it. We're losing so many species at an alarming rate."

"Oh, that's heartbreaking. I hate hearing that."

They sat in reflective silence, and then, to break the gloomy mood that threatened to overtake them, Colin looked toward the bar where Ward, his back to the room, was now engaged in conversation with the woman serving behind the bar. "That fellow at the bar. He looks familiar."

Penny turned to see whom he meant. "That's Bill Ward. He's leading the painting group. He's fairly well known in this country, but more as an actor than a painter. He played a really despicable villain on a popular soap. *Jubilee Terrace.* Have you heard of it?"

Her companion nodded. "Everybody's heard of it."

"True. Anyway, that was a few years back. His character was so hated that women actually stopped him in the streets and whacked him with their handbags. The producers had to ask people to stop attacking him."

"Good publicity for the show, though."

"Yes, I suppose it was. But it was probably a relief to him when his character was killed off. After that, he didn't do much acting, and he focused on his painting career. He's done really well with it. His work is in all the big galleries in Manchester and Liverpool. Expensive, too. Well out of my price range."

"What kind of paintings does he do?"

"Wildlife, like you, actually. I've seen them at various exhibits, and there's one series he did of foxes that was absolutely beautiful."

"That may be how I heard about him, then—through his paintings. Someone I was on assignment with probably mentioned him. How did you hear about him?"

"I belong to a sketching and painting group in Llanelen, and he came to us in March as a guest speaker. He mentioned this painting weekend he organizes, and my friend and I decided to sign up for it. We'd been talking for ages about a painting getaway, so coming here, with meals included and hotel accommodation all sorted, seemed like an easy way to do it. And besides, it's not too far from home."

"So you're here with a friend?"

"Yes, my painting pal, Alwynne Gwilt. She looks after our local museum and is a keen amateur painter. But I think she's really here to get away from her husband for a few days."

Colin raised an eyebrow and Penny laughed.

"No, not like that. He can be a bit, well, dependent on her. She was dreading his retirement, when he'd be under her feet all day, but it hasn't worked out too badly. He spends all day in his garden, and when it rains, he bakes. The whole town loves his Welsh cakes. And she spends much of her time at the museum, so all in all, it hasn't been as bad as she thought it would be."

Colin laughed, and then gestured at the half-full glass Penny had been nursing.

"Can I get you another one? I'm ready for a refill, and the bar's so busy we don't want to make any more trips than we have to."

"No, I'm fine, thanks. This'll be my last one."

He returned a few minutes later, and just as he sat down, a young woman holding a glass of cloudy cider approached their table. She wore a blue-and-white-striped, long-sleeved top over jeans, and scuffed trainers that had seen many miles. She smoothed back shoulder-length blonde hair.

"There seems to be a chair going spare at your table," she said, gesturing at it with her glass, "and if you're not expecting anyone else, since there's no place else to sit, I wondered if I might join you. I've had a couple of long travel days, and I could do with a sit-down."

"Of course," said Penny. "Oh, you're one of us. You're wearing one of our painting group name tags." She tapped her own, then read the name on the young woman's. "Hello, Jessica Graham."

"Oh, that," said the woman, touching her badge with a sunburned hand that looked as if it spent a lot of time outdoors. "I'm not really a member of the group, at least not as a painter. I'm a journalist, but they gave me a name tag anyway." She slipped the straps of a hefty black backpack off her shoulders, hoisted it away from her body, and leaned it against the wall, tucking its straps behind it. "So you might say it's like press accreditation." She pronounced the last two words with gilt-edged pride.

"That's interesting," said Penny. "You're doing a story on Bill Ward, I take it."

"That's right. *Jubilee Terrace* is huge back home, and he's made an unusual career change, from actor to artist, so it'll make a good feature story." She reached into a side pocket of her backpack, and the three exchanged business cards. "I couldn't believe my luck when I found out he was here and he agreed to give me an interview."

"When you say 'back home,'" Colin said when she was seated, "would that charming accent be from Australia?"

"No, the other one. New Zealand. And you two—Americans, are you?" She gave them a youthful grin, revealing two rows of perfect white teeth.

"No, we're the other one as well," said Penny. "Canadian."

"Oh, I see." She took a sip of cider, set her glass on the table, and allowed her eyes to wander over the crowded room. As the woman who had been serving behind the bar made her way from table to table, collecting empty glasses and loading them on a tray, Jessica leaned forward and said in a conspiratorial voice, "But besides the Bill Ward story, I'm actually here in the U.K. to investigate a murder."

# Chapter Two

"Oh my goodness," exclaimed Penny, her wine glass frozen in place halfway to her lips. She lowered it and asked, "Whose murder?"

"Well, I *say* murder. That's just Dave's opinion. He's my editor and he likes to sensationalize things to try to sell more papers. Besides the Bill Ward story and a few travel features, I'll be looking into the disappearance several years ago of a New Zealand man. Something must have happened to him. People don't just drop out of sight for no reason, do they?"

"Actually, sometimes they do," said Colin. "Every now and then, you read a newspaper story or see an item on the television news about a person who wanted to start a new life someplace else, so they stage a disappearance, usually involving a pile of clothes and a pair of shoes abandoned on a beach so it will look like they drowned, and then they move to a third-world country where their money will go farther, and assume a new identity."

"Well, that's probably what happened to him, but whatever it was, I intend to get to the bottom of it. His parents are getting on a bit now, and they're desperate to know what happened to their son, and if he's alive and well somewhere, it would be nice to be able to put their minds at ease."

"Have you spoken to the police for your story?" Penny asked, and then she answered her own question. "Of course you have. You're a newspaper reporter, and you know what you're doing. That's probably the first place you started."

"The police!" Jessica let out an exasperated sigh. "They don't want to know. I spoke to the police in New Zealand almost every week for a while. Finally, they got irritated with me. Said the British police could find no evidence there was anything suspicious about the man's disappearance and that if anything turned up, they'd be sure to let me know. Naturally, I never heard back from them." She took a sip of cider. "There's only so much you can do, trying to investigate something from eleven thousand miles away. But it cost my paper a lot of money to send me here, and newspapers just don't have the budgets they used to. So, now that I'm here, I intend to make the most of it. I'm going to find out what happened to him."

"Well, I'm sorry to hear that he's gone missing," said Colin. "I can understand how not knowing what happened to him must be a terrible burden for his family."

"It was very worrying for his family at first," agreed Jessica, "when they stopped hearing from him. No emails or phone calls. But gradually they came to accept that something bad must have happened to him, and with the parents getting older, as I said, and for legal reasons, it's time to get some answers."

"But why here?" Penny asked. "Was he last living on Anglesey?"

"Oh, I don't know that *he* was ever here," Jessica said. "But I did discover that he was close to someone with a connection to this area, so there might be something there. I don't want to say too much about that. Don't want to jinx my story, as we say." She drained the last of her cider and fixed first Penny and then Colin in the beam of her bright blue eyes.

At this natural break in the conversation, the barmaid reached their table, and the three sat in silence as she lifted empty glasses onto her tray and gave the table a quick wipe. When she'd moved on to the next table, Jessica spoke.

"I'm very lucky, you know. Would you believe this is my first time out of New Zealand? And to come all this way and have the chance to work on such great stories. I can't believe it. And to get to see all these beautiful places. Did you know there's a lighthouse here? How wonderful it would be to see it by moonlight."

Having done a lot of travelling herself when she was about Jessica's age, Penny returned Jessica's irresistible grin with an understanding smile.

The three talked for a few more minutes, and then Jessica stifled a yawn, muttered something about jet lag, gathered up her backpack, and left.

"You have to admire the enthusiasm of youth," said Colin. "She's just getting a taste for all the adventure that lies ahead."

"She seems so keen and enthusiastic. It's inspiring."

Finally, as people began to trickle out of the bar, Penny indicated that she, too, was ready to call it a day, and after a breezy, "Well, I'm off. Goodnight, then," she headed upstairs.

As soon as her door was closed, she switched on her phone and Googled Colin Campbell. His biography was impressive, but his photographs were stunning.

* * *

Penny checked the time: just after midnight. She'd been asleep for about an hour before she awakened, disoriented, to find her room unbearably hot and stuffy.

She threw back the sheet and the light blanket, and groped about in the dark until her hand found the switch on the unfamiliar bedside lamp. In its soft light, she climbed slowly out of bed and padded across the room to the window. She drew back the heavily patterned curtains, allowing a bright beam of bluish-white moonlight to pour through the pair of mullioned windows. She turned the latches and pushed the casement windows open, and was rewarded by a welcome rush of night air. She closed her eyes and raised her face to it, allowing the light breeze to cool her flushed and perspiring face.

Her room overlooked the garden at the rear of the hotel, and beyond the eerily empty promenade she could make out the Menai Strait, the narrow tidal waterway that separates the island of Anglesey from the North Wales mainland. As she admired its sparkling waters dancing under the full moon set against thin, grey clouds draped across the night sky, strident voices gusted out into the rich quiet and floated up to her. She couldn't hear clearly what the speakers were saying, but she could make out that there were two of them, a man and a woman, and from the volume and intensity of their muffled words, it was clear that they were arguing.

She turned her head to try to catch what they were saying, but without success. She placed one knee on the window seat and leaned out to see Bill Ward, whom she recognized from the distinctive red plaid sleeves, make his way unsteadily through the hotel's back garden to the road that ran alongside the promenade. A minute or so later, the sound of a car's engine starting up shattered the calm of a midsummer's night, and a minute or so after that, quiet once more descended on the hotel.

# Chapter Three

"This looks like a good spot," said Alwynne the next morning. The last of the pale pink streaks of sunrise were long gone, leaving a milky blue sky dotted with a few fluffy clouds. "And we've got a beautiful day for it."

People carriers had been laid on to convey the artists and their bulky equipment to various scenic possibilities for their *plein air* painting sessions, and Alwynne and Penny had hopped off at Black Point, a jagged limestone headland on the most easterly end of the island, close to the sea-washed Trwyn Du Lighthouse. With its distinctive three black bands painted on a white background, the lighthouse, standing guard in the narrow channel that separates Anglesey from Puffin Island, attracted artists and photographers from all over the world.

"This spot looks just fine," said Penny. "It's such a clear morning, and we're high enough up on this cliff that we can see all the way across the Irish Sea to the Great Orme at Llandudno." A gust of wind caught her scarf and lifted the fringed edge. "It's a bit breezy, though. If the wind picks up, that could be a problem for us."

"I'm surprised we're the only ones who chose to paint the lighthouse today," said Alwynne as she clattered about setting up her portable stool and unfolding the slim wooden legs of her easel. "I would have thought there'd be more of us here. What is it about a lighthouse that's so appealing, anyway?"

"The romance? Smugglers? Danger? In any event, artists have loved painting them, probably for as long as they've been around. I expect the other painters are saving it for tomorrow or Monday. But it's nice to have this vantage point all to ourselves this morning."

"And another thing," said Alwynne as she positioned a sheet of lightly textured paper on her easel and fastened it in place, "have you ever noticed that lighthouses are almost always round? I wonder why that is. Surely round ones must have been more difficult to build than square or rectangular ones."

"I don't know," replied Penny. "Are they almost always round? I guess they are. Do you know, I never thought about that." She remained standing with her arms folded, her painting gear unpacked.

"Aren't you going to get started?" Alwynne asked. "You do know that we're supposed to have something ready this afternoon for the critique session."

"In a minute. I'm just going to have a little wander round and see if I can find another view point to make my painting a little different from yours."

"Well, mind how you go, now. Don't go near that steep cliff edge. It's a long way down."

Penny retied her billowing scarf to shorten the ends, and then, her hands thrust in the pockets of her jacket, walked a few paces away. She breathed in the salty tang of the fresh air, listened to the cries of the sea birds, possibly curlews, as they called to one another, and noted the choppy waves breaking against the base of the lighthouse. Its black and white bands appeared sharp-edged, and the whole of the structure was infused with the kind of sparkling radiance much loved by photographers and artists, as if large bodies of moving water had a magical power to disperse light in new ways.

*I've got to find exactly the right spot to make this work,* she thought. In tune with the gentle shoreline rhythm, she walked a little further, keeping well back from the cliff edge but occasionally hazarding a glance down at the rocky coastline far below.

And then, on the stretch of pebbly beach where the headland, eroded by centuries of wind and waves, jutted out into the sea, a blur of blue and white caught her attention. Unable to make out what it was from this height and distance, she stepped back a couple of paces, then turned and sprinted back to the spot where she'd left her painting supplies.

Alwynne, her eyes focused on the lighthouse in front of her, moved her head slightly at the sound of Penny's return, and then her mouth opened as if to say something when Penny dropped to the ground and began rummaging through her painter's case. Pulling out the small pair of binoculars that had proved useful on more than one occasion, Penny scrambled to her feet, and aimed them at the beach.

"There's something down there. I can't quite make it out, but it looks like it could be a person," Penny shouted, pointing with one hand as she handed the binoculars to Alwynne. The wind snatched at her words and carried them away. "I'm going down there. If you can get a mobile signal, ring nine-nine-nine."

Penny raced along the top of the promontory. She paused just long enough to take in the yellow and black DANGER sign showing an unfortunate stick figure flying off a cliff and scattering rocks and stones beneath it. Then, deciding she had no choice but to take her chances, she launched herself down the precipitously steep path that led to the beach. Her sturdy boots caught on the uneven stones that protruded out of the packed soil, and she clutched at the tall grass that sprouted along the sides of the rough path, to steady herself as she scrabbled her way down. Just as she reached the bottom, her feet slipped out from under her, and she slid the last few feet on her back. She coasted to a stop and struggled to her feet, brushing the dirt off her stinging palms. Her heart racing from the roughness of her descent, and her throat filled with the dreadful anticipation of what she was about to find, she scrambled over the rocks at the base of the cliff and staggered across the shingle beach.

The pallor of Jessica Graham's cold, grey skin confirmed what Penny feared, but nevertheless she dropped to her knees beside her and felt for a pulse. There was none. She rocked back on her heels and looked up to the top of the cliff, where Alwynne stood, binoculars shielding her face.

Penny turned her attention back to the young woman's body. From the thighs to the feet, it was immersed in water, and as each wave lapped at it, then receded, it gently rocked and shifted a tiny bit. A thin line of foam, white against the dark browns of the rocks and pebbles on the beach, showed the shifting demarcation between land and sea. *The tide's turned and it's on its way out,* Penny thought. This was followed a moment later by the realization that if she didn't do something, the tide could take the body with it, carrying it out to open water and handing it over to merciless currents that would bear it away on a watery journey to parts unknown. She rose and stood behind the woman's head. Then, she bent over, and grasping the body under the arms, she lifted, then pulled as hard as she could. But the body, small as it was and light as it had been in life, didn't move. With the weight of the water in the woman's clothes and her feet digging into the wet soil beneath the surface of the water, the task was impossible.

Penny gently lowered Jessica's body back onto the wet ground and considered what to do next. She might be able to turn the body so she could roll it higher up on the beach, but a couple of reasons why she shouldn't do this flashed through her mind. When the authorities arrived, they would prefer the body to be positioned exactly as she'd found it, and more importantly, if the woman's death were suspicious, turning the body would mean immersing more of it in the water, and that could wash away even more material that might be of forensic interest.

She decided the best thing—in fact the only thing—she could do would be to leave the body where it was, and hope that help arrived soon. She didn't envy the police officers and paramedics having to carry the body up the rugged cliff face that she'd just climbed down, but perhaps they knew a better way.

She pulled her mobile phone from her jacket pocket but in the sheltered bay was unable to get a signal. She moved away from the body and waved at Alwynne, who waved back. Hoping that response meant Alwynne had been able to get a signal from her higher vantage point, and the authorities had been summoned and were on their way, Penny crouched beside the body to wait.

Until this moment, she had managed to avoid looking at the woman's face, but now she forced herself to. Lifeless blue eyes gazed unseeingly at a sky that was only a few shades bluer. Her blonde hair, darkened by the water and clumped with sand, hung in wet, matted strands.

Tears beading in the corners of her eyes, Penny reached for Jessica Graham's hand and held it. Where last night it had been young and free of blemishes, lightly tanned by long days in the sun, this morning it was discoloured and wrinkled from having been immersed too long in water.

Her thoughts were interrupted by the hum of the engine of an approaching boat. As the sound grew louder, she raised her eyes from the body, hoping that the help she so desperately needed was arriving by water, not land.

But the small craft rounded the lighthouse and turned away from her, headed in the direction of Puffin Island. It was too far away for her to make out the occupants, and as it ploughed its way through the waves, she wondered if Colin Campbell was on board.

# Chapter Four

The hotel coffee shop was doing a brisk business in tea and coffee, cakes, and scones as the members of the painting group picked up a little something to see them through the rigours of their first critique session. Having purchased their refreshments, they then carried them into the adjoining lounge to await the arrival of their mentor, Bill Ward. Framed prints of inoffensive, well-known paintings like Gainsborough's "The Blue Boy" adorned walls painted a soothing Wedgwood blue, and conversational groupings of deep, button-back sofas and armchairs in burgundy or green faux leather combined to create the comfortable atmosphere of an old-fashioned gentlemen's club or the shabby chic of a country house that had been in the same family for a very long time.

Penny placed two steaming cups on the low table in front of Alwynne and then settled herself into the comfy chair opposite her, beside one of the floor-to-ceiling windows that overlooked the car park at the rear of the hotel.

"Thank you," said Alwynne. "Goodness knows we earned that." She picked up her cup and took a small sip. "I wonder what's going to happen now."

"I expect the police will investigate," said Penny. "To determine the cause of death, and so on."

"No, I meant about us. Our painting group. Will we be allowed to stay and paint, do you think, or will we be sent home?"

"I see no reason why the painting weekend shouldn't continue." Penny gestured to the opposite wall, where about half a dozen paintings on easels awaited the arrival of Bill Ward, and the anxious artists who had painted them braced themselves for his commentary. "Everyone else seems prepared to carry on."

"It's too bad you didn't get a chance to paint today."

"Oh well, there's always tomorrow."

"If you'd like to go back to the lighthouse, I'd be happy to go with you. Or maybe, in view of what happened there today, you might prefer that we tried another spot." Alwynne referred to the schedule they'd been sent when they registered. "There's Moelfre, the fishing village along the coast. Colourful little boats and so on. That might be nice."

"Yes, it might. What else is there?"

"There's the ruins of the old priory."

"I want to paint things we can't get at home. We've got lots of sheep and stone walls, but we don't have lighthouses and ruins. And while we've got rivers and streams and waterfalls, we haven't got a wide open expanse of water like the Menai Strait. You can't tell where it ends and the Irish Sea begins."

"True."

Alwynne tucked the painting weekend information documents back in her handbag. "I daresay the police will want to interview you, and sooner rather than later."

"Yes. I spoke to them this morning when they arrived on the beach, but Bethan texted me to let me know she's on her way. In fact, she should be here soon."

As Penny finished her coffee, a woman in her early forties, dressed in a navy-blue trouser suit, followed by a uniformed police officer, entered the lounge. She ignored the heads turning in their direction as she scanned the room's occupants, and then, spotting Penny, headed over to her. After greeting her and Alwynne, the two officers sat down, the uniformed officer in the chair beside Penny, and the plain-clothes policewoman on the sofa beside Alwynne.

"So Penny," Detective Inspector Bethan Morgan began. "Trouble does have a way of finding you, doesn't it?"

"I don't go looking for it."

Penny and Bethan Morgan had met several years ago, when Penny, who had been friends with Bethan's supervisor, helped solve a Christmas murder. The friend had since retired and moved to Scotland, and Bethan, now an inspector, was in charge of her own investigations. Although eager to help the police solve crimes, Penny had learned to tread carefully around Bethan and to wait to be asked before offering suggestions or insights.

"But first things first," said Bethan. "Discovering a dead body always comes as a terrible shock. How are you doing?"

"All right, I suppose."

"I'd say she's holding up remarkably well," said Alwynne, "considering what she went through this morning."

"We're just beginning our investigation, of course, and I don't want to go into any great detail here, but I do want you to know we're treating this death as unexplained," said Bethan.

"Oh, but you don't think there's anything suspicious about it, do you?" Alwynne asked. "Of course, I know nothing about what happened, but those cliffs are so steep and dangerous, and the edges can be rather crumbly. I even warned Penny about getting too close to the edge, didn't I, Penny? There are warning signs posted everywhere."

"It's just standard operating procedure until we know more," Bethan assured her. "We have to keep an open mind until we're satisfied that we know exactly what happened. One way or another."

PC Chris Jones, the uniformed officer, shifted slightly in his chair, eyed Alwynne's and Penny's cups on the table in front of him, then raised a questioning eyebrow at Bethan. She gave a little nod.

"Yes, Jones. I know you're gasping for a cup of tea."

"I'll get it for you," said Alwynne, rising from her chair.

"Just milk, please," said Jones. "No sugar."

"Well," said Bethan, "I can tell you this much. Based on his initial examination, the pathologist said it was a good thing you discovered the body when you did. He's something of a sailor, and he said there's this phenomenon called wind over tide. It's physics, apparently. Opposing forces. So the tide was going out and wanted to take the body with it, except the wind was blowing the other way." She placed her hands one above the other and moved them in opposite directions to demonstrate.

"So the two opposing forces work against each other, and the wind kept the body on the beach long enough for you to find it," Jones added. "But in the end, unless something intervenes, the tide usually wins."

"And then the body is washed out to sea," Penny finished. "I'm glad that didn't happen to her. To Jessica."

"About her," said Bethan. "You told the first responders at the scene that you were able to identify the body because you were talking to her in the bar here last night. Is that correct?"

"That's correct. Her name is Jessica Graham, and she's a reporter for a newspaper in New Zealand." Penny corrected herself: "She *was* a reporter. She was here this weekend to do a feature story on Bill Ward. And she also mentioned she was looking into the disappearance of a New Zealand man. Apparently his family hasn't heard from him in years and naturally they'd like some answers.

"But to be honest, it was the clothes I recognized first, not the person. I took the usual amount of notice of her when we were talking last night, but the tables and chairs are laid out in the hotel bar so you sit more beside someone rather than across from them, if you know what I mean, and then she'd been in the water. . . ."

"Of course. Being immersed in water for even a short time can change a person's appearance."

Alwynne returned with a cup of tea and two biscuits on the saucer that she placed on the table in front of Jones. "There you go," she said cheerfully.

The police officer nodded his thanks, leaned forward, and picked up the cup. Just as he was about to take a grateful sip, a middle-aged couple approached. The woman wore a floaty, ankle-length, floral-patterned skirt, and a pale blue, wispy scarf was draped around her neck. A cumbersome-looking, crossbody, black handbag divided her torso in two, and a broad-brimmed, beige, cotton hat tied under her chin completed her ensemble. The anxious-looking man beside her held in front of him, by its brim, a similar-looking hat.

"Excuse me," he said, addressing PC Jones. "Wondered if I might have a word."

"Of course," the policeman said, setting down the cup and getting to his feet. He pulled out his pocket notebook, flipped it open, and gave the man a little nod to indicate he should go ahead.

Bethan leaned forward to hear what the man had to say.

"It's just that we heard there was an accident today. That someone fell off the cliff at the lighthouse site."

"Yes?"

The woman gave her husband an encouraging nod, and he continued, slowly twirling his hat by moving his fingers along the brim.

"Right. We were at the welcome party in the bar last night, and, well, it's probably nothing, but we thought we should tell you."

"Go on," said Jones.

"Just before closing time, see, the barmaid got into an argument with a man," said the woman when the man hesitated. He then picked up the story.

"Normally, we'd never stay in a pub until closing time, but we're here on this painting course with another couple as part of our fortieth celebrations, so we stayed up a bit later than usual. Our friends had already gone up to their room. But when the argument kicked off, we felt uncomfortable and decided to leave."

Bethan stood up and showed him her warrant card. "I'm Detective Inspector Bethan Morgan, North Wales Police. Did you hear what they were arguing about?"

The man seemed surprised by her question, and he and his wife exchanged an anxious glance. "The bar was very crowded earlier on," the woman said, "but by the time the argument started, it was late and many of the guests had already gone upstairs or left. And to be honest, the man had had a fair bit to drink, and that's what they were arguing about. The barmaid was telling him that he'd had enough, and she refused to serve him. We were sat a little too far from the bar to catch every word, but we got the gist of it. You could tell from the body language that it was getting a bit heated, and as I said, at that point we felt uneasy and decided to leave."

"And do you know who the man arguing with her was?"

"Well, it was . . ." the man paused as Bill Ward entered the room. "It was him. Mr. Ward. The painter. And then another man appeared, and he spoke to them. Trying to calm things, down, probably."

"And do you know who this other man was?"

"Well, no, not exactly, but he was wearing a suit and something about him made me think he was in a position of authority here in the hotel."

"Like he worked here," the woman added. "Had a kind of take-charge manner, if you know what I mean."

"How old would you say this man was?" The couple looked at each other, and the woman asked her husband, "Early fifties, would you say, dear?" The man nodded and turned to Jones. "That sounds about right. Early fifties."

Jones read out the couple's names from their name tags. "And you are Gerald Thorpe and Betty Thorpe—is that correct?" When they nodded, he wrote their names in block capital letters in his notebook and then asked where they lived. "We live on the Wirral," Thorpe replied, and gave his home address and telephone number.

"Anything else you'd like to add?" asked Jones.

"I don't think so," said Thorpe, turning to his wife. "Can you think of anything?" The woman shook her head.

"Right, well, we'll be in touch if we need anything more from you. Thank you," said Jones.

The couple retreated to the other side of the room to rejoin their friends, and as the two police officers were about to sit down, Bethan's phone rang. With a brief, "Excuse me she stepped away, listened to what the caller had to say, then returned to the group.

"That was the pathologist. He's had a closer look, and says the woman's injuries could be consistent with a fall from a considerable height, but he's not entirely certain. He'll know more after the post mortem, when he's had a proper look."

Penny frowned. "What's the matter?" Bethan asked.

"About that argument last night," said Penny. "That the couple just described."

"Did you hear it?" asked Bethan.

"I wasn't in the bar when it happened, no, but I did overhear something from my bedroom. Loud voices disturbed me, just around midnight. My room overlooks the back of the hotel"—she gestured to the window beside them—"it faces this way, toward the strait—and I looked out the window and saw Bill Ward leaving the hotel, headed to the car park, possibly. But I couldn't see who he was shouting at or arguing with. And then I heard a car start up and drive off. If it was him, he was in no fit state to be driving, judging from the way he was walking."

Bethan surveyed the lounge and then spoke to the uniformed constable. "You'd better ask around and get the names of everyone who was in the bar last night. And see if you can find out who the man was who spoke to Ward and the barmaid." She turned to Penny. "You can give us a proper statement later. I'll be in touch."

When the police officers had left to set about their tasks, Penny asked Alwynne if she'd spoken to her husband about the discovery of the body.

"No, I haven't, and I'm not going to. He'll hear all about it soon enough. And when he does, he'll only insist I come home, and I want to stay. What about you?"

"Oh, I'm definitely staying."

"I thought you'd say that. I can almost hear the wheels turning in your head. What are you thinking?"

"Well," said Penny, "I'm wondering what Jessica Graham was doing out there on that steep, dangerous cliff. And it was early when you and I got there this morning, just after eight. I'm no expert, of course, but I'd say she'd been on that beach for a good few hours. So what was she doing out there, in such a dangerous spot, in the middle of the night? When she left Colin Campbell and me in the bar, she said she was tired, and I assumed she was going to bed. And how did she get out there by the lighthouse? Did someone drive her there?"

"I wonder if she'd had something to drink," said Alwynne. "In the dark, in that dangerous place at night, it would be easy

31

to lose your footing if you ventured too close to the edge of the cliff. Heaven knows, it's dangerous enough during daylight hours, as we saw for ourselves this morning."

"Well, the toxicology report will tell how much she'd had to drink. But she didn't seem in any way incapacitated when she left the bar. She just had the one glass of cider when she was with us. Alcohol could have been a factor, but not from what I saw. But who knows? She could have had more to drink later, of course. She might have picked up a duty-free bottle on her travels."

The artists had started to gather around the easels, signalling that the critique was about to start. Penny got to her feet. "Right. We've come all this way, so we might as well get over there and hear what Bill Ward has to say."

"It's funny," Alwynne remarked as they crossed the room. "How disappointing it can be when you see someone in person that you know from the telly. When I first saw Bill Ward in March at our Stretch and Sketch Club meeting, he looked shorter than I expected, and he seems even more so now. And of course, he's older than his *Jubilee Terrace* days, and to put it kindly, he's added a few pounds."

# Chapter Five

The critique session wrapped up shortly before five o'clock, leaving the participants free for the rest of the afternoon and evening. After agreeing to meet in the bar for a drink at seven o'clock and to decide then what they wanted to do about dinner, Penny and Alwynne went to their separate rooms.

Desperate for a shower and a lie-down, Penny made her way upstairs to her room. She crossed over to the open window and peered out. The area below looked different in daylight, but she recognized the spot where Ward had been standing when he turned around to shout something to someone in the hotel. Penny hesitated for a moment, pulled the curtains shut, and then hurried back downstairs, along the main corridor, past the coffee shop, and out the rear entrance of the hotel. She walked along the pavement until she reached the spot where she was sure Ward had been, then turned around and looked up at the first floor. She recognized her room by the open window and closed curtains. She imagined herself in Ward's shoes and turned slightly to her left, to be in the same position he must have been when he spoke to whoever it was. Penny had expected to find herself facing the rear entrance, but instead she was looking just to the left of it, at the coffee shop window. She returned to the hotel to take a closer look at the layout of the coffee shop.

Situated off the main corridor at the rear of the hotel, the coffee shop consisted of a long serving counter with an attractive display of wrapped sandwiches, scones, cakes on glass stands, and biscuits. A screened window beside the coffee machine—the window Penny had just been looking at from outside—was open for ventilation.

"What can I get you?" asked the young woman behind the counter.

"Oh, nothing right now, thanks," said Penny. "Just looking around. But tell me. Is the coffee shop for hotel residents only?"

"Oh no. Anyone can come in here. In fact, we get a lot of tourists wandering in, especially for morning coffee."

Penny thanked her and was about to leave when something occurred to her.

"Just one more thing. What time do you close?"

"Close at eight."

"Right, thanks very much."

*Well, that was a long walk for a short drink,* thought Penny as she returned to her room. After a shower, and feeling somewhat better, she had barely finished drying herself before she was sound asleep.

\* \* \*

"My turn to get the drinks in," said Alwynne. "What would you like?"

"No, I'll go," said Penny. "You can get the next one."

"Oh well, in that case, a red wine, please."

The bar was nowhere near as crowded as it had been the night before, and Penny soon returned with two glasses of wine.

"I spoke to Medwyn," Alwynne said as she reached up for her glass. "He heard on the radio about the body at the lighthouse. It was on the news."

"Oh, so the news is out. Does he want you to come home?"

"No, surprisingly enough, he doesn't. He asked if I was enjoying myself, and I said I was. I asked him what he's getting up to, and he said he's tried out that new recipe for rhubarb cake he got off some woman at church a couple of weeks ago, and tomorrow he's going to weed his vegetable garden." She raised her shoulders and grinned. "He seemed perfectly happy. Funny, isn't it? You can be married to someone for a very long time, and you think you know them well enough to predict how they're going to react to something, and then they completely surprise you."

"I'm glad he's enjoying himself. But really, there's no reason for you to return home if someone accidentally falls off a cliff. There's no danger to you."

"True," said Alwynne. "But I thought he might use it as an excuse to ask me to come back, because he was missing me. But apparently not. Hmm. Now I don't know whether to be relieved or insulted."

Penny laughed. "It's only for a couple more days, so if I were you, I'd leave him to his tomatoes and make the most of your holiday."

Alwynne smiled back. "That's exactly what I intend to do. Now let's talk about dinner. I'm starved. How about you?"

"Ravenous. But you know, I think it would be nice if we left the hotel, had a little walk, and ate dinner somewhere else."

"I agree. If only to get away from the painting crowd. I've heard enough about slanted shadow and composition for one day. I don't want to overhear people talking about that over dinner. There'll be plenty of time for that tomorrow when we all have dinner together."

"We're having dinner together?" Penny asked as her eyes wandered around the room, stopping at the doorway.

"That's what it says on the schedule. Dinner together in the hotel dining room on the last night. Haven't you read it?"

"Not as closely as you have, it would seem." Her eyes slid toward the doorway again.

"Are you expecting someone?"

No. Why do you ask?"

"That's the second time you've glanced at the doorway, so I wondered if you were hoping to see someone."

"No, of course not."

# Chapter Six

"It's a pretty little town, Beaumaris," observed Penny as they walked along Castle Street, pausing every now and then to admire an article of handmade clothing or a hand-sewn stuffed toy on display in a window of one of the independent boutique-style shops.

"It is," agreed Alwynne, "but Beaumaris Castle isn't as impressive as some of the others."

"Probably because it was never finished, so the walls don't have the imposing height, and it lacks grandeur. But it does have a proper moat with actual water in it, and you don't see that every day."

"No, you don't. In fact, it was interesting that several artists chose to stay in town and paint the castle today."

"Poor things, they probably come from places where they don't have an abundance of castles like we do here in Wales."

They reached their destination, a bistro that specialized in seafood. Although dinner service was in full swing and the small restaurant was nearly full, they managed to squeeze into a small table for two at the rear. A waiter brought menus, and the women studied them for a few minutes.

"I'm leaning toward the Scottish salmon in watercress sauce with Pembrokeshire potatoes and fresh carrots," said Alwynne.

"That sounds delicious. And shall we have some white wine with it?"

"Yes. I'll get the wine. I owe you for earlier. And what about a starter?"

"Not for me," said Penny. "The salmon will do me just fine."

They placed their order, and just as their wine was brought to the table, the door opened and in walked Gerald and Betty Thorpe, accompanied by another couple. The four hesitated in the doorway, surveying the crowded room, and then Gerald Thorpe acknowledged Penny and Alwynne with a gentle wave.

"Looks like they had the same idea we did about trying a different restaurant for dinner," remarked Penny as she acknowledged their greeting with a brief wave of her own. When he had finished pouring their wine, the waiter led the foursome to a table in the centre of the room with a RESERVED sign on it.

"What did you make of the Thorpes coming over and speaking to the police about the argument they overheard in the bar last night?" asked Alwynne.

"It did seem rather strange. Why would they think an argument between Bill Ward and a barmaid was connected to a young woman's death? Do they know something we don't?"

Alwynne took a thoughtful sip of wine while eyeing the Thorpe couple and their friends. The two women were chatting while the men were engrossed in the menus. "Of course, they might have just been trying to be helpful."

"That's possible. Bethan always says the police want people to report everything, no matter how trivial or inconsequential it might seem. The police will decide what's relevant. People often withhold information that turns out to be useful because they didn't think it could be important, but they don't have the big picture. They don't know what the police know," said Penny.

"True."

"And there are also people who just like talking to the police because it makes them feel important. The Thorpes could belong in that group."

"Or they might just be civic-minded folk who thought it their duty to report something they thought was unusual or suspicious to the police," said Alwynne.

"That's certainly a possibility."

"And then, some people just have a morbid curiosity about death, and when the police get involved, they just want to be close to the action."

"I can see why they wanted to speak to Constable Jones, since he was the one in uniform, but poor Mr. Thorpe was thrown for a bit of a loop when Bethan identified herself as the senior police officer."

Alwynne smiled. "I know what you mean, but to be fair, she was in plain clothes, and PC Jones was in uniform, so Mr. Thorpe wasn't to know."

The waiter appeared with their entrees, and despite their intention of avoiding any topic to do with art, they soon found themselves discussing how to capture the rough texture of stone walls and buildings in their paintings.

They decided to pass on dessert, and as they were preparing to leave, Penny remarked, "That argument the Thorpes overheard at the bar—it would be nice to know more about it."

"Why? Do you think it matters?"

Penny arranged the strap of her handbag on her shoulder. "I don't know. It might."

* * *

"This is my favourite time of day," Alwynne remarked as they left the restaurant and set off on the short walk back to the hotel. "It's a relaxing time. Just before sunset as you notice the light's beginning to change. And then comes twilight."

"'Twilight.' Such a lovely word."

"Yes, it is. You start to get a sense that the day is ending, but it's not quite over yet. There's still time for something interesting to happen."

"In that case," said Penny, "since it's a lovely evening, why don't we take the longer way round to the hotel's rear entrance so we can have a little stroll along the promenade?"

They retraced their steps in the direction of the castle, but instead of entering the hotel as they passed its main entrance on the high street, they walked on a little further until they reached the open space across the street from the castle adjacent to the seventeenth-century courthouse. Here, they turned right toward the seafront, passing a B&B painted a soft blue, with a joyful display of red and yellow azaleas in window boxes and pots. The sun cast a scattering of light in the palest of pink across everything it touched, and the air felt thin and light.

They turned right again and passed a circle of standing stones that had been set up on the green for an arts festival in the 1990s. A little further along, Penny paused to admire a magnificent limestone Georgian terrace with sashed windows, a hipped slate roof, and its east and west wings resolved in a grand pedimented central block. A FOR SALE sign was affixed to the end house.

"Imagine living here"—she gestured at the grandly designed property—"and getting to look out at that every day." She pointed across to the green with the Menai Strait and Snowdonia mountain range beyond it and then turned to face her friend. "Do you ever do that? See a unique or beautiful property and wonder what it might be like to live there? Or wonder about the lives of the people who are fortunate enough to live there?"

"I do," said Alwynne with a touch of wistfulness. "And I envy everyone who lives in that beautiful terrace. To my mind, Georgian buildings are the most beautiful."

"Oh, absolutely. The proportions, the elegance." Penny pointed toward the third storey. "You can often tell a Georgian building because the windows on the top floor are smaller than the windows on the lower floors. Servants slept in the attics, and the architects thought their rooms wouldn't need as much light as the main rooms, where the owners lived."

"It makes sense, really. The servants were out of their rooms all day working, so they wouldn't have needed large windows to let in light. And of course it was a cost-saving measure. Glass was very expensive, and smaller windows were cheaper."

Dusk was now closing in, and they set off toward the beckoning light coming from the rear entrance of the hotel. They entered to find the coffee shop closed and the lounge, so busy during the day, almost deserted.

"It's been a long day, and after all that's happened, you must be exhausted," said Alwynne. "Are you coming up?"

Penny hesitated. "I'm just going to pop into the bar, but you go on up, if you want to."

"Well, it's still early. I'll come with you."

The bar area, located just off the lobby, was an open, rectangular space consisting of two long walls and a shorter one. Comfortable brown leather club chairs and small round tables were lined up along the two longer walls. The third wall was taken up with a carved wooden bar, complete with brass rails, and the fourth wall was open to the hallway.

Behind the bar, a young man busied himself attaching a sign that read GIN OF THE WEEK to a display.

As Penny hesitated in the entranceway, Colin Campbell leapt out of his chair and reached her in a couple of long strides.

"I heard what happened, and I was hoping to see you," he said. "I'm just here if you'd like to join me." He gestured to a table about halfway down the room. All the other tables were occupied. Penny introduced him to Alwynne, and the three of them made their way to his table. "What can I get you?" Colin asked when they were seated.

"We had some wine at dinner, and I feel as if I've had enough to drink," said Penny. "Maybe just a—oh, I don't know, a . . ."

"What about a tonic water with a slice of lemon for each of us?" suggested Alwynne.

"Yes, that would be fine," said Penny. Her eyes followed him to the bar.

Colin returned a few minutes later and placed a glass in front of each woman. He lowered himself into the chair beside Penny, and the two angled their bodies toward each other so their knees were almost touching. "Cheers," said Penny.

"I heard what happened this morning," Colin repeated, "and I was so sorry you had to go through that. It must have been a terrible shock. I wish I'd been there to help you. How are you doing? Are you all right?"

"I'm doing all right," said Penny. "And how about you? Did you have a good day? Did you make it to Puffin Island?"

"I did. Got some good photos. I think the magazine editor will be pleased."

Alwynne, seated on Penny's other side, had to incline her body forward to see them. Her head moved from side to side as she followed their conversation.

"Where do you think you'll go tomorrow?" Colin was asking.

"We discussed that briefly, but we didn't settle it," said Penny. She turned to her friend. "What do you think, Alwynne?"

"Well, there's just the one day left to paint, and I'd rather like to paint the boats at Moelfre."

"I don't know," said Penny. "I'm leaning toward staying in Beaumaris. There are some interesting shops, so I thought maybe a streetscape." She brightened. "Or what I'd really love to paint is that beautiful Georgian terrace at the seafront we were just looking at. Remember I said I want to paint something I can't get at home? Well, that definitely fills the bill."

"Then I'll stay in town, too," said Alwynne. "I don't think you should be left on your own."

"I'd be happy to look after her," said Colin.

"I don't need looking after," protested Penny, "although it's very kind of both of you."

"Keep you company, then." Colin corrected himself. "Sorry, wrong choice of words. Made you sound like an elderly aunt. Not at all what I meant."

"I know what you meant." As they smiled at each other, Penny smoothed her hair and tucked a strand behind her ear.

"That sounds like an excellent idea," said Alwynne. "I'll go to Moelfre, then. And now that we've sorted out tomorrow, I'm suddenly feeling terribly tired." She got to her feet. "I'm going to take my drink up to my room, and maybe I'll see you in the morning, or maybe not. It's an early start for me, but there's no need for you to get up, Penny. In fact, after what happened today, a lie-in might do you good."

As Alwynne walked across the hardwood floor and through the entranceway into the green-carpeted corridor, Colin and Penny turned back to each other and were soon deep in conversation. One by one, and two by two, the other customers in the bar left, until they were the only two who remained.

"Miss Brannigan?"

It was the woman who had served behind the bar the previous evening.

"Yes?"

"Good. I was told I'd find you in here. I'm Sarah Spencer, assistant manageress here at the Beaumaris Arms. I'm sorry to interrupt, but I wonder if I might have a moment of your time."

"Yes, of course."

As Colin half-rose from his chair, Sarah gestured that there was no need for him to step away.

"I just wanted to thank you for what you did this morning," she said. "As you know, the woman whose body you found was one of our guests. The police told me that you stayed with her, and in fact, if it hadn't been for you, I understand that she might even have been washed out to sea, so we're all very grateful to you for what you did."

She reached into her jacket pocket and withdrew an envelope. "I just wanted to thank you personally." She held out the envelope. "I understand you're here with Bill Ward's art group. On behalf of the hotel, I'd like you to have this voucher for an all-included weekend for two. We hope you'll come back another time for a more pleasant stay under better circumstances." Penny accepted the envelope and thanked her. "And here's my card. If there's anything you need for the rest of your stay, please, just ask." She checked her watch. "I'll let you get back to your drinks. The bar'll be closing early this evening, so may I get you one last drink? Complimentary, of course."

Colin and Penny thanked her but declined.

"That was decent of her," said Colin after Sarah left to speak to the barman. "But given what happened, and what you did, I guess it's the least the hotel could do."

"I do appreciate the gesture, though," Penny said.

A few minutes later, the dimming of lights and clattering of the metal grille as the barman sealed off the bottles behind the bar signalled the end of the evening.

"I'd like to walk you to your room, if that's all right with you," Colin said as they left the bar and entered the main corridor. They walked comfortably together upstairs, and Penny stopped outside her door. As she prepared to put her swipe card in the lock, he placed a light hand on her shoulder and, without any awkward hesitation, bent down and kissed her softly on the cheek. He lingered, giving her a moment to breathe in the clean, soapy smell of him, and then, with a warm smile, he said, "See you tomorrow."

# Chapter Seven

Alwynne and the rest of the painting group were long gone by the time Penny entered the dining room the next morning. As she hesitated in the doorway, Colin Campbell looked up from the menu he had been pretending to study for the last fifteen minutes, and waved her over.

"Have you ordered?" she asked as she slid into the chair across from him.

"I was just about to." He handed her a menu, which she left unopened beside her place setting.

"Thanks, but I know what I want. I have the same thing almost every morning. Creature of habit, me."

With their order taken, Colin asked Penny how she had slept, although her puffy eyes hinted at the answer.

"Not that well, if I'm honest. I managed quite well throughout the day, got through dinner, and last evening in the bar with you, but last night when I closed my eyes, I kept having flashbacks to Jessica's body on the beach." She swallowed hard as she reached for her water glass. "I kept seeing her there. So young. Remember how excited and enthusiastic she was on

Friday night? All that energy, all that"—she held up her hands in a gesture of despair—"all that future. Just gone. And what really made me sad, and what I couldn't stop thinking about last night, was how cold and wet she was. It all just seemed so terribly wrong." She dabbed at the corner of her eyes with the snowy linen napkin and offered a weak, apologetic smile. Colin reached across the table and gave her hand an encouraging, sympathetic squeeze.

"But something didn't seem right. Beyond the obvious, that is—that she was dead." Colin said nothing, giving her the time and mental space to gather her thoughts. "What bothers me is where the body was located. It seems to me it was too far away from the cliff for her to have fallen. She was half in the sea by the time I got there. The tide was going out, so . . . oh, I don't know. I can't think clearly until I've had coffee."

"Neither can I." A few minutes later their server placed a silver coffeepot on the table, along with two steaming bowls of oatmeal, a bowl of fresh raspberries, and a jug of cream. Penny held out her cup and Colin filled it with fragrant coffee.

"You know," he said, as he picked up his spoon, "I've been on assignments and expeditions with a lot of scientists over the last couple of years, and I learned from them that science governs just about everything to do with the coastal environment—currents, waves, tidal forces, and so on. It's too complicated for me, but if you think Jessica might not have fallen off the cliff, is it possible that her body was left on the beach by someone hoping the tide would take it out to sea?"

Penny thought for a moment. "That's entirely possible. A really easy way to get rid of a body, when you think about it. As long as whoever put the body there gets the timing right, of course, and the body isn't discovered before the tide can do its work."

"As might have happened in this case, but didn't, thanks to you." He took a sip of coffee. "It's odd, though, that we were discussing something along that line with Jessica on Friday night. The scenario where someone who wants to disappear leaves their shoes and clothes in a neat pile on the beach, hoping the authorities will assume they went in for a swim and drowned, and then their body was swept out to sea. And then this happens."

They looked at each other for a moment, and then Penny broke eye contact to stir a little cream into her oatmeal.

"So, to change the subject," said Colin. "If you're still planning to paint in town today, as I said last night, I'd like to come along. If that's all right with you, of course. I wouldn't bring too much camera equipment, so I could help carry your painting gear. And I promise you I won't get in the way."

"I'd like that," said Penny. "As long as you don't look over my shoulder. I find that terribly distracting. It makes me so self-conscious. Can't stand people creeping up behind me and watching while I'm trying to work."

"Neither can I. Or when people ask questions."

"Oh, I know! That's even worse. It completely destroys your concentration."

"But worst of all is when they offer opinions. 'Why don't you just try this? Have you thought about doing that?'"

They both made a little groaning noise at the same time and then grinned at each other.

\* \* \*

By mid-morning, Penny had set up her easel on the green facing the Georgian terrace. As she sketched, Colin wandered along the waterfront in the direction of the pier, watching the little boats bobbing along in the sparkling blue waters, and photographing black and white oystercatchers wading about in the shallow water, poking the shoreline mud with their strong, red-orange bills.

As Penny set down her pencil and compared her half-completed sketch to the building in front of her, a shadow fell across her easel. She turned her head slowly, expecting to see an interested passerby, but when a flash of red flannel appeared in the corner of her eye, she realized who was standing behind her.

Before she could respond, Bill Ward placed a hand on her shoulder, gave it a little squeeze, and leaned over to examine her sketch. As the side of his chest brushed against her upper arm she shrank away from him.

"I heard you were out here, so I just came to see how you're doing," he said. As he leaned in for a closer look at her sketch, she caught the unmistakably sour smell of stale alcohol on his breath and immediately sprang up off her stool. She took a step back and folded her arms. He darted a questioningly sharp look at her, gave her a sly smile, and then turned back to the sketch. "You've made a good start. You've got the angles of the receding planes of the roof extended to the horizon line exactly right. I'll be very curious to see how it looks when you've finished painting it." He pulled a packet of cigarettes out of his pocket, took out a cigarette, but didn't light it. "Why did you decide to paint this terrace?"

"I love Georgian buildings," said Penny.

"I know a little about this terrace," Ward replied. "Built in 1833, Grade 1 listed. Designed by architects Welch and Hansom. Yes, he of the Hansom cab."

"I imagine it must be beautiful inside," said Penny, with a hint of wistfulness in her voice. "If the houses haven't had all the charm modernized out of them."

"Yes, that's often the terrible fate of beautiful old buildings. They don't suit modern living. Originally the terrace consisted of ten townhouses, but in the 1930s, I believe it was, they were converted into eighteen apartments. Smaller, more manageable, to better suit the way we live now. Not many of us have the benefit of servants anymore."

He turned his attention back to Penny's sketch and gestured at it with a stubby finger. "Now just here, what were you thinking of doing about the windows? By the time you come to paint these in, the light will be completely different."

They discussed her artwork for a few more minutes, and then Ward asked if he might take her to lunch. "And we'll see where that leads. Who knows? I have friends with art galleries."

*Where that leads? Nowhere,* thought Penny. *That's where all this is leading.* She scanned the promenade in both directions and was relieved to see Colin Campbell had finished his expedition and was ambling back to her.

*Walk faster, Colin,* she thought. And as if he heard her, he sped up, and she put off answering Ward as long as she could, pretending to give his invitation to lunch the careful thought it deserved.

"Oh, thank you, that's very kind," Penny said as Colin joined them, "but I, er, promised Colin here that I'd give him lunch today. My treat." She threw a pleading look in his direction. "Fish and chips, we thought."

"That's right," he replied without missing a beat. "Fish and chips. Been looking forward to it all morning."

"Well," said Ward, following Penny's awkward introduction of the two men, "Enjoy your fish and chips, and I'll see you later at the critique session, but unless you get a lot more done this afternoon, I doubt I'll have much to add to what I've just told you. And don't forget it's our artists' dinner tonight. I'll save the seat beside me for you. And now I'll leave you two Americans to enjoy your fish and chips."

"Canadians," they muttered together as he left, and then turned to each other and laughed.

Penny folded up her easel, tucked her sketch in her bag, and slung it over her shoulder as Colin picked up the easel.

"I suppose we should get some fish and chips, after all that," said Penny.

"Yes, we definitely should."

"And it is my treat, just like I said. We could make a picnic and eat them in the little square across from the castle beside the courthouse. There are lots of benches there."

"Good idea."

And half an hour later, lunch on their laps, that's exactly where they were.

"How well do you know that guy, Bill Ward?" asked Colin as he broke a piece of crispy batter off the end of a piece of deep-fried cod.

"Not well at all. Friday night was only the second time I'd met him."

"There's something kind of creepy about him."

"Yeah. I know what you mean."

He picked up a chip. "After you left the bar on Friday night, he got into an argument with Sarah Spencer. I recognized her when she gave you the hotel voucher last night. She was working as the barmaid on Friday night."

Penny took a sip of water. "Oh, that's right. I heard about that." This was the argument the Thorpe couple had made a point of mentioning to the police officers on Saturday afternoon. "Were you able to catch what they were saying?"

"It didn't last very long. She lit into him about drinking too much, and then he said something about clearing her stuff out, and then a man stepped in and spoke to them, and Ward left. It was almost closing time anyway."

"So this would have been about eleven?"

"Yes, right before the bar closed."

It had been midnight when Penny had observed Ward from her bedroom window, standing in the hotel parking lot below, shouting at an unseen person in the hotel. When she had placed herself yesterday where Ward had been, Penny had realized that that person must have been in the coffee shop. And a person in the coffee shop, long after it had closed, must have been an employee.

She wondered where Ward had been and what he'd been doing between eleven, when he'd been seen in the bar, and that midnight encounter.

# Chapter Eight

"I think you should stay for a few more days," said Alwynne on Monday morning. "This little break is doing you a world of good."

Penny finished buttoning a red cardigan, folded it neatly, and set it on top of the pile of clothes already arranged in her suitcase.

"Maybe the room isn't available."

"Oh, it is. I asked at reception."

"Now why would you do that?"

"I just told you. Because I think you should stay. I've never seen you like this. Your eyes are positively sparkling, and you seem so happy."

"I am happy. I like it here."

"I think it's the company of a certain gentleman you like."

"Certainly not Bill Ward's company. It was really good of you to switch places with me last night so I didn't have to sit beside him at the dinner."

Alwynne laughed. "The look on his face! He sat there and scowled for the rest of the evening, like a spoiled brat who'd just been told he couldn't have any ice cream. Barely said a word to me. I must say, he's been rather a disappointment. Personally, I mean. You'd think he could have made more of an effort to dress for the dinner last night; the rest of us certainly did. I thought you looked very smart, by the way. Still, his critique sessions have been helpful, and I've picked up some good painting tips, but he doesn't come across as a particularly likeable man, does he?"

"No," said Penny. "Not in the least. I suspect he's used to being admired and getting his own way, and he finds it difficult to cope when he doesn't." She sat on the edge of the bed, her hand resting on top of the clothes in her suitcase. "If I did stay, would you still go home today?"

"Yes. Medwyn's decided he's been on his own long enough, and he's coming to fetch me just after lunch, as planned. Of course, you're welcome to come home with us, if that's what you want to do."

Penny pinched her bottom lip and glanced out the window.

"What's the matter? I thought you liked him," said Alwynne. "He's obviously interested in you."

"I do like him. But the thing is, Alwynne, I'm worried that he might be married."

"Well, he isn't," Alwynne said with a hint of triumph in her voice.

"How do you know that?"

"Because I bumped into him in the lobby about an hour ago, and he was wondering the same thing about you. He asked me if you're spoken for, and I told you aren't. And then I asked him if he's got a partner, and he said, 'There was someone, but we broke up some time ago.' Those were his very words. So you see, if you . . ."

But Penny was already reaching for the telephone beside the bed, and after exchanging a few words with the hotel receptionist she stood up and replaced her red cardigan in the bureau drawer.

"Two more nights. I'll stay two more nights."

\* \* \*

After waving Alwynne and Medwyn off, Colin turned to Penny. "Anything special you'd like to do this afternoon?"

"Let's talk about that over a drink."

When they reached the bar, Colin gestured to a table and asked Penny if she wanted a white wine.

"I do," she said, "but I'd like to get the drinks in. I need a word with the barman. What can I get you?"

"Better make it something non-alcoholic in case we decide to drive out somewhere. A diet cola would be fine, thanks."

The barman was in his early twenties, with neatly combed black hair and wearing a smart striped waistcoat over a white shirt. When he set the drinks she had requested on the bar, Penny asked if he was "young Llifon," the person Sarah had mentioned as the one who had been scheduled to work Friday night. "It's just that Sarah was working and she seemed really put out that the regular barman—and I'm guessing that's you—wasn't there."

"Yeah, it was meant to be my shift," he said, "but I couldn't make it in. Wasn't feeling well, if you must know." He folded his arms across his chest and tilted his head back.

"Oh no, no," said Penny. "Sorry, I didn't mean it like that. I'm not implying at all. Nothing against you. It's just that she was busy—the bar was very crowded, and she was run off her feet—but a man, Martin I think she called him, stepped in and said he'd be glad to help her out, but she declined his offer. She seemed rather short-tempered about it all. Not usually what you think of when you think of people serving behind bars, who are usually so friendly. And in the hospitality industry, things happen all the time, and you just have to roll with them, don't you?"

The young man's face relaxed. "You do. I'm surprised to hear that she was put out, actually, because she's really good at springing into action. Or maybe I'm not so surprised. She was flexible—until recently, that is. She changed."

"Oh? How recent was that, would you say?"

"The last month or so, maybe. Lately, she's been impatient and hard to please, where she used to be quite easy going. We used to like working for her. Now, not so much." He took a swipe with a white towel at a couple of water rings on the highly varnished surface of the bar. His face seemed on the verge of crumpling, but he gathered himself up. "I really shouldn't have spoken about her like that with a customer."

"Don't worry," said Penny with a reassuring smile. "Anything you tell me goes no further."

"Well, I'm not surprised that Martin stepped in and offered to help her. That sounds like something he'd do."

"And who's Martin?"

"Oh, Martin Hewitt, the hotel manager. He's a really decent sort. Always takes the time to speak to the staff, and if you need anything, you can go to him. Kind. I'd say he's a kind man. Nothing flashy, but just, well, steady and decent. I never heard a staff member say a bad word about him, and as far as I know, everybody likes him."

"I'm sure you're thinking that I'm asking an awful lot of questions," Penny said, "but it's just that I'm the one who discovered that young woman's body on Saturday morning at Black Point. I'm curious about what was going on at the hotel in the time leading up to her death."

"Oh, it was you who found her body, was it? I heard it was someone staying in the hotel, but I wasn't sure who." He thought for a moment. "So maybe that explains why Sarah spoke to you on the Saturday night when you were in here."

He glanced around the room, as if to make sure no one could hear him, and then leaned forward and in a conspiratorial tone added, "Things are a bit up in the air here, and I think that's one of the reasons why Sarah's been taking it out on the staff lately. On Thursday afternoon she and Mr. Hewitt had a closed-door meeting. It didn't last too long, but she looked really upset when she came out, and she went home right after that. To be honest, I thought she'd been fired."

Another guest approaching the bar was a signal that their conversation was over, and Penny held out a bank note to pay for the drinks. Llifon made change, handed it to her, and moved away to serve his waiting customer.

"That was rather a long chat you had with the barman," said Colin when she rejoined him. "Did you learn anything useful?"

Penny set the drinks on the table and slid into the chair beside him. "Sorry it took so long. I wanted to see if I could find out a little more about the hotel operation. Apparently, things haven't been going great here lately, and something happened last week. The bartender's called Llifon, and he said Sarah left the manager's office on Thursday afternoon looking so upset he wondered if she'd been fired. But he doesn't know for sure what happened in there."

"Does it matter?"

"I don't know. Probably not. But it seems a little unsettling somehow."

"Well, it could have been anything—a customer complaint; they didn't meet a sales target." He reached for his cola. "Of course, the big work problems usually involve incompetence, harassment, or money."

"Money as in fraud? Embezzlement? That kind of money?"

"Yeah."

They each took a sip of their drink and said nothing until the sound of Penny's ringing mobile broke their thoughtful, melancholy-tinged silence.

"It's Bethan Morgan," she said. "The police officer in charge of the Jessica Graham case. Also a friend of mine. I should take it." She kept her eyes on Colin while she listened, making little noises every now and then to indicate she was listening, and wrapped up with, "Right. I'll be home on Wednesday. Talk to you then, if not before." After thanking Bethan, she ended the call.

"The postmortem analysis confirms that Jessica suffered massive blunt force trauma to the back of the head and neck, consistent with a fall from a considerable height, and that fall was responsible for her death," she said. "The report makes no mention of any other abrasions or cuts to the skin pre-mortem."

"Pre-mortem. So that means no defensive wounds?"

"Correct. No fibres or skin were found under her fingernails, which would indicate there'd been a struggle. The police are waiting for lab results and forensics, but at this time, they believe that Jessica died where her body was found. And they're treating her death as accidental. Bethan said they have no reason to think otherwise."

"Can I ask why she would reveal all that to you? It seems like a lot of information for a police officer to share with someone who just—"

"Who just found the body? Well, yes, I can see how it would look like that. But the thing is, there's a bit more to it than that. I've helped her with a few cases in the past." Penny closed her eyes and tilted her head back.

"What's the matter?" Colin asked. "Are you feeling all right?"

"I'm fine. I'm just trying to picture what I saw on the beach that morning." She opened her eyes. "When I found the body, it was half immersed in water, and I'm no expert, of course, but it seems to me it was further away from the base of the cliff, where presumably it would have been if she'd fallen off the cliff."

"So what are you suggesting? That someone placed the body where you found it?"

"I'm not really sure what I'm suggesting. This whole thing has got my brain tied up in knots."

"But the tide was going out," said Colin. "If the tide was in when she fell off the cliff, her body could have been further up on the beach, and as it started to go out, it would have taken the body with it, just as we discussed at breakfast yesterday. So the tide could have moved the body."

"Yes, that's definitely possible, said Penny. "That's pretty much what the pathologist suggested." She took a sip of her drink. "I had a terrible time getting down to the beach on that rough, dangerous path, so I can't see anyone managing to carry a body down it, even a small person like she was. So yes, I guess it could have happened the way the police think it did."

"But just for the sake of argument, let's say it didn't happen that way. Is the path you took the only way to the beach? Maybe there's another way that isn't so steep and rough. Maybe you took the hard way down, but further along there's an easier way. A better path that a local would know."

"There could be," said Penny. "I didn't see one on Saturday morning, but I wasn't looking for one. My only thought was to get down to the beach as quickly as possible, to see if there was anything I could do to help."

"Well, we could go back this afternoon and look for another access point to the beach, if you want to."

"No, I don't think I want to revisit that place right now, thanks all the same.

"Of course not. I'm sorry. It was insensitive of me to suggest it."

"No, you're all right. It's just that I'd rather we do something fun."

"Apparently there's an interesting gaol in the town that we could visit. Or we could make it a double. Visit the court house and then the gaol."

"Another time I might really enjoy that, but I'm not in the right mood today."

"In that case, what you need—what we both need—is nature. I know where some red squirrels live, not too far from here, and if we're lucky, we might be able to spot a few."

"That sounds perfect," Penny replied. "Exactly what I need. Let's drink up and be on our way."

# Chapter Nine

A fternoon sunlight filtered through the canopy of treetops, casting dappled shadows on the woodland path that was part of the grounds of Plas Newydd, a stunning neo-Gothic country house located on the north bank of the Menai Strait, about eight miles west of Beaumaris.

Penny and Colin had arrived in time to join a guided red squirrel walk. Treading quietly, they passed several feeding stations filled with sunflower seeds. The group paused to listen for activity in the tree branches overhead, but the woods remained stubbornly still and silent.

The red squirrel ranger gave a brief account of the red squirrel reintroduction program after their numbers went into serious decline in the 1990s. And now, after careful and loving management, their numbers were on the upswing, and the squirrels were once again beginning to thrive.

"And in case you were wondering," said the guide, "a nest of squirrels, that is, the mother and her young, is called a drey. And a group of squirrels is called a scurry, but because squirrels are solitary creatures, you don't often see one. A scurry, that is. I haven't given up hope we might yet see a squirrel today."

The group walked on, hoping for a sighting, until they reached a clearing where some seeds had been scattered on top of a tree stump. Amid the bracken, ferns, sticks, and branches, the guide spotted something and at the exact moment she pointed to a bushy red tail, Colin raised his camera. The group watched, entranced, as the squirrel scampered up the tree stump, picked up a seed, and ate it. And then, with a saucy flick of his tail, he vanished up a tree and was gone.

The walk was soon over, and the group emerged into the open parkland, flooded with bright sunlight.

"Would you like to see the interior of the house now?" Penny asked, referring to the guidebook they had purchased in the gift shop. "There are some lovely 1930s-style rooms, and a serious collection of Rex Whistler paintings."

"I'd rather walk round the front of the house," Colin said. "And after that, we could wander around inside and then have a cup of tea and a scone in the café."

They walked down the path that led to the house. "It's interesting, this house," remarked Penny, "because unlike most grand houses, you approach it from the rear, through the grounds and gardens, and the main entrance is saved for the spectacular view over the strait and on to the Snowdonia mountain range."

They walked at a moderate pace, in a smooth, steady gait, with their bodies close together, and as Penny's hand swung past Colin's, he caught and held it. Hand in hand, they rounded the corner of the building and strolled along the terrace with the beautiful views Penny had just mentioned. When they reached a bench, Colin gestured at it and they sat. They maintained their closeness, and he tucked her arm under his as he continued to hold her hand.

"We haven't known each other very long, but I'm going to miss you," he said.

"I'll miss you, too. But I suppose it had to end sometime."

"Tomorrow. I heard from my agency that I'm booked on a flight that departs Manchester Airport at noon, so I have to leave early in the morning."

"Where are you off to?"

"Botswana. The client wants photos of critically endangered black rhinos." He let out a little sigh and looked at her. "If it had been someplace closer, like Scotland, I would have asked if you'd like to come with me."

"They don't have too many black rhinos in Scotland." Penny's face relaxed into a soft smile. "But if you'd asked me to go with you, I might have said yes."

"I would have offered to give you a lift home in the morning, if there'd been more time. You don't drive here in the U.K.?"

"No, I never had the desire to. I like public transportation. I'll just take the bus to Bangor, where my friend and business partner is going to pick me up. Not a problem."

"I think you said you live in Llanelen. Is that right?"

"That's right."

"How did you come to be there?"

So Penny told him how she'd left Canada with a degree in fine arts, to go backpacking around Europe, visiting the galleries and museums. And how she'd stopped off one afternoon in Llanelen on her way to Holyhead to catch the ferry to Dublin, met a lovely woman who had taken her under her wing, and stopped the night. And that night turned into one more day, and soon she had begun to put down roots. Tiny and weak at first, but over the years those roots had strengthened and deepened, and now Wales was her home and she loved it dearly, from the bottom of her heart. She couldn't imagine living anywhere else.

"And you?" Penny asked.

"I grew up in Toronto in what was then a pretty shabby neighbourhood, but now, of course, it's gentrified, and those red brick, three-storey Victorian row houses where several families used to live are now home to a young couple in their early thirties—he's a lawyer and she works in marketing or public relations—and somehow they can come up with the million dollars or so they need to buy the place."

"Did you have brothers and sisters?"

"No, only child. You?"

"Same."

"Your childhood, was it happy?"

"No, I can't say that it was. I grew up with my grandparents in Nova Scotia, and we didn't have much. They sacrificed a lot for me."

"And your parents?" he asked gently. Her eyes clouded over, lost in a private pain from a time long ago. "Or maybe you'd rather not talk about that."

"No, it's okay. But you're right. It isn't something I normally talk about. My mother was severely depressed, and my father left us to find work in Toronto. That's what a lot of men from the Maritimes did back then. I think the plan was that once he was settled, he would send for us. But after a while, we stopped hearing from him, and then my mother died, so I went to live with my grandparents." She hoped she wasn't revealing too much, too soon, in a way that signalled she was desperate for intimacy.

"Oh, I'm so sorry." He squeezed her hand.

When the moment passed, they talked some more, eagerly discussing their interests and describing how their travels and experiences had led them to where they were today.

Across the strait, as dark clouds rubbing against one another began casting deepening shadows over the mountains, Colin stood up and extended his hand to pull her to her feet.

"The weather looks like it's closing in." He checked his watch. "We'd better go in, if we want to see the interior. The house is going to close in an hour." They wandered from room to room, not saying much and not taking in much of what they were seeing, either. Even the massive Rex Whistler mural in the dining room failed to capture Penny's attention the way it might have at another time, and had she been with someone else.

They drove back to the hotel through a gentle, misty rain. Wrapped in an easy, comfortable silence, neither spoke on the journey until they reached the Beaumaris town limits, and as they passed a row of terraced houses painted in pretty pastel colours, Colin asked Penny what she'd like to do about dinner.

"It looks like we could be in for a rainy night, and we've been out all afternoon, so how would you feel about just having dinner at the hotel?" she replied.

"Sounds like a good idea."

\* \* \*

When they reached the hotel, Colin said he needed time to prepare for his upcoming assignment, and after agreeing to meet in the restaurant in a couple of hours, and a brief embrace in the lobby, they went to their rooms.

After notifying reception that she would be checking out in the morning, Penny lay on her bed, thinking about the time she'd just spent with Colin. Then, ambushed by a contented tiredness, she rolled over on her side, tucked her hands under the pillow, and closed her eyes. Twenty minutes later she awoke refreshed, and after a gentle soak in a leisurely bath, she wrapped herself in a white towelling robe, and sifted through her limited selection of clothes. Mostly casual outdoor wear, they were perfect for *plein air* painting and walking, but not suitable for dinner in the formal dining room of a lovely hotel. Wishing she had time now to pick up an evening outfit with a bit of style or sparkle in one of the local shops, she had to settle for the simple dress she'd worn to the artists' dinner on Sunday evening.

Once dressed, she studied her hair in the mirror as she brushed it, and wondered if it was time for a change. She touched the smooth, even ends of her tapered blunt cut, coloured in a soft, sophisticated, natural-looking red and meticulously styled by Alberto, the Spa's resident hair specialist. She made a mental note to ask him when she got back if he thought a change in hair style would be a good idea. Should she try something shorter? A lighter colour?

While she applied her lipstick, she allowed herself to think about how the evening might end. Although she knew how she wanted it to end, she wasn't sure that would be for the best in the long run. Something was telling her it didn't feel quite the right time. It was early days. And all that, of course, was assuming he felt the same way.

She decided not to let the fact that they would be going their separate ways in the morning cast a gloom over dinner. Resolving to be cheerfully upbeat and to make the most of their remaining time together before they had to drag themselves back to their everyday lives, she let herself out of her room and made her way to the restaurant.

As she passed through the lobby, a glimpse of Bill Ward shouting into his mobile made her rethink her route. But as she paused, wondering if she could avoid him by going the other way round to the dining room, he caught sight of her and gave her an airy wave. So she felt she had to keep going; if she changed her route, it would be awkwardly obvious that she was avoiding him.

"Well, yeah, but hopefully this means I can at least sell the property now without her getting in the way again with all her ridiculous legal claims," he said. "I mean, we weren't married, and we broke up well over a year ago, so why she thought she had any right to keep living in my house is beyond me. But now she says she wants to buy it, and all that money she's been waiting for is coming soon. . . ."

His agitated voice faded away as Penny left him behind. *Why do some people conduct what should be private conversations on their mobiles in public places,* she wondered. *Especially when it's about their domestic troubles. Do they think they're in some kind of bubble, and no one can hear what they're saying?*

At the sight of Colin waiting for her at the entrance to the restaurant, all thoughts of Bill Ward and his telephone conversation vanished, and she focused on the man she was there to meet. They were shown to a table by the window, away from the rest of the diners.

"I'm sorry I'm not better dressed," Colin said. "I don't even have a tie with me, although I could have borrowed one, I suppose, but nobody wears them very often anymore. At least my shirt is clean."

Over dinner they continued exploring each other's pasts.

"How did you get started on a photography career?" Penny asked. "No, let me guess. It started as something you really enjoyed doing and then grew into something more."

"That's exactly what it was. It was a hobby, and then it became my second career."

"What were you doing before?"

"I worked for a Bay Street investment firm. We promised our clients we'd make a lot of money for them, and we did. But the truth is, we made even more money for the firm and for ourselves. And after twenty years or so of that, I wasn't happy anymore and couldn't see myself doing it any longer."

"Was it the hours?"

"That was part of it, certainly, but ultimately it was the ethics. We made money investing in organizations with questionable business practices. Oh, they were legal, but that didn't make them right. At least, not the way I came to see it. So I got out. And I had what I thought was a decent portfolio of wildlife photos that I'd taken on holidays around the world, so I applied to a few photo agencies and started getting assignments. And now I'm doing what I love. Of course the money's not nearly what it used to be, but that's not the point. I've got enough money. More than enough."

"That's interesting about your career change," said Penny. "I've started to feel a bit restless myself. I was in Dublin recently, and after a visit to the national art gallery, I realized I've been missing that kind of experience. Small-town life is good, but there are times when it feels like the world has so much more to offer, and I'm missing it."

"Maybe you need to get out more."

"Yes, I do. In fact, when I left Dublin, I told myself that's exactly what I was going to do. I had a friend who died a few years ago—Emma Teasdale she was called, the one I inherited my cottage from, actually—and she and I used to go to art exhibits and concerts in Manchester and Liverpool, and I definitely need to do more of that."

"That should be easy enough. And your Spa? Do you like running a business?"

"I don't have much to do with the day-to-day running of it. My partner looks after the operational side of things, although we make all the important decisions together. But the actual work part, the manicures—to be honest, I'm getting bored with that."

"Sounds like you're ready for a new challenge."

"I'd like to spend more time painting. Or maybe getting more involved in some other way in the art world."

Happy and relaxed in each other's presence, and each pretending that it wasn't their last evening together, they conversed easily and smoothly, diving eagerly into the other person's life.

"Tell me about your ex," said Penny.

"She was a corporate lawyer for one of the big firms, and boy, did she work hard. I saw for myself how much harder women in positions like that have to work than men, to get ahead. But when I began to lose interest in that high-stress life, our relationship was in trouble. I wanted less, and she wanted more. And finally, when I just couldn't live like that anymore, it became apparent to both of us that our relationship had run its course. We didn't have anything important in common anymore."

"So you're divorced, then?"

"No, we never married. And now it's your turn." He speared a forkful of salad. "Have you ever been married?"

"Not quite," said Penny. "But there was someone once. Tim, he was called. We were both in our early thirties. We were engaged, but he drowned, saving a child's life, before we could marry. He was a police officer, and if he'd lived, I'm sure my life would have turned out very differently."

Colin put his fork down and reached across the table to take Penny's hand. "I'm so sorry," he said as he gave it a gentle squeeze.

"It felt as if something inside me died. I just never experienced that depth of feeling again." She took a sip of wine, to which she had added a generous splash of mineral water. "Of course I was younger then, so perhaps that added to the intensity of my feelings of loss and grief. I think we become a little more accepting of what life throws at us as we get older, and we're able to handle setbacks better."

"And no one after that?"

"More recently, there was another police officer. Bethan's former boss, in fact. I was very fond of him, and we were good friends, but that bit of chemistry was missing, so that's really all we ever were."

"And are you still friends?"

"Well, he met someone and moved to Scotland, so it all worked out well for him." She smiled at Colin over her wine glass. "He's a good man, and I'm glad he's happy."

They lingered over coffee until, finally, there was no putting it off any longer.

"It's getting late, and I've got to finish packing," said Colin, placing his napkin on the table. "I've got an early start in the morning. I don't know how you feel about all this, but I'd feel better knowing that I'll see you again as soon as we can arrange to get together."

"I'd like that," said Penny. "Earlier I told you that if you'd been able to invite me to go to Scotland with you, I might have said 'yes.' If I were to invite you to Llanelen, what would you say?"

"Yes. I'd say yes, thank you."

"Then consider yourself invited."

The evening just felt over, so they decided not to prolong the inevitable with a farewell drink in the bar. They walked together upstairs, and outside Penny's door, he took her in his arms and held her. She closed her eyes and rested her head against his chest. Her heart was hammering. She desperately wanted to ask him in, but was afraid to. What if they had this one night together, and she never saw him again?

He gently released her and took a step back into the corridor as she opened the door to her room.

"Good night."

"See you soon."

"How soon?"

"You'll be hearing from me."

# Chapter Ten

"You look refreshed, considering," said Victoria Hopkirk the next morning when she greeted Penny off the bus in Bangor. Tall, slim, in her early fifties, and with shoulder-length blonde hair, she was Penny's best friend as well as her business partner. "A few days away on a painting break seem to have done you good."

"I had—well, it was definitely a busy and interesting time."

"So I hear. Let's put your gear in the car and then go for a coffee and you can tell me all about it before we head home."

When they were settled in the coffee shop of a department store overlooking the busy bus station, Victoria wrapped her hands around her mug and leaned forward. "Well, we heard you found a body, and of course we're dying to hear all about it. What happened?"

"She was a young woman. A newspaper reporter from New Zealand. I found her on the beach on Saturday morning. We spoke to her the night before, and she was so young and eager, and excited about her future, and there's something about her that makes it all just terribly upsetting. I've been trying not to think too much about her, and do you know, what with everything else, I've almost managed to put finding her body to the back of my mind."

"What? You can't mean that. I'd have thought you'd be sleuthing all over the island and asking questions like nobody's business."

"Well, the police are treating the death as accidental, and Bethan and the police have everything in hand, so I left them to it."

"That doesn't sound at all like you." Victoria tipped her head. "It looks like you're having a hard time emotionally with this. But is there something you're not telling me? Did something else happen?"

"Yes," said Penny, spooning a bit of foam off her latte, "I guess it did." She locked eyes with her friend. "I might as well tell you. I met somebody. That's why I decided to stay a bit longer. I was going to stay two more days, but then he had to leave today, so there wasn't any point in my hanging about in Beaumaris."

"Oh, how exciting. What's his name?"

"Colin Campbell."

Victoria grinned. "Ah, the first bloom of a new romance. Just the way your eyes lit up when you said his name tells me everything I need to know. Well, not quite everything. What's he do? Where's he from? What's he look like? How old is he?"

Penny held out her phone so Victoria could see a photo she'd taken of Colin at Plas Newydd on the red squirrel walk. "That's him. He's Canadian, and he's a couple of years younger than I am."

Victoria leaned across the table. "Oh, he's quite nice looking. Tell me about him."

Penny described the days she and Colin had spent together and ended by saying she hoped to hear from him soon about his coming to visit her in Llanelen. "And then you can meet him for yourself."

"Well, I'm really happy for you, and I hope it works out the way you want it to." They finished their coffees, gathered up their handbags, and were soon on their way.

"I've got a couple of boxes of supplies to pick up at the Cash and Carry," said Victoria, "so we'll go into Llandudno on the way home."

"Fine with me."

The Irish Sea, blown into tight little waves by a friendly wind, sparkled in the morning sunshine. Penny allowed herself one last look over her shoulder as they drove past Puffin Island, then settled herself in her seat.

"I'd still like to hear about that body you found, though," said Victoria. "If you feel like talking about it, that is."

"How much do you already know?" Penny asked. "Alwynne's husband heard about it on the news. Is that how you heard about it?"

"No."

Penny smiled. "Ah, Mrs. Lloyd."

"Apparently Alwynne bumped into Mrs. Lloyd at the supermarket and told her all about it."

"And then Mrs. Lloyd told everybody."

"That's about the size of it. She popped into the Spa to ask when you'd be back, and immediately changed her appointment so she could see you this afternoon instead of having to wait until tomorrow. She's eager to hear every last detail, as you can imagine."

75

"Well, the body I found isn't that of a local person, so I don't know how interested Mrs. Lloyd will be. Jessica Graham was her name, and as I said, she was a journalist from New Zealand. This was her first time on an international trip, and she was just bursting with life and all its possibilities. Colin and I spoke to her in the bar on Friday night, and then I discovered her body first thing Saturday morning on the pebbly little beach at Black Point. Alwynne and I were there to paint the Penmon Lighthouse. Apparently she died from injuries suffered during a fall, but what on earth she was doing there—that's the mystery."

"And Bill Ward, what was he like? Did he live up to your expectations?"

"He was fine as far as the art went, but on the personal side, well, a little creepy." Penny described what had happened while she was painting the Georgian terrace at Beaumaris.

"He said that? He actually said, 'Let's have lunch and see where it goes?'"

"He did."

"You're right. That is so creepy." Victoria kept her eyes on the road ahead but made a little moue of disgust.

"And he's not even all that attractive," Penny said. "But he probably had women lining up when he was a big television star, and he still thinks he's God's gift."

"Could be. Is he with anyone, do you know? Has he got a wife or girlfriend?"

"I don't know. I didn't see him with anyone, and he was on his own for the weekend, as far as I could tell."

"Of course, you probably weren't giving him your full attention, your mind being occupied elsewhere."

Penny took this with a good-natured smile. "You might be right about that. But Ward's profile says he lives on Anglesey, and he seemed at home in the hotel. I wonder if he lives there. Or is at least staying there temporarily."

"It's possible, I suppose," said Victoria. "And did your Colin meet him? What did he think about him?"

"He's not *my* Colin!" protested Penny.

"Well, maybe not yet, he isn't. Give it time."

As they approached the Victorian seaside resort of Llandudno, Victoria suggested they have lunch there after they finished picking up their order at the Cash and Carry.

"And then, we could leave all your gear in the car, go straight to the Spa for the afternoon, and I'll drive you home after work."

"Sounds good. And how's Harrison?" Penny asked, referring to her grey cat. "Behaved himself, did he?"

"Oh, he was very good. I spent a couple of evenings sitting with him so he wouldn't be lonely. We're quite fond of each other, but I'm sure he'll be glad to see you."

* * *

The Llanelen Spa is beautifully situated on the bank of the Conwy River in the picturesque market town of Llanelen. The two-storey, grey stone building had been abandoned and left to decay for decades until, against everyone's advice, Penny and Victoria bought it, renovated it, and converted it into a light, bright, airy space offering a full range of relaxing and refreshing rejuvenation treatments, including facials, massages, manicures and pedicures, and hair styling. Their investment had proved wise, providing a profitable business, a sound real estate holding, and—for Victoria—a spacious flat on the first floor.

After receiving a warm welcome back from Rhian, the receptionist, Penny made her way to the nail studio at the end of the corridor. Eirlys, her assistant, was taking a half day but had left everything laid out for Mrs. Lloyd's manicure.

A flurry of greetings in the corridor let Penny know that Mrs. Lloyd was on her way, and a moment later she entered the nail studio. The town's former postmistress, now in her late sixties, she was a robust woman who took good care of herself. She had her hair and nails done every two weeks and dressed smartly in sensible shoes, pleated skirts, tidy blouses, and woollen cardigans. She prided herself on keeping up with all the latest news in Llanelen, which some townsfolk referred to as gossip, and some even went so far as to say that she relished every delicious morsel of other people's troubles and indiscretions.

"Penny, my dear," she said as she eased her ample bottom into the client's chair. "I've been dying to hear all about your time on Anglesey. You have so much to tell me. The painting excursions with a famous actor and, of course, discovering a body. How thrilling it all must have been for you! What dull little lives the rest of us lead in comparison to yours."

Penny placed a soaking bowl filled with lavender-scented water on the worktable and lifted Mrs. Lloyd's right hand into it. Just before her fingers broke the surface of the water, Mrs. Lloyd gave Penny a steely look. "Now, it's not too hot, is it? With you, the water's always too hot. Eirlys knows exactly how I like it, and she always gets it just the right temperature."

"Try it and see. If it's too hot, I'll add some cold water. We'll make it just the way you like it."

Mrs. Lloyd slid a tentative two fingers into the bowl, breathed a sigh of relief, and allowed the rest of her hand to follow.

"It'll do. Now then, off you go. Tell me all about your painting holiday, and don't leave anything out."

"Anglesey's lovely this time of year. You really must go."

Mrs. Lloyd laughed. "You know that's not what I meant. You'll have to do better than that. Oh, and by the way, before I forget, Morwyn asked me to pass on a message. She wants to interview you for a story she's working on for the Saturday edition of the paper. She'd like to speak to you this evening, if possible."

The local reporter, Morwyn Lloyd, was Mrs. Lloyd's niece. Penny could only imagine how many stories she'd written over the years that had started with a tip from Mrs. Lloyd as a result of the keen interest she took in local affairs.

Penny finished shaping Mrs. Lloyd's fingernails, removed the wet hand from the soaking solution, and replaced it with the one she'd just finished working on.

"I'm sure it was upsetting for you, discovering that young woman's body," said Mrs. Lloyd as Penny dried her wet hand. "Although to be fair, this isn't the first time you've done that. Still, if you'd rather not talk about it, of course I understand. But I would like to hear all about your meeting that famous actor from *Jubilee Terrace*. I've watched that program since it began, and that must be, oh, forty years ago now. I'm sure every actor and actress in Britain wants to appear on that show, so really, only the very best make it. Tell me, what was he like?"

"I didn't think much of him personally, if I'm honest, but he is knowledgeable about painting, and I picked up a few useful tips in the critique sessions."

"You 'didn't think much of him personally.' It's always a shame when we meet someone who doesn't live up to our expectations. What was wrong with him?"

"I found him a bit creepy."

Mrs. Lloyd's lips pinched together in a disapproving frown. "Did he pester you?"

"Yes."

Mrs. Lloyd made a little tsking noise. "Oh, Lord. Why do some men do that? Do they ever look at themselves in the mirror in a good light? How do men like that manage to convince themselves that women find them irresistible?"

"I'm sure lots of women did find him attractive when he was younger, in better shape, and working on a hugely popular television show," said Penny. "He would have been a real star back then, but his star is somewhat dimmer now."

"Well, other than that, though, and finding that poor girl's body of course, you had a good time?"

"Oh yes."

"I thought so because Alwynne told me you decided to stay on for another couple of days." She gave Penny a shrewd look through narrowed eyes. "I wondered what the attraction was."

"Squirrels. I decided I absolutely had to see the red squirrels at Plas Newydd."

Mrs. Lloyd let out a merry little peal of youthful laughter. "Oh, go on. Pull the other one! Alwynne's already told me all about that photographer chap you met. Or as much as she knows, anyway. She said he was very keen on you and that you like him. You didn't think you could keep that a secret around here, did you?"

"Not for a minute, Mrs. Lloyd. At least, not from you. But it's early days, so let's wait and see what happens, shall we?"

The manicure continued, and as she was preparing to leave, Mrs. Lloyd reminded Penny to ring Morwyn about that newspaper story.

"She's eager to hear from you."

# Chapter Eleven

After ensuring her wrought-iron front gate was securely latched behind her, Cilla McKee unclipped the lead on her elderly brown and white boxer and followed him up the path that led to the front door of her modest house in Betws-y-Coed.

She put the kettle on, and while she waited for it to come to a boil, she put away the few groceries she'd just bought, and tidied up the kitchen. Then, with a mug of coffee just the way she liked it, and a fresh cream bun from the local bakery beside her, she unfolded the local newspaper. A headline on the front page leapt out at her, and with her mug poised halfway to her lips, she skimmed the brief article. She took a tentative sip as she reread the item, this time taking in every word and occasionally going back to reread a sentence.

Local artist describes finding murder victim on
Anglesey beach
by Morwyn Lloyd

*The local artist who found the lifeless body of journalist Jessica Graham, 27, on an Anglesey beach a week ago describes the experience as "shattering."*

*Penny Brannigan, 54, who was on a painting retreat with a group of other artists, made the grisly discovery Saturday morning whilst preparing to paint the iconic Penmon Lighthouse at Black Point.*

*"You never expect to come across something like that," Ms. Brannigan said. "I can't tell you how shocked I was. I spotted the body from the cliff top, then scrambled down to the beach. But unfortunately, she was beyond help, so all I could do was stay with her body until the first responders arrived."*

*A postmortem determined that Ms. Graham died from injuries consistent with a fall from a great height, and although the police believe the death to be accidental, they urge anyone who might have information to come forward. The deceased woman was a visitor from New Zealand, and her family have been notified.*

*Sarah Spencer, assistant manageress at the Beaumaris Arms Hotel, where Ms. Graham had been staying, expressed condolences. "We were shocked and saddened by the sudden death of one of our guests, and our thoughts and prayers are with her family."*

*The painting retreat was led by former Jubilee Terrace actor Bill Ward, now an acclaimed artist, who himself lives on Anglesey. Ms. Graham had been in the U.K. to work on a feature story about Ward's mid-life career change, along with other stories, for the "Auckland Spectator."*

*Ms. Brannigan is co-owner of the Llanelen Spa and is becoming well known in the area for her landscape watercolours.*

A grim moue of distaste played at the corners of Cilla McKee's lips as she pulled a pair of scissors from their slot in the knife rack.

*Who'd want thoughts and prayers from that nasty piece of work Sarah Spencer, as she calls herself now,* Cilla thought as she cut out the article. She read it through one more time, then checked her watch and, letting out a little gasp of dismay, hurried upstairs to get ready for work. She'd dawdled this morning over the newspaper, and she'd have to get her skates on if the gallery was to open on time. Saturdays were the busiest day of the week, especially in summer with so many tourists visiting the area, eager to take home a painting by an established or up-and-coming Welsh artist.

Dressed and back in the kitchen, she tucked the newspaper clipping in her handbag, gave her boxer an affectionate goodbye pat, and let herself out of the house. She usually walked to work, but because she was running late, decided to take the car. She liked to arrive at least twenty minutes before opening time to do a walk-through, making sure everything was clean and tidy and the staff were ready, set, and on their marks for the day.

A few minutes later she pulled into the car park of the Oriel Snowdonia and locked her vehicle. On the short walk from her car to the gallery's back door, she picked up two discarded coffee cups and, with a little grimace of disgust, dropped them in the bin near the rear entrance. She let herself in, entered the code on the keypad to switch off the security alarm, flicked on the lighting system, and unlocked the door to her office.

She pulled the newspaper clipping out of her handbag, Googled a telephone number, and listened to the options. When there was no answer, she left a brief voicemail message.

*Excellent,* she thought. *That's two birds with one stone.*

\* \* \*

It was lunchtime before Penny had a chance to check her voicemail, and when she had, she put the phone down and did an over-the-moon little twirl in her office. Cilla McKee from the Oriel Snowdonia had left a voicemail asking to meet with her the next day to discuss the possibility of including Penny's paintings in an upcoming exhibit featuring local artists.

As she walked home after work, rooting about in her mind for paintings she might include, she realized that the first person she wanted to share her happy news with was Colin Campbell. And besides, he had lots of experience showing his work in exhibits, so he'd be sure to have some good suggestions. She'd ask him about this when they video-chatted that evening, as they did every evening.

Not so long ago, it would have been Victoria she rushed to tell.

# Chapter Twelve

Colin advised Penny to choose paintings that evoked an emotional response in her and that she considered or knew to be technically good. And then, he reminded her to present them with confidence, as if she truly believed they deserved to hang in this gallery.

So the following afternoon, with twelve of what she considered the best examples of her work tucked flat in her portfolio case, she walked up the rough lane that led to the main entrance of the Oriel Snowdonia. Built in the mid-nineteenth century as the summer home of a prosperous Liverpool merchant, the grand house had been a nursing home before being converted into its present use as an art gallery displaying the work of sought-after contemporary Welsh artists working in all media. Penny had visited the gallery many times over the years, as someone who enjoyed and appreciated art. Today, she was here by invitation, as a creator. She was here as an artist.

She took a deep breath, practised a smile, squared her shoulders, and pushed open the door. She found herself in a cream-coloured hallway with flooring of brightly coloured

Victorian Minton tiles. As Cilla had instructed, she followed the hallway to the centre of the house, crossed in front of the grand staircase, and then turned left. A solid wooden door marked PRIVATE stood ajar, and Penny tapped lightly on it.

"Come in."

Penny found herself in a spacious, high-ceilinged room painted a rich, warm burgundy, with natural wood trim. An imposing fireplace featuring a marble surround stood against one wall, and above it hung an oil on panel painting depicting the rugged Welsh landscape. The room was bathed in natural light from a tall window overlooking the car park, and below the window stood a long, highly varnished table, its surface clear.

A large brown and white boxer resting in a dog bed got to his feet and wagged his tail as a woman turned away from her computer, stood up, and held out her hand across her desk.

"Cilla McKee. And you must be Penny Brannigan. Thank you for coming in."

She gestured at the dog beside her desk. "This is Chris York. He's allowed to come to work with me today. He's big, I know, but he's perfectly gentle. I hope you're all right with dogs, but if you're not, we'll go somewhere else."

"He's just fine," Penny replied. "I love dogs."

When they were seated, Cilla folded her hands together and placed them on her desk. "Right. Well, let me just explain why I asked you here. I thought we might be able to include a few of your watercolours in our Christmas mixed exhibition, if you'd be interested in participating." When Penny indicated she was, Cilla continued. "Good. Then let's start by having you show me what you brought. You can use that table to display them."

Penny opened her portfolio case, removed a selection of unframed paintings, and spread them out on the table beneath the window.

Cilla concentrated as she examined Penny's paintings, placing most of them in a pile and setting two to one side.

"Well, they're lovely," said Cilla. "You certainly know watercolour techniques. Your work on the bridges and stone walls shows you know what you're doing. And you've included open gates, which is good. I like to see open gates. They invite the viewer into the painting. Otherwise, it all feels closed off."

"Oh, it's great to hear that you like them. I wasn't sure if you would. To be honest, I contacted the gallery a couple of times about the possibility of showing my work here. You and I even spoke on the phone, and there never seemed to be any interest, so I wondered why you called me now." Fearing that might sound too assertive, Penny added, "But I'm so glad you did. I was really excited to hear from you."

"Like most things in life, it's all about timing. The thing is, an artist I was going to include had to back out, and I thought you might be the solution to my problem." She gestured at Penny's paintings. "And I was right. You are. I'm sorry I didn't have you in before. I should have—I can see that now— but we were always booked up. But then I saw your name mentioned in a newspaper article. You were described as a talented local artist, or something like that, and I remembered that we had spoken about your exhibiting here."

"This article you saw in the newspaper, am I right in assuming it was about the painting weekend on Anglesey?"

Cilla nodded. "It said you were the one who found that poor girl's body."

"Yes, I did."

"And the article included condolences from Sarah bloody Spencer, of all people." Cilla spat out the words.

Penny's eyes widened and her mouth opened slightly. "From the way you say her name, I'm guessing you know her, and not in a good way."

"Oh, I know her all right."

"Would you mind telling me how you know her?"

Cilla indicated that they should return to their chairs near the desk. "I usually have a cup of tea about this time. Would you like one? Or a coffee?" When Penny opted for coffee, Cilla picked up her phone and called the café. A tray arrived a few minutes later, and Cilla held out a cup to Penny, glanced at her sleeping boxer, and then settled back in her chair.

"Sarah worked at a country house hotel outside Manchester, where my husband and I liked to go for Sunday lunch. The food was delicious. Fresh, local ingredients, beautifully prepared and presented. The staff were well trained—so polite, and nothing was ever too much trouble. The whole place was all about creating the perfect illusion of how the other half lives, so guests can imagine they're living that life, too. Gracious rooms, curtains and soft furnishings in lovely floral patterns, antique furniture, soft lighting. Occasionally, we treated ourselves to a romantic weekend. Four-poster bed, working fireplace. And then, my husband stopped taking me there. Except he kept going without me, if you see what I mean."

"Oh, he . . ."

"Yes, apparently Sarah took the bit about the staff being at your service to a whole new level. He and Sarah started up an affair, and then he announced that he was leaving me and moving in with her. She was married to someone else, too, but they didn't let that stop them. Her husband and I got together a couple of times for a coffee, to talk about the situation. Misery loves company, and all that. He was determined to fight for his marriage, although God knows why he'd want to have anything to do with her after the way she treated him, but he must have changed his mind about her, because after a while someone told me that he'd moved away. I decided that would be best for me, too. My family's from Wales, so I moved here and started over. And then three or four years ago, I heard the two of them were living together on Anglesey."

She took a sip of tea and eyed Penny over the rim of the cup.

"Ever heard that old saying about the man who marries his mistress creates a job vacancy? It was like that with my ex. I'm sure as soon as he got together with Sarah, he was looking for the next one, although to be fair, they never legally married. And I doubt very much he would have married her, anyway."

"And how long ago did all this happen?" Penny asked.

"Seven years."

"Gosh, I don't really know what to say," said Penny. "But I can certainly see why the newspaper story stirred up a lot of bad memories for you."

"Oh, it did, but it felt quite therapeutic getting all this out just now," Cilla said. "It took me a long time to get over what they did, and I haven't really spoken of him or her"—she said the word "her" as if it had curdled on her lips—"in some time. But I must admit I'm a little curious to know something. Did you meet her?"

"Yes, I did."

"And?"

"I'm not sure what you're asking."

"What was she like? How did she seem?"

Penny thought carefully before answering. "Well, I only saw her a couple of times. She was busy in the bar on the Friday night, and the next day she made a point of thanking me for, well, my role on the Saturday morning in what happened with Jessica Graham. I found her professional, actually." *If you want me to start slagging her off, you're going to be disappointed,* Penny thought.

If she was disappointed that Penny hadn't been more critical of Sarah Spencer, Cilla took care not to show it.

"Well, enough about them and their sordid little lives," she said with a tight smile. "Back to business—your paintings and the reason we're here." Indicating that the topic was now closed, Cilla opened her desk drawer and pulled out several pieces of paper clipped together and handed them to Penny. "Here's our contract. The show opens November thirteenth and runs to the twenty-second of December."

"The twenty-second? Oh, of course," said Penny. "It closes just before Christmas, to give people enough time to pick up the purchases they bought to give as gifts."

"Exactly. And you get to set your own price, but all work for sale in this exhibit must be priced under five hundred pounds. Is that all right with you? It should be. It's quite a generous price for an amateur painting. You can take the contract home with you to read at your leisure, and if you're in agreement with the terms, sign it and send it to me in the post, let's say by the end of next week.

"If you don't want to participate, let me know ASAP so I can ask someone else. I don't need to tell you that many local artists would love to have this spot. I'll need the framed art-work by November sixth. Nice, simple frames work best. If you take them to the framer in Llanelen and tell him it's for a show-ing here, he'll know what kind of frame to put on them. Now, let's take one last look at your paintings."

They moved back to the table under the window, where Penny's paintings were spread out. "So which ones would you like for the exhibit?" Penny asked.

"All of them except those two." She pointed to the two most recent paintings, the Georgian terrace Penny had painted during the weekend retreat in Anglesey. Of all the paintings, Penny liked them best because they were her most recent and because they reminded her of the time she'd spent with Colin. "It's not that those paintings aren't good. They are. It's just I don't care for the subject matter, and I don't want to have to look at it."

"May I ask why not?" Penny asked, trying to keep the prickle out of her voice.

"My ex owns a flat there, and very nice it is, too. More like a house, really, or so I'm told. Or maybe I should say owned. Past tense. I saw it was for sale. Anyway, he was living there with his fancy woman, but apparently he was the one who moved out when they broke up."

The conversation she'd had with Bill Ward outside the ter-race sprang into Penny's mind, and she remembered that he'd seemed to know quite a lot about the history of the property. Penny's brows drew together as her head tilted slightly to one side. "Are you talking about Bill Ward? Is he your ex-husband?"

"Yes, he is. Didn't I say? I thought I told you that. And as for him, of course I was the one, with my gallery connections, who got him started on his brilliant painting career. Which he's done very well out of, by the way. He was always one to make good use of people. Except maybe with Sarah Spencer, it was the other way round. He got caught up in her sticky web, and I expect he'll pay dearly for that one way or another, if he hasn't already."

She picked up her almost empty cup and forced down a sip of tepid tea, as if she could wash away the taste of the bitterness that filled her mouth.

*   *   *

"I was gobsmacked when Cilla McKee told me that Bill Ward, of all people, is her ex-husband," Penny said to Colin that evening as they video-chatted.

"I can imagine."

"I never bothered to Google Bill Ward because I thought I knew enough about him, but if I had, I suppose his ex-wife's name would have come up, although I'm not sure I would have realized that she's the same woman who runs the Snowdonia art gallery."

"Well now that you know about the relationship between Bill Ward and Sarah Spencer, are you going to do anything about it?"

"What do you mean, 'do anything about it'?"

"Well, like, tell the police."

"Why would I want to do that?"

"I don't know. Do you think it could be important?"

"I'm not sure if whatever's going on between Sarah Spencer and Bill Ward is connected to Jessica Graham's death, but there certainly seem to be bad feelings between the two of them.

When I was on my way to meet you for dinner in the hotel restaurant, I overheard Bill, on his mobile, saying something like, 'Now maybe she'll finally move out,' and it certainly sounds as if he was referring to Sarah. Several people, including you, overheard the two of them arguing in the hotel bar that Friday night, and I think it was Sarah he was shouting at from the car park at midnight, because the person he was speaking to was in the coffee shop, and that could only have been an employee. And given everything else, the logical person for that to have been is Sarah."

"She was probably locking up or making sure all the appliances were switched off or something like that. Doing one last check to make sure everything was shut down for the night."

"That makes sense. But the timing of their argument, the night before Jessica died—well, it may not have anything to do with her death, but it makes you think, doesn't it?"

She mulled all that over for a moment. "I should tell Bethan if I happen to be speaking to her. She always says to tell her everything, no matter how small or inconsequential it might seem, and she'll decide whether it's important or not. But the police aren't treating Jessica's death as suspicious. As far as I know, they're not even investigating it, so I don't think this really matters."

Colin's eyes flicked to the top of the screen to check the time. "I'm going to have to go in a minute. But before I do, congratulations again on being offered a place in the art gallery's Christmas exhibit. I'm so happy for you."

"I've been wanting to show in that gallery for a long time, so I'm really chuffed."

"I'll bet you are," said Colin. At that moment, the screen posted a "Connection lost" message, and he disappeared. She waited for him to ring her back, and a few minutes later he did.

"I've got to make this quick before we get disconnected again," he said. "The Wi-Fi's terrible here. I'll be wrapping up in a few more days," he added. "And then I'm between assignments. I thought I might stop off in the U.K. on my way home to Toronto. Would you like to meet up?"

"I'd like that very much."

"Good. Maybe take you up on that invitation to visit you in Llanelen?"

Penny indicated that would be fine with her, and Colin just had time to say, "Then I'll see you soon," before the connection was lost again.

# Chapter Thirteen

"Checking your watch every thirty seconds won't get his train here any faster," said Victoria. Penny lowered her wrist with a sheepish grin.

She'd insisted that she and Victoria set off from home to arrive at the Junction railway station with plenty of time to spare. Now, holding takeaway cups of coffee from the station buffet, they paced along the platform.

"How do you feel about seeing him again?" Victoria asked.

"A little nervous, but excited."

"But you like him, though?"

"I do. But it's early days."

"And he's stopping at the hotel?"

"We're both more comfortable with that arrangement. We've only known each other in person for a few days, although we video-chat almost every day, so it seems like longer. We don't want to rush into anything."

"Very wise."

"I thought I might invite him round to mine for dinner one evening."

"You? Make dinner?" Victoria grinned.

"Stop that. I can heat up ready meals and open a bottle of wine with the best of them."

Victoria laughed. "Well, that's true. Oh, and just to save any discussion later, I'm completely fine with you taking as much time off as you like whilst he's here. You deserve a bit of fun."

Finally, Penny was rewarded with the sight of the train coming into view. It slowed on approach to the platform, then stopped, and after a moment the doors slid open and passengers began to alight.

She scanned them anxiously until she saw the man she was looking for. His face lit up when he caught sight of her, and after allowing a woman with two small children to go ahead of him, he adjusted the camera bag on his shoulder and made his way along the platform toward her.

When he reached Penny, he set down his case and took her in his arms. After giving her a warm hug, he released her and stepped back, turning his attention to Victoria. After a casual but cheerful introduction, the three made their way to the car and set off for Llanelen.

Penny and Victoria were eager to hear about Colin's recent trip to Africa, and once he'd described the animals he'd photographed in great detail and answered their questions, he settled back to drink in the rolling hills and neat parcels of land in varying shades of green, stitched together with drystone walls, hedgerows, and stands of trees.

"They say the grass is greener," remarked Colin, "and in Wales it really is."

Penny followed his gaze. Everything they passed—granite cottages and farmhouses with slate roofs, streams, woodlands, bridges—was drenched in late summer sunshine, and she saw the beauty of it all through fresh, appreciative eyes.

Finally, the narrow, twisting country roads brought them to Llanelen's bridge spanning the River Conwy, and Victoria slowed the car as they approached it.

"Here we are," said Penny. "My favourite teahouse is just there on the left, and right across from it there"—she pointed to the other side of the river—"is our Spa, where Victoria and I work." Colin made all the right admiring noises, and a minute later they pulled into the car park of the Red Dragon Hotel.

"No need to come in with me," Colin assured them. "I'm looking forward to a shower and a nap, and then I might take a stroll around the town." After thanking Victoria for the lift from the station, he and Penny got out of the car.

They stood there, Colin holding his bags, as Victoria drove away to return her car to its parking place.

"I'll see you after work," he said to Penny, then gave her a light kiss on the cheek. Just as he straightened and they stepped apart, Penny caught sight of Mrs. Lloyd and her companion, Florence Semble, watching them from the pavement.

"Oh, Mrs. Lloyd won't let that go," she whispered to Colin, and sure enough, a moment later the two women walked toward them.

"Hello," said Mrs. Lloyd, her blue eyes twinkling as she looked from Penny to Colin. Penny introduced them, and Mrs. Lloyd asked, "And how long will you be staying here in Llanelen?"

"Not exactly sure," Colin replied. "Depends. A few days anyway."

"Oh well, we'd love to have you for dinner whilst you're here," said Mrs. Lloyd. "Wouldn't we, Florence?" When

Florence indicated that, yes, they would, Mrs. Lloyd said, "Well, what about tomorrow evening? We'd love to hear all about your adventures."

"Didn't I hear Alwynne Gwilt was with you on this painting excursion?" Florence asked.

"Yes, that's right," said Penny. "She was."

"Well, what if we invited her and Medwyn and a few others, and instead of dinner, we had a little get-together at a drinks party?"

"Oh, that's a lovely idea!" exclaimed Mrs. Lloyd. "I'm sure Thomas and Bronwyn Evans would love to meet Colin. He's our local rector, see," she explained, addressing Colin directly, "and very interested in wildlife, he is. Used to be out birdwatching in all kinds of weather. Of course, she's only interested in their little cairn terrier, but no matter. And Victoria would come, of course, and one or two we haven't thought of yet."

"Oh, but we wouldn't want to put you to any trouble," protested Penny.

"It wouldn't be any trouble," said Florence. "A few bottles of wine and some cheese straws. In fact, it would be less trouble than a dinner. But why don't we say Monday evening, if you're free? That'll give us more time to get organized, and we can give our guests a bit of extra notice."

When Penny and Colin agreed to the date, Mrs. Lloyd said, "Well, that's settled then. We'll get the invitations out and look forward to seeing you Monday evening."

The two women set off for home to put their party plans in motion, and Colin and Penny turned to each other.

"I'll have to buy a new shirt for that," said Colin, "although I really don't want to because I keep the clothes I travel with to a minimum. I could always donate it to a charity shop when I leave, I suppose, or maybe the hotel has a laundry service."

"I doubt it runs to that."

"Well, I'm sure there's a laundromat."

"Laundrette we call it here." Penny thought for a moment. "But look. Here's the easy answer. Why don't you come to mine for dinner tonight, bring your laundry, and we'll do it there. That'll save time and bother, and you'll have clean clothes for the rest of your stay."

"That would be great. Even though most of my work clothes are the kind that don't need washing very often, I'd like to be wearing a clean, decent shirt when I meet your friends."

"Well, enjoy your nap and I'll meet you in the hotel reception just after five. But if you feel like doing something between now and then, there are some swans down by the bridge that would probably enjoy having their picture taken."

# Chapter Fourteen

"I don't know about you, but I don't like eating stodgy stuff in summer," said Penny as they walked along the riverbank on the way to her cottage. "So I just got us some cheese, cooked ham, lovely fresh bread rolls from the bakery, and a couple of salads."

"Perfect," said Colin. "I got beer and wine."

It had been an unusually warm day, and a light breeze made walking pleasant. Colin adjusted his stride to match Penny's, and they fell into an easy rhythm, chatting comfortably, until they reached fields hemmed in by drystone walls with stones on the top, laid on their edges to give the wall a finished appearance.

"That's where the agricultural show is held each autumn," Penny remarked. "Not much further to go now."

A few minutes later they arrived at Penny's door, which had recently been painted a hazy grey-green. She unlocked it and stepped aside to allow Colin to enter. He glanced at the cozy sitting room with its calm, quiet colours, and then turned to Penny.

"It's beautiful. It's exactly what I imagined your place would be like."

"Go through. Let's get all your stuff in the kitchen." They unpacked the food, placing most of it in the refrigerator, and then loaded Colin's laundry into the washing machine.

"Right," said Penny, taking a wine glass and a tall tumbler from the cupboard. "Why don't we take our drinks outside, and we'll think about eating in a few minutes."

She unlocked the back door, and Harrison, her grey cat, led the way to a secluded area with a table and two chairs. Climbing roses in a soft shade of pink contrasted with the grey stone wall that supported them.

"I'm envious of your beautiful home," said Colin when they were seated.

"Tell me about your home in Toronto."

"We lived in a condo on the forty-eighth floor of a downtown tower. It was what you'd expect. Open concept, with lots of glass, a couple of terraces with tables and chairs like these ones. We had panoramic views of the city, and to the south you could see all the way to Lake Ontario. At night, with millions of lights in the high rises and sky scrapers all around us lit up, it was breathtaking."

"So what happened to the apartment? Did you sell it when you broke up?"

He shook his head. "She still lives there. It's close to her work, and she just didn't have time to deal with trying to sell it. Now I keep a little place in the west end of Toronto, near the airport. I still have friends in the city, and I like going home when I can. In fact, my next assignment is in Canada, with a team of British and Canadian scientists studying the changing habitat of our polar bears on the Hudson Bay coast. But I'm spending more time in Europe and Africa, so I'm starting to think a base here would be a good idea, too."

He drained the last of his beer, stood up, and gestured at her wine glass.

"Going to get another. Would you like more wine?"

"I'll come with you. The wash cycle should be finished, and we can start thinking about supper. I'm sure you're hungry." After dealing with the laundry and helping themselves to the food Penny had bought, they carried fresh drinks and laden plates back to the table and settled in for dinner.

"You've done a brilliant job of making a life for yourself here in Wales," said Colin. "I envy you. Your friends, your cottage . . ."

"Oh, but I didn't earn this cottage," said Penny, with an appreciative glance at it. "I was fortunate, very fortunate, to inherit it from the first friend I made here in Llanelen. Emma Teasdale, she was called. I miss her. There's a lovely painting of her in the sitting room."

Colin reached for a bread roll. "Speaking of painting, how are your preparations going for the art show?"

"I've taken the paintings Cilla accepted for the exhibit to be framed. To be honest, I was surprised so many made it in. She only rejected two."

"Here's a tip from one who knows. Don't use the word 'reject.' Not a word creative types like us need to hear."

"You're right. She excluded two paintings. Better?"

"Better. Did she give you a reason?"

"She said she didn't like the content. Said she didn't want to look at it."

"Really! Everything here seems so beautiful. What was it?"

Penny leaned forward. "Now this is really interesting. They were the paintings I did of the Georgian terrace in Beaumaris. The ones I was working on that Sunday morning when Bill Ward crept up on me and I used you as an excuse to get out of going to lunch with him by saying you and I were going for fish and chips. Remember?"

Colin tipped his head slightly to one side. "I do remember, and very good fish and chips they were, too. But it's odd she didn't like those paintings. I thought you did a terrific job, and I liked them very much."

"The terrace stirs bad memories for her."

"How's that?"

"I didn't have the chance to go into all this with you the other evening when we were chatting, because the Wi-Fi was disconnecting, but the apartment that's for sale belongs to none other than Bill Ward. That's why he knew so much about the building's history when I was sat in front of it, painting, and he came along."

"That is interesting."

"It gets better. Listen to this. He left his wife—that's Cilla McKee, the gallery manager, remember?—for Sarah Spencer, now assistant manager at the Beaumaris Arms Hotel. Or manageress, as they say over here."

They took a moment to reflect on that, and then Colin brought out his phone. "Let me check something." He tapped a few times, then replaced it in his shirt pocket.

"How would you feel about an outing to Anglesey tomorrow? I just checked the weather, and it's meant to be perfect."

"I'd love that."

"And while we're there, what if we were to look over that apartment that's for sale?" Penny's eyes widened and a slow grin spread across her face.

"There's a bus we could take," she suggested.

"No, I'll rent a car and we'll drive. That way we'll have more freedom to go where we like. And how would you feel about spending a night or two at the Beaumaris Arms Hotel?"

"That sounds lovely."

"Good. I'll make the arrangements."

Penny, wearing only a light pullover, shivered as they finished their meal. The sunshine of earlier in the day was losing its warmth as the sun sank lower in the sky. A dusty shaft of mellow gold shone through the clouds, lighting up their faces, indicating that evening was drawing in.

Penny suggested they have coffee in the sitting room.

When she had laid out a coffee tray, Colin picked it up, carried it through to the sitting room, and set it on the low table in front of the sofa. As he leaned back into the sofa, he extended his arm, and she sank into the warm curve of his body. He wrapped his arm around her and pulled her closer as she rested her head lightly on his shoulder.

"I know we haven't known each other very long," he said, "but I missed you. The whole time I was away, I couldn't stop thinking about you." She turned her face to him, and he leaned forward and kissed her. When they released each other, their coffee was almost cold.

Finally, Colin stood up. "It's getting late. I'd best get back to the hotel. I'll aim to pick you up in the morning about nine, but if there are problems with the car arrangements, I'll call you."

"Oh," said Penny, "your laundry. But since you're coming back in the morning anyway, there's no point in bothering with that now unless you need something. Sure you can find your way back to town?"

He held up his phone. "I can find my way through jungle, forest, savannah, any terrain you care to name. A friendly Welsh town is a piece of cake."

One last, lingering embrace later, Penny reluctantly closed the door behind him, and after putting away the leftover food and tidying up the kitchen, she opened the door of the washer/dryer and removed his clean, dry clothes.

She set them on the table and sorted them. She picked up a shirt, looked at the label, and then did something she hadn't done in a very long time—she plugged in her iron. While she waited for it to heat up, she bunched the shirt in both hands and held it to her nose. She breathed in the fresh laundry scent but was searching for something deeper. Him. And then, she placed the shirt on the ironing board, smoothed it out, and ironed it. But instead of folding it and placing it with the rest of the clean clothes in the carryall, she carried it upstairs and hung it in her wardrobe, where it lined up perfectly with her own clothes.

# Chapter Fifteen

"What's the strangest or most interesting vehicle you've driven?" Penny asked the next day as they sped along the A55 on their way to the Isle of Anglesey. "And where was it?"

Colin focused on the road ahead while he considered his reply. And then he said, "Africa. And someone told me it was a World War Two Jeep that the Americans had left behind. And based on the grinding of the gears, it very well could have been. The thing was so loud, the seats were so hard, and I'm sure it had no shock absorbers. Those African tracks are so rough, I was afraid the whole thing would collapse at every pothole. It was the noisiest, smelliest, roughest, most uncomfortable ride I've ever had. But the great thing was, there was something really special on the back seat that made the trip so memorable."

"Oh? What was it?"

"A lion cub."

"Really? How did that happen?

"Long story, but the cub was being transported to a sanctuary for orphans, and I volunteered to drive it."

"So you had your own *Born Free* moment?"

He grinned. "I did."

They approached the magnificent Telford suspension bridge that connects the North Wales mainland with the Isle of Anglesey, and joined the slow-moving queue of traffic. Finally, they crossed the bridge, drove through the Victorian town of Menai Bridge, and headed toward Beaumaris. The winding country road offered stunning views of Snowdonia on their right, and the sun filtering through the hedgerows that flanked the road cast patterns of shifting light and shadows.

"What time is our viewing of the apartment?" Penny asked.

"Two. Plenty of time for lunch. What are you in the mood for? Fish and chips again?"

"No, not today, thanks. Actually, I rarely eat fish and chips. I don't know why I suggested them that day when I was trying to get out of having lunch with that awful Bill Ward. For some reason, it just popped into my head."

"So what would you like to do then?"

"It's such a beautiful day, I'd like to just pick up a sandwich and eat outdoors and maybe walk around for a bit until it's time to see the apartment."

"Sounds good. We might just as well park at the hotel. We can walk everywhere from there."

\* \* \*

"I can't wait to see it," Penny whispered as they walked up the short, flagged path that led to the stone steps at the entrance of the end house on the terrace. "I love the symmetry of Georgian houses. Show me a fan light over a front door, and I'm beside myself with excitement."

Colin pointed to the glossy black door with its knocker in the shape of a lion's head and then raised his hand to the fan light above it.

As Penny laughed, a man with a freshly scrubbed face and a youthful cowlick, wearing a pair of summer trousers, a casual shirt, and an eager-to-please expression, opened the front door, which was flanked by two bay trees in concrete pots. He held out his hand and introduced himself as Dylan Rees, and after the usual exchange of pleasantries about how far they had driven and, "Isn't the weather fine, but we might get some rain later," he offered each a brochure.

"It's my honour and great pleasure to show you over this desirable property this afternoon," he said. "And once you've seen it, you'll understand why it completely deserves its Grade One heritage designation. Although," he added as he stepped to one side to allow them to enter, "judging from your accents, you're Americans, so you might not know what that means."

Penny and Colin exchanged an amused glance. "I've lived in Wales for quite some time, so I'm familiar with listed buildings," said Penny. "It means a building or structure of historical or architectural significance," she added for Colin's benefit.

"And we're Canadians," he told the estate agent. "But lots of people mix us up. The difference between a Canadian accent and some American accents can be subtle."

"Right. Well then, here we are." They found themselves in a beautiful, airy entrance hall, where the temperature was several degrees cooler than outside. After pointing out the details of the intricate plaster molded ceiling, he led them into what he described as a "superbly proportioned drawing room."

The room was flooded with light from tall windows. After allowing Penny and Colin a few minutes to take in the lofty ceiling and then admire the view from the arched window to the village green, and across the Menai Strait to the majestic mountains of Snowdonia, he indicated their next stop would be the dining room.

"It's a good thing you're interested in viewing this property now," he said. "It's been tied up for a while."

"Oh? Was it taken off the market?" Colin asked.

"Not exactly." He adjusted a pair of candlesticks flanking a photograph in a silver frame on a side table. "No, it's just there's been an ongoing dispute about possession between the woman who's been living here and the actual owner of the unit. It's owned by her former partner, and they had been living here together, but when they broke up, she refused to move out." And then, unable to resist adding in a bit of sales promotion, he added, "Well, you've only to look around this beautiful period property to understand why she would be so attached to it. But because she was the equivalent of a sitting tenant, the sale became, well, let's just say complicated. But apparently they've now reached an agreement, and although she hasn't moved out yet, the sale can go ahead with no further problems anticipated."

"Problem solved," said Colin.

"Well, yes. But the thing is, their personal effects haven't been removed, so the apartment doesn't show as well as it might. Her furniture might not be to your taste, so please try to look beyond that, to the beautiful elegance of the apartment itself. Originally this end unit was one grand house, and now it's three apartments, but to my mind, this unit is the best of the lot because it's spread out over two floors."

As they prepared to leave the room, the photograph on the side table caught Penny's attention. It showed a couple standing in front of a heavy door, and while she was sure the woman was a younger Sarah Spencer, the man was definitely not Bill Ward. She was about to pick it up for a closer look when the real estate agent cleared his throat. "We'll just have a look in the butler's pantry and kitchen before we head upstairs," he said. "And the kitchen will seem a little dated, but the vendor has advised that he intends to have it renovated to a high standard, along with the butler's pantry, before contracts are exchanged."

The kitchen was dated, but Penny took one look at the cream-coloured Aga cooker and remarked, "I do hope the Aga stays."

"Oh, I'm sure it will," the estate agent assured her. "Who wouldn't want one of those? Now, as we head upstairs, I want you to take particular note of the turned staircase and the mahogany handrail. It's one of the most beautiful features of this property." He stepped aside. "After you."

As they ascended the stairs, Penny paused to run her fingertips over the smooth handrail, allowing the estate agent to pass her. As she did so, she caught Colin's attention by touching his hand, and with her back angled to the estate agent, she mouthed, "That photo." He gave her a quick nod of understanding, and when they reached the top of the stairs, Colin exclaimed, "Oh, I must have left my brochure downstairs. I'll be right back. You go on ahead and I'll catch up with you." He bounded lightly down the stairs, and Penny and the estate agent entered the first room. "Now this is currently being used as an upstairs sitting room, but it would make a beautiful office, or of course it could be used as an additional bedroom. It's situated right above the main sitting room, and it features the same tall, arched windows."

Penny glanced out the window at the view of the Menai Strait, and as she turned back to the room, Colin entered, holding his brochure and wearing a conspiratorial smile. The viewing continued with two more bedrooms and a tastefully remodelled bathroom with a roll top tub, and then they made their way down a set of backstairs to the ground floor and a look at a private, enclosed garden, similar to the one at Penny's cottage.

"Well, thank you very much for showing us the property," Colin said as they retraced their steps through the kitchen to the entrance hall.

"I've got to run along to my next appointment," said Dylan Rees, handing each a business card, "but here's my contact information if you have any questions or you'd like to request a second viewing. And especially if you want to make an offer."

"What did you think?" Colin asked as they walked toward the hotel. "Did you like it?"

"I loved it," Penny said. "It's beautiful. What did you think?"

"What really shocks me is that that lovely two-storey apartment, in a building that was beautifully constructed almost two hundred years ago, costs less than a condo in downtown Toronto with glass walls that will start falling out in about fifteen years."

"Do you know what's the best thing about Georgian buildings?" Penny asked as they entered the hotel.

"What's that?"

"Real Georgian people once lived in them." She paused. "I loved the feeling of placing my hand on the very same spot on that banister where, two hundred years ago, a Georgian lady placed hers. To feel that living connection to the past."

# Chapter Sixteen

When they'd checked in and were settled on a sofa in the hotel lounge, with cups of coffee and a slice of cake to share, Colin took out his phone and opened it to the photo he'd taken in the dining room of the apartment. Penny nestled into his shoulder, and the two of them studied it.

"That's definitely her," Penny said. "Sarah Spencer. Even though she's younger and her hair is lighter there. Or maybe it's just the way the light is. But who's that man she's with?"

"I have no idea," Colin said as they continued to peer at the image. "But then I don't know many people here. Does he look familiar to you?" Penny lifted her head and their eyes met. When she returned to her comfortable position resting against him, Colin used his thumb and forefinger to enlarge the image so they could focus on the man's face.

"Possibly," said Penny. "But if I've seen him before, I can't place him." She thought for a moment. "I wonder if he could be her husband. Cilla McKee mentioned that Sarah had been married, and her husband moved away, leaving her free to take up with Bill Ward. But if that is her husband, I haven't a clue where I would have seen him."

Colin shrank the image back to its normal size. "What kind of door is that? If we can work out the location, that might help."

"It looks like a solid door, with that arch at the top, and fancy red brick work around it," said Penny. "And with those raised panels it looks substantial."

"The paintwork has that thick glossiness that comes from many coats," said Colin, "So the door is probably old. But it doesn't look like it belongs on a typical private home, does it? What kind of building would have an important-looking door like that?"

"A National Trust property?" Penny suggested.

"Or a hotel?"

"That could be it," agreed Penny. "In fact, that makes sense. Cilla said that Sarah was working at a country house hotel when she and Ward met. Country house hotels tend to be old, so this photo could have been taken at that hotel. Let's see if we can get a closer look at her face." Once again Colin enlarged the image, and Penny peered at the screen. "Yes, she looks younger here. What do you think?"

"I can't really say. I've only seen her a couple of times, and I didn't take too much notice of her in the bar that first night, to be honest. I bought a drink, and then I met you, and after that, you were all I could think about."

"Really? That's so sweet."

"Of course, really." He shifted away from her to free his arm. "Here, I'll email you the image." After he had sent it, he placed his arm around her shoulder, pulled her into him, and settled her back into the sofa. They settled back into the sofa. Penny gave him a warm smile, then turned her attention back to the image. "So perhaps this man she's with was someone she was involved with when she worked at that other hotel, before she came here."

While they pondered that, two boisterous boys bounded into the lounge, followed by their parents. The man, carrying a laden tea tray, looked about for a place for them all to sit, and the woman just looked exhausted. The children jumped on two facing sofas, and the man set the tray down on the table between them. The woman then took care of pouring tea, buttering scones, handing everything round, and when she'd made sure that everyone else had something to eat and drink, she leaned her head against the back of the sofa and closed her eyes. After a moment she rallied, picked up a cup, and took a sip of tea.

"She looks as if she could do with a relaxing massage or a bit of pampering in your Spa," remarked Colin, "while dad looks after the kids."

"She could do with a nap first, I think," said Penny. She stiffened and then sat up.

"You've just given me an idea, and I don't know why we never thought of this before. There's a great business opportunity here. I need to speak to the manager." She stood up. "Wait here. I'll be back."

"If I'm not here, I'll be in the bar."

"Good idea. I'll see you there."

\*   \*   \*

"Well?" Colin asked half an hour later as a smiling Penny slid into the chair beside him. The bar was almost empty.

"I talked to the manager," Penny said, "and he's interested in the idea of our operating a capsule spa in the hotel, so I've sent his details to Victoria, and she'll follow up and get things rolling."

"Well, that sounds good." He gestured at the glass of white wine at Penny's place. "I got that for you. Hope it's what you wanted."

Penny picked it up. "It's perfect, thank you. But listen, as soon as I saw the manager just now, I realized he looked a bit like the man in that photo with Sarah. I just saw him briefly here in the bar on the Friday night when he offered to take over from Sarah, so maybe that's why I thought he looked familiar. He looks older now, though, so it's hard to say, and I can't be sure."

"I don't suppose you mentioned the photo to him?"

"I didn't get a chance. I wanted to get to the business about the Spa service in the hotel. And besides, I wouldn't have been sure what to ask or how to position it. When you think about it, it's strange displaying a photo of you with your boss in your home. I mean, I'm Eirlys's boss, and I'd be shocked if she put up a photo of the two of us."

Colin laughed. "Thinking about some of the idiots I've worked for, you're right. The last thing I'd have in my dining room would be a photo of some guy I worked with. But maybe he was more to her than just her boss."

"An office romance, you mean?" She thought for a moment. "Could be. He's the manager here at the hotel, and she reports to him now, but back then they could have been just colleagues. Of course there could be a perfectly innocent reason why she'd have a framed photo of him in her home. If it really is him. I'm not sure that it is."

Colin took a sip of beer as he contemplated young Llifon behind the bar drying glasses and putting them away. "I wonder if he knows anything about the relationship between Sarah and the manager. If you've told me his name, I don't remember it."

Penny took a business card out of her pocket and showed it to him. "Martin Hewitt, manager." She tucked the card in her handbag. "And actually, Llifon did tell me something interesting about the two of them. I'd forgotten about it until just now."

"What was that?"

"Llifon said that on the Thursday afternoon before the painting weekend, Sarah and Hewitt were in his office together, and then she came out looking upset. So much so that he— that's Llifon—thought maybe she'd been fired."

"Oh, right. I remember your saying that now."

"I wonder what happened in there."

Colin glanced at Llifon, who was engrossed in his phone. "He doesn't seem terribly busy, so now might be a good time to speak to him. He might have heard something since you last spoke to him."

"Let me think. I need to find a way into that conversation that he won't find alarming or that will shut him down."

"Maybe mention that you've spoken to Hewitt about opening a spa service here?"

A moment later Penny was at the bar. Llifon glanced up and placed his phone on a shelf, out of sight.

"Hi Llifon. Could I have a packet of crisps, please?"

"Yeah, sure. What flavour?"

"Oh, just the regular lightly salted kind, please."

Penny accepted the packet and handed Llifon a coin. As he stepped toward the cash register to ring in the sale, she walked along her side of the bar to keep even with him and said, "I just had a brief chat with Martin Hewitt about the possibility of my partner and me opening a spa service in the hotel."

"A spa service? For the ladies, like? Cool."

"Yes, we think it could prove really popular. But now, there's just something bothering me. It's probably nothing, but when you and I spoke earlier, you mentioned that Sarah looked upset when she left the meeting with Martin Hewitt on the Thursday afternoon before the painting weekend. Naturally, if we're going to be doing business with the hotel, I just wondered if everything's okay here, and if you'd heard anything more about what happened during that meeting."

Llifon frowned and sucked in his breath. "Something's going on, that's for sure. The food and beverage manager told the staff that the auditors are coming in early next week but that we shouldn't worry about it, we should just keep doing our jobs. But I don't know if that had anything to do with what happened between Sarah and Mr. Hewitt."

"Oh, I see. Well, it's probably just routine."

She returned to Colin and set the bag of crisps on the table. "Well?" he said.

"An audit's going to take place next week, and it doesn't sound as if it was planned. I wonder if some irregularities have been discovered and that's why Sarah looked so upset when she left the manager's office that Thursday."

"But that was weeks ago. Believe me, at the slightest whiff of any financial impropriety, any employee suspected of wrongdoing would have been on immediate leave, and the auditors would have been on the doorstep first thing the next morning."

"Well, that couldn't have been what upset her, then."

They sipped their drinks, and then Colin said, "There's a sunrise boat cruise around Puffin Island, and I wondered if you'd like to do that. It would mean getting up early, but if the weather's fine, the views should be spectacular, and they serve coffee and a continental breakfast on board."

"That sounds like fun. Let's do it."

\* \* \*

The next morning, just as the stars were fading and the blackness of night was giving way to the deep blues that signalled the coming dawn, the night porter unlocked the hotel's back door, and Penny and Colin slipped out into the quiet, empty street.

At the sound of a light humming, swooshing noise, they turned to see a milkman making his early morning deliveries in an electric-powered vehicle. He glided past them and then slowed to a stop at one of the units in the Georgian terrace. The glass bottles in the metal rack he carried made a gentle clinking sound as he crossed the road, deposited two full bottles on a doorstep, picked up two empty bottles, returned to his vehicle, and with a friendly little wave as he passed Penny and Colin, continued on his round.

"I didn't know home milk delivery is still a thing," Colin said. "I thought that service disappeared years ago, when people started shopping at supermarkets."

"It's making a comeback here," Penny replied. "There's a real nostalgic appeal to it. Plus, the glass bottles are recyclable, and some people are willing to pay a bit more to avoid plastic. Some shops even have milk stations where you fill the bottles yourself."

"I'm glad to hear that."

# Chapter Seventeen

"Penny, Colin. Welcome! Do come in," said Mrs. Lloyd on Monday evening as she threw open the door of her home on Rosemary Lane. "A few of our friends are already here, so please, go on through."

They entered the sitting room to find the rector offering glasses of wine to Penny's friends and neighbours, and a moment later Florence appeared with a plate of cheese straws and warm, puffy mini quiches.

"Please, let me pass these around," Colin said to Florence, holding out his hands. "It'll make me very popular with everyone."

Florence handed over the plate, and with Penny at his side, introducing him, they circled the room. When the last cheese straw had been snapped up, he set the plate down and was immediately approached by the Rev. Thomas Evans, who was taking a break from his wine-pouring duties. As the two struck up a lively conversation about the joys of birdwatching, Penny spotted her painting partner, Alwynne Gwilt, across the room and joined her.

Just as she was about to describe the most interesting aspect of the boat ride around Puffin Island, Detective Inspector Bethan Morgan appeared in the doorway. Her turquoise trousers paired with a bright pink jacket, loose hair, and red lipstick indicated she was off duty.

Nevertheless, all heads turned in the policewoman's direction, and as conversation stilled, she and Penny locked eyes.

"Excuse me, Alwynne," Penny said. "I get the feeling Bethan wants a word with me."

The conversation in the room resumed as Penny made her way over to Bethan, who remained just inside the doorway.

"How's it going?" Penny greeted her.

"Good, good. Are you enjoying the party?"

"Oh yes. You haven't met Colin yet, have you? Come and let me introduce you."

"In a minute. Okay if we just have a quick word first?" She ducked into the hallway and indicated that Penny should follow her. "It's about Jessica Graham. Something's not quite right and it's bothering me. We found a suitcase in her room, just as you'd expect, and we've examined the contents. But I would also expect a journalist on foreign assignment to have another bag with work materials in it. Notebooks, photocopies, research documents, maybe a file or two, newspaper cuttings and definitely a laptop. Important stuff. But we didn't find anything like that in her room or anywhere near where her body was found. And believe me, we searched the area near the lighthouse thoroughly, looking for it."

"She did have that," said Penny. "When Colin and I spoke to her on the Friday evening in the bar, she had a backpack. A black one. She leaned it against the wall, and she was most particular to tuck the straps out of the way. The bar was full, and I guess she did that to prevent anyone tripping over them. I thought that was considerate of her. And she kept her business cards in a side pocket."

"Ah. That would be it, then. I knew there had to be a bag like that. And her passport was probably in it, too, because it wasn't in her room, and that's usually the one thing travellers are careful to keep safe."

"Maybe she had the backpack with her when she . . . I don't even know how to put this into words," said Penny. "I can't bring myself to say 'when she fell off the cliff' because I'm having a hard time accepting that she did fall. I think something more sinister happened."

"I know you think that," said Bethan, "but we haven't got anything to support that theory."

"Something about where the body was lying when I found it just wasn't right. It wasn't where I would have expected it to be if she'd fallen, but then as Colin and I discussed, it's possible the tide could have moved it further out."

After a pause, Bethan replied. "If there's nothing to indicate something sinister happened, I can't allow myself to speculate. Speculation and conjecture just mean guessing. I have to be precise and exact, and go where the evidence leads. And so far we haven't been able to turn up anything to show that Jessica Graham's death was anything other than a tragic accident. The forensics and the postmortem both point to that."

"Then apparently my weakness is guess work. I tend to leap to conclusions."

"Look, Penny, here's the thing. We've spoken to her work colleagues and her family, and there's nothing to suggest that she had any reason or was in a state of mind to take her own life. So we can rule that out."

"We can agree on that," said Penny. "When Colin and I spoke to her on Friday night, she was positively fizzing with excitement and looking forward enormously to working on stories."

"So that leaves either accident or murder. And if you're talking about murder, it's not like there was a long list of people who knew her and hated her and wanted her dead. There wasn't even a short list. How could there have been? She'd only just arrived in the country, and she didn't know anybody. So I'm really stretched to think of a motive."

Bethan glanced through the doorway at the guests in the sitting room, and when Penny did not reply, she continued. "Right. So we have to go with the pathologist's finding that her death was accidental, unless we can find some evidence that would open up a new line of inquiry."

"What kind of evidence?"

"A witness would be helpful. Someone who saw or heard something suspicious. Or material evidence—something tangible. The thing is, the pathologist didn't find any evidence of a struggle. Everything he found was consistent with injuries she would have sustained in a fall, and that's really all we have to go on. I can't make this case into something it's not.

"But still, having said all that, the backpack bothers me, and I keep coming back to it. It's a loose end, and detectives don't like loose ends. I need to find out what happened to it." She let out a defeated sigh. "Still, it's possible that Jessica was carrying the backpack on the beach, and the tide managed to take it, so we may have to accept that's what happened. We may never know."

"You just said you weren't going to speculate," Penny muttered.

"You've given me a lot to think about, I'll give you that," said Bethan just as Mrs. Lloyd joined them in the hallway.

"You've probably come right off your shift and haven't had your tea," Mrs. Lloyd said to Bethan. "Would you like me to ask Florence to make you something? She does a lovely creamy scrambled eggs on toast, and we might even have some smoked salmon to go with it. I'm sure she wouldn't mind making something specially for you."

"That's very kind, but I'm all right."

"Oh well, if you're sure." Mrs. Lloyd disappeared into the kitchen and emerged a moment later with a tray of warm canapés that she held out to Bethan, who selected a cheese and spinach mini quiche. She popped it in her mouth and said, "Oh, that's good," then reached for another.

"Well, I'm sure you two were discussing important matters," said Mrs. Lloyd, "so I'll leave you to it." She looked from one to the other, as if hoping one of them would fill her in on what they'd been discussing, but when nothing was forthcoming, she drifted away with her tray into the sitting room.

The sound of Bethan's mobile ringing broke what could have become an uneasy silence had Colin not caught Penny's eye. Just as she was about to excuse herself to rejoin him, Bethan glanced at the number and said, "Sorry. I have to take this." She listened for a moment and then took a step in the direction of the front door. She paused, then said to Penny over her shoulder, "I have to go. But I also came here to tell you that you should expect a visitor."

\* \* \*

125

"Expect a visitor?" said Victoria when Penny recounted her conversation with Bethan as the party was drawing to a close. "Is she channelling the ghost of Jacob Marley?"

"I don't know," said Penny. "She got a phone call and left before she could give me any details. But we'll see what happens, I guess."

"You look troubled," said Colin. "Did she say something to upset you?

"Not really. We were discussing how Jessica Graham died. Bethan said the police don't have anything to go on beyond that it was an accident, but I can't shake the feeling that there's more to it."

"Then she should listen to you," Victoria suggested. "You have good instincts about these things. Maybe the police need to dig deeper."

"I think they do."

"Do the police listen to you?" Colin asked.

"I offer insights and suggestions when I can," said Penny, "and sometimes they listen to me."

"Oh, Penny, you're being much too modest," said Victoria. "You've helped the police solve, what, six or seven murders?"

"That's astonishing," said Colin. "I thought you were just interested in what happened because you found the girl's body. You did mention that you'd helped out with a few cases in the past, but I had no idea there was rather more to it than that."

"Does it bother you?" Victoria asked. "That Penny's into solving crimes?"

"No, not at all. It just seems such a—well, I wouldn't use the word 'strange,' but it is unusual. Isn't it? I mean, I've never met anyone else, who wasn't a police officer, who does that. So you're, what, an armchair detective?"

"You could probably call me an amateur sleuth," said Penny.

"She doesn't go looking for it," said Victoria. "Murder just has a way of finding her." She threw him a sly look. "You might just have to get used to that."

\* \* \*

"Our guests stayed a little longer than I thought they would," remarked Mrs. Lloyd as she and Florence tidied up after the party. "We should have little get-togethers like this more often. Everyone seemed to be having such a good time."

"It was lovely to see Penny enjoying herself," said Florence as she stacked used plates and glasses on a tray. "I don't think she stopped smiling the whole time, except after her conversation with the policewoman. She was positively lit up. And him. He seems like a nice chap. What did you make of him?"

"Made for each other."

"He seemed a little taken aback when he learned that she's solved some murders."

"Oh, that. Pfft." Mrs. Lloyd dismissed Penny's accomplishments as she tossed a bunch of crumpled paper napkins on the tray. "The police would have got to the bottom of those cases anyway, without her help." Florence responded by giving her one of her looks over the top of her glasses. "Yes, all right, Florence, point taken, but to be fair, she wouldn't have got nearly as far as she did solving those murders without the benefit of my local knowledge. But enough about that. Did you see the way he looked at her? When she was over by the window, talking to Alwynne, and he was stood over here with Thomas, he couldn't take his eyes off her. His eyes followed her everywhere."

"She did look rather pretty the way the light fell on her," said Florence. "And that green frock she had on was so becoming. It must be new; I don't think I've seen it on her before. She really is looking rather remarkable. There's something about her eyes—there's a sparkle in them. When she smiles, she looks so young and fresh. She's positively glowing."

"Oh, Florence. There's no mystery there! It's as plain as can be. Can't you tell? They're in love." Mrs. Lloyd rubbed her hands together as a broad smile lit up her face. "We're going to be shopping for new outfits and fancy hats, you and me. You mark my words: those two will be married within a year."

"They've only known each other a few weeks, so it's early days," said Florence.

"Sometimes all it takes is a few weeks. Or even less. The very first time I laid eyes on my Arthur, stood outside his fruit and veg shop in his green apron, I just knew he was the man for me."

"He didn't stand a chance," said Florence. She folded her arms and surveyed the now tidied-up room with some satisfaction.

Mrs. Lloyd laughed. "No, I suppose he didn't. But, oh, what wonderful times we had, Florence. We were so happy together. It's on days like this I miss him terribly." Florence did not reply, but gave her friend a soft, sympathetic smile, then set the laden tray on an old-fashioned tea wagon and trundled off with it into the kitchen.

# Chapter Eighteen

"So he's gone," said Victoria as she and Penny made their morning coffee in the Spa's staff kitchen.

"Yes. Left early this morning. He had to return the hire car, and then off to the airport."

"When will you see him again—did he say?"

"He's going to be out of touch for at least a couple of weeks. He'll be working in the far north, and there probably won't be Wi-Fi and masts for mobile phones, and all the rest of it. So I have to wait to hear from him."

Victoria removed her cup from the coffee brewer and then stepped aside to allow Penny access to the machine. "Well, I'm sure he won't be gone a minute longer than necessary. And in the meantime, we've got lots to do here to keep you busy, including a meeting with Sarah Spencer today about our offering a spa service at the Beaumaris Arms. Which was a great idea, by the way. We're going to do really well out of it."

"I'd like to take credit for it, but actually it was Colin's idea. But we're meeting her today? Why didn't you tell me?"

"I just found out myself a few minutes ago, when I checked my email, so I'm telling you now. She's coming here for a site visit and to see what kinds of services we offer. And really, to see if the hotel wants to partner up with us."

"Well, can we suggest she get her hair done? It's so dry and needs a professional colour. Alberto could do wonders with it."

"That's not a bad idea. Let's give her a voucher for hair and a manicure."

"A voucher's a great idea. After all, she gave me a voucher for a couple of nights at the hotel." Penny pressed the "Start" button on the coffee brewer. "But in this case, instead of giving her a voucher, why don't we offer to give her a manicure and haircut and colour today, after she's had a tour? That way, she'll leave feeling extra positive about us."

"Good idea. Manicure first, then hair. Is Eirlys free around, say, four this afternoon?"

"Oh, I wasn't thinking Eirlys would do her manicure. I'd like to do this one myself."

Victoria raised a perfectly shaped eyebrow. "I have no idea what you're up to, but go on then. I'll ring her now and see if she has time today."

By the time Penny's coffee was brewed and she'd unwrapped a muffin from the bakery, Victoria was back.

"Sarah was thrilled. She says she never has time for herself, and presented with the offer of getting hair and nails done at no cost to her, and on company time, how could she say no?"

*Right,* thought Penny. *Now I just have to work out what I'm going to ask her.*

\* \* \*

"You do have a lovely place here," said Sarah as Penny ushered her into the manicure studio after the tour of the premises. "I can see why the Spa is so popular, and your business is thriving. Everything is immaculate, and the colours are so calming. Do you think you'd use the same colours in the capsule spa at the Beaumaris?"

"I don't know. We haven't thought that far ahead. I suppose it depends on how much space we have. But for now, let's think about what colour of nail varnish you'd like." She gestured at the wall of bottles of lacquer arranged in colours ranging from white to black, with every shade and hue in between.

"Well, nothing too outrageous. Something safe for work, I suppose." Penny pointed her to the section of deep pinks and reds, and after careful consideration, Sarah selected a brownish taupe.

"Very smart," said Penny. "Sophisticated."

Over the course of the day Penny had pondered how to open her conversation with Sarah, and had settled on the words she spoke now. "The hospitality industry is so demanding I'm sure you don't get much time for a little pampering for yourself. On the Friday night of the painting retreat, as I recall, you were called in at the last minute to take over bar duties."

"That's right," said Sarah as Penny placed her hands in a soaking bowl. "Sorry—did I serve you? If so, I don't remember. I was run off my feet that night and barely had time to look up, let alone chat with customers. Friday nights are always busy in the summer, plus that night we had the painting party in."

"And then, of course, the next morning Jessica's body was found."

"Well, I could have done without that, let me tell you," Sarah said, emphasizing the word "that." "Oh, I'm sorry, I didn't mean it to sound the way it did. Of course, I'm terribly sorry for what happened to the poor girl, but it was really the police all over the place, asking their endless questions, that annoyed me. And of course her room was tied up for a couple of days while they poked around. And on top of all that, we've got a lot of internal stuff going on."

Penny decided not to respond to her comments on Jessica's death. "If there's a lot of internal stuff going on, is this the right time for us to be discussing opening a spa at the hotel?"

"Oh, absolutely it is. There's a couple of hair salons and a nail bar in town, but there isn't a proper spa where you can get everything done in one place. And I visited those other places recently, and if I'm honest, they're all looking a bit tired. One of the hair salons is painted the most hideous candyfloss pink. Can you imagine?

"And just think about all the trade we'll do over the Christmas season. All the ladies getting ready for the festive parties, family dinners, and so on."

"And weddings," Penny reminded her. "June is always our busiest time. The bookings start the year before."

"Not to mention the add-on benefits for the hotel. They'll all be taking tea. We were thinking about offering a champagne service. A glass of champagne to go along with your pampering. What do you think about that?"

"That would certainly make it special," said Penny. "Sounds like a lovely idea. Unfortunately I didn't think of that today, so no champagne for you, I'm afraid."

"Well never mind. I forgive you this time."

Penny continued shaping Sarah's nails, and then, without looking at her, asked, "Did you happen to meet Jessica Graham when she stayed at the hotel?"

Sarah hesitated for what seemed just a fraction too long before replying. "No, I never spoke to her. I wouldn't have had any reason to. She didn't complain about anything, so the hotel staff looked after her. Why do you ask?"

"Oh, no particular reason. Just curious, that's all. We chatted with her on the Friday evening and she seemed so excited about her first visit to the U.K. and the stories she was working on."

"Well, I wouldn't know anything about that. Spent the whole night behind the bar getting the drinks out as fast as I could, and then there's always so much to do after the bar closes. Well, you've got a business, so you know all about that. Running the end-of-day sequence and making sure everything's in order for opening the next day. It never ends."

"Oh yes," agreed Penny. "I know all about that. Not complaining, though. Our business would be in serious trouble if we didn't have takings to total up at the end of the day."

"True. Though I suppose it's different when it's your own business than when you work for someone else. I expect you care just that little bit more."

Penny reached for a bottle of base coat and began applying it in swift, smooth strokes. Thinking about the photo she and Colin had seen in Sarah's apartment, with Sarah and a man standing in front of that glossy black door, and remembering what Cilla had told her about Sarah and Bill Ward meeting at the country house hotel where Sarah worked, she asked, "Have you always worked in the hospitality industry?"

"Yes, I have. Different hotels, of course. Some better than others."

Penny took a gamble with her next question. "What was the nicest hotel you worked at?"

"Well, I'm sure you're expecting me to say the Beaumaris Arms, but not quite. I worked at a beautiful country house hotel just outside Manchester called Langdon Hall. It was really beautiful and had such a warm, inviting atmosphere. I loved it there."

"Oh, was there any particular reason you left?"

Sarah gave her a piercing look. "It was just time to move on. Pastures new. Judging by your accent, I'm guessing you know a little about that yourself."

"Yes, I do. Although I've been very happy in my current pasture for the last twenty-five years or so."

She finished the base coat and picked up the bottle of nail varnish Sarah had chosen.

"Last chance to change your mind. Are you sure this is the colour you want?"

Sarah examined it, pursed her lips, and then glanced at the array of bottles arranged so neatly on their shelves. "I might just have another look, if that's okay."

"Perfectly fine. Clients often change their minds. Take your time."

Sarah browsed the bottles, and after selecting another one, she handed it to Penny and the manicure continued. Just as Penny applied the last few brushstrokes of the top coat, Rhian, the Spa's receptionist, poked her head around the door.

"Penny, Alberto's almost ready for Sarah. Oh, and you have a visitor waiting for you in the quiet room."

# Chapter Nineteen

For the briefest of moments, her heart soared. And then, when she remembered that Bethan had told her to expect a visitor, it landed back in her chest with a deflated thud. *Of course he isn't here. How could he be? He's thousands of miles away by now and soon he'll be somewhere in the dense, inhospitable bush of Northern Canada.*

"All done," Penny said a few minutes later as she screwed the top back on the bottle of clear top coat and set it to one side. "You'll have to be careful for the next little while until they're dry." Sarah remained where she was, her hands flat on the work top, while Penny tidied up, and when she was finished, she indicated it was time to leave for the hair salon. After handing Sarah over to Alberto, Penny made her way down the hallway to the quiet room.

A small space reserved for private conversations or a reflective moment alone, it was decorated in soothing, sophisticated neutral colours of cream and taupe and featured two deep, squishy chairs upholstered in chocolate-brown faux suede, facing each other, with a low coffee table between them. On a small floating shelf mounted under a watercolour of the Spa building as it had been before its renovation, painted by Penny herself, a grouping of LED candles flickered away.

A woman seated in one of the chairs turned a pale, drawn face to Penny, and placing her hands on the armrest for support, she rose. She was about Penny's age but seemed much older.

"Hello," she said. "Are you Penny Brannigan?"

Seeing a family resemblance and sensing who she was, Penny held out her hand. "Yes, I am."

The woman grasped her hand. "I'm Louise Graham. The police told me it was you who found my daughter, Jessica."

"Yes, I did. Mrs. Graham, I cannot tell you how deeply sorry I am for your loss. Please, let's sit down. May I get you some tea or coffee?"

"Your receptionist offered me something to drink, but I don't want anything right now. I've come a very long way, and all I really want to do is talk to you. I have so many questions. I hope you don't mind."

"No, of course not. Please, make yourself comfortable." Penny gestured to the woman's chair, and when she was seated again, Penny closed the door and sat opposite her, on the edge of her chair, with her hands resting lightly on her knees.

Mrs. Graham took a deep breath and looked around the room. "I still can't believe this is really happening, and yet, here I am, so it must be."

"I cannot imagine." Penny reached over the coffee table between them to take her hand. Instinctively and wordlessly, both women rose, and Penny pulled the coffee table out of the way. When Louise began to weep, Penny held her for a moment, and then, as her tears began to subside, she offered the box of tissues from a side table, and they sat again.

"It's just that the police told me that you were talking to our Jessica in the hotel the night before she died and that you must have been one of the last people to see her alive," Louise said, her voice thick with grief. "So I wanted to see you. I feel close to you. Because you were there, and you spoke to her. Please, tell me where you were and what you talked about."

"It was on the Friday night. We were in the bar of the Beaumaris Arms Hotel," Penny began. "I was chatting with a man I'd just met—a really nice man, as it turns out—and there was an empty chair at our table, and because the room was so crowded, Jessica asked if she could join us. She was such delightful company, so . . ." Penny almost said "full of life," but deciding Jessica's mother might find that too distressing, she said, ". . . so enthusiastic about her first trip abroad, and she was really excited about the stories she'd be working on for her newspaper. We were really taken with her and looking forward to seeing her again and learning more about her. She was just a lovely young woman, and you must have been so proud of her."

"Oh, we were." Mrs. Graham choked at the use of the past tense and dabbed her eyes with her sodden tissues. She steeled herself and continued. "And then it was on the Saturday morning that you found her on that beach."

"Yes. A friend who was on the painting retreat with me, she and I went to Black Point to paint the lighthouse. We were on a headland, so it's quite high up. I spotted something on the beach below, and when I got down there, I realized it was Jessica. We rang the emergency services, and I waited with her until help arrived. And I hope this is a bit of comfort to you, but I held her hand, and she wasn't alone."

"Yes, the police told me if it hadn't been for you, we might have lost her to the sea. I can't tell you how grateful I am."

"I'm just glad I was there."

They sat in silence for a moment, and then Penny asked how the family had heard about the tragedy.

"The Auckland police came to the door. Two of them. A man and a woman. They asked if I was Jessica Graham's mother. When I said yes, they asked if they could come in. And in that moment I knew that something terrible had happened to Jessica. My legs turned to jelly, and how I got to the lounge, I don't know. And when they insisted that I sit down, I knew that the news was the worst possible. They said they'd received a call from the Welsh police and that"—she paused and gathered herself—"and that the body of a young woman believed to be Jessica had been found on a beach on the island of Anglesey, North Wales. They asked for the name of her dentist, to get her dental records as there was no one here who was close enough to her to formally identify her. And then the room started spinning, and I think the woman officer made tea, but I don't remember any more after that. I was in such shock that I couldn't take it in.

"But they must have notified my husband at work because he arrived home soon after that, and the woman police officer stayed with us."

"Let me ask Rhian to get us some tea now. Shall I do that?" Louise nodded, and Penny darted down the hall to the reception desk. When she returned, Louise was a little more composed.

"And did the North Wales police suggest that you come here, to the U.K.?" Penny asked.

"They said it would be helpful if I could but that it wasn't absolutely necessary. But I wanted to. To bring her home. But before I do that, I want to visit the place where she died. I don't know, but I feel it might help me somehow. All this is simply unimaginable. You drive your daughter to the airport, you hug her, wave goodbye, and then this happens? She should have been safe here. How is this even possible? In your wildest dreams, nothing like this would . . ."

"Louise, are you here in this country on your own?" Penny asked. "Your husband isn't with you?"

"No, he had to stay home. It was very expensive for me to come here because everything had to be arranged in such a hurry. We had to borrow the money for my flight. Friends and family chipped in, but their generosity could only go so far. The newspaper would have liked to help, but they didn't have the funds, and although they offered to launch an appeal among the readership, we really didn't want that kind of charity."

"I can understand that."

Penny knew what she had to do. "Would you like me to go to Anglesey with you? To show you where I found Jessica?"

Louise raised puffy, tear-filled eyes to her. "Oh, I was hoping you would. I wanted to ask you, but it seemed too much. But yes, I would like that very much."

"We can go tomorrow, then." Penny had a sudden thought. "And is this your first time here in the U.K.?"

"Yes, it is."

"And do you have someplace to stay?"

"Well, I was going to stay at the hotel where she was. Is it far from here?"

"Not if you're driving. But it would be expensive in a taxi, and it will take quite a while on the bus, and the buses don't run that often." She met the woman's tired eyes. "It's too late now to go there today."

"Oh well then, I'm not sure what I . . ."

Penny leaned forward. "Louise, I have a spare room, and I'd be happy if you would stop with me for the night. Perhaps after a bath, something to eat, and a good night's sleep, you'll feel a bit better. And then we can go together to Beaumaris in the morning, after you've had a chance to rest. You must be utterly exhausted."

"That's very kind of you. And I don't think I've ever felt this exhausted. Just drained. Everything has been so stressful, and on top of that, there's the jet lag. I don't even know what day it is, let alone what time. I barely know how I got here. The doctor gave me some sleeping tablets in case I needed them, so I might take one tonight, and then hopefully I'll be out like a light."

"Right. Well, that's settled then."

Rhian knocked on the door and entered with a tea tray. After a quick glance at Penny, she set it down on the low table and left.

"Louise, I'm going to leave you for a few minutes while I make some arrangements. You can relax and have your tea. Is that all right?"

Louise gave Penny a grateful nod and then added a splash of milk to her tea. Assured that her visitor would be all right for a few minutes, Penny walked down the hall and peered into the hair salon, where Sarah was admiring her newly trimmed hair.

"You look terrific," Penny said as their eyes met in the mirror.

"Yes, it's a great improvement. I shouldn't have let it go so long."

"Listen, Sarah, I need to ask you something. It's about that voucher you gave me for the hotel. The mother of Jessica Graham has arrived, and she'll be spending a couple of nights in Beaumaris. Money's a bit tight. I wondered if she could use the voucher to cover the cost of her stay at your hotel."

A look that Penny read as concern flashed across Sarah's grey eyes.

"Never mind the voucher," she said. "You keep it. We can comp Mrs. Graham. Two nights, did you say? Has she registered?"

"No."

"And when is she arriving?"

"She's here now."

Sarah's eyebrows shot up. "She's here? Where? In the Spa?"

"Yes."

"Well, as I'm driving back to the hotel anyway, I could give her a lift."

Penny considered that before replying.

"No, she's had a very long journey, and she's drained. She's had more than enough travel for one day. I offered her my spare room for the night, and she seemed glad of it, so the best thing is if she stays with me and I bring her to Beaumaris tomorrow, when she's had a chance to rest and is better prepared for what lies ahead of her. Just so you know, she wants to see where her daughter's body was found, so it's going to be an emotional time for her. Even more emotional, I should say, because it's been very difficult for her getting this far."

Sarah adjusted the zebra-patterned hairdressing cape on her shoulders.

"Yes, of course. Well, I'll notify the front desk, and we'll expect her sometime tomorrow. Do you know if she wants to stay in the room Jessica had, if it's available? Sometimes people like to do that when they are retracing a loved one's final journey. Other times, they don't. But we wouldn't offer it to her without knowing that's what she wants."

"I don't know if she wants to stay in it, but she may want to see it."

After thanking Sarah, Penny went in search of Victoria, and then, arrangements sorted for the next day, they tidied up, and when the last customer had left, they closed the Spa.

"I think this must be what they mean when they talk about the kindness of strangers," said Louise as the three women made their way to Victoria's car for the short drive to Penny's cottage.

"I was a stranger here myself once," said Penny, "and someone was very kind to me."

# Chapter Twenty

The salty tang of the sea and the calling of sea birds greeted Penny and Louise as they approached Black Point the next afternoon. Louise hesitated as they neared the edge of the cliff that overlooked the beach, and then, clutching Penny's arm, took a step forward and peered over.

"She was just down there," Penny said, pointing.

"Can we get down there?"

"I used that rough path, just there, but it's steep and dangerous. I was in a hurry to get to her, of course, so I just charged ahead. But we might walk a little way and see if there's an easier way, and if not, we'll use that path. We'll just have to take our time and be careful."

They walked on and, a few hundred metres away, discovered several stone steps built into the side of the cliff face that were the start of a well-trodden dirt path that led to the beach on a kinder, gentler slope.

They descended to the beach and picked their way across the pebbly beach until they reached the spot where Penny had found the body of Jessica Graham.

"She was just here," Penny said softly, and then took a few steps back.

Louise sank to her knees and caressed the cold wet sand. Then she fell forward, buried her hands in it, and moved them back and forth with increasing desperation until her fingers were as raw as her grief. "Jessica," she wailed. "Oh, Jessica, my darling girl."

\* \* \*

Penny handed Louise a cup of tea in the quiet of her hotel bedroom and then, at the ping of an incoming text alert, glanced at her phone.

"Inspector Bethan Morgan of the North Wales Police is downstairs with Jessica's personal effects. Shall I tell her to come up? Are you ready to meet her?"

Louise took a sip of tea, set the cup down, and folded her hands in her lap. Five minutes later came a soft tap on the door.

Penny opened it and Bethan entered, pulling a wheeled black suitcase behind her.

Louise gasped when she saw it, then raised a hand and covered her mouth. Bethan set the suitcase to one side as Penny introduced them, and Bethan offered polite and formal condolences.

"I'm glad Penny's looking after you, Mrs. Graham," Bethan said. "You couldn't be in better, kinder hands."

"Yes, I know. She's been wonderful and I'm beyond grateful."

"What would you like to do now? Would you like to be alone to go through the suitcase? There's a police security seal on it, but I can remove that, if you wish."

Louise frowned.

"A security seal? Why?"

"To show that the contents were examined and then to prevent anyone from opening it or tampering with the contents. It's just routine."

"You went through her things?"

"Yes."

"Why? What were you looking for?"

"We weren't looking for anything. We examined the contents to make sure there was nothing there to indicate that her death was anything other than a terrible accident."

"And that's it? That's all you have? Just the suitcase?"

"Yes, I'm afraid so."

"But when she left, she also had a backpack. Where is that?"

"We didn't recover a backpack," Bethan replied. "Just this suitcase that was in her room."

"Well, what happened to her backpack?"

"I really don't like to speculate, but we think she had it with her when she fell, and as the tide was going out, it took the backpack with it."

Louise's mouth opened slightly, and she slumped forward.

"I'll go through the suitcase later, in my own time. I'm not ready to do that right now, and I don't know when I will be. I might even wait until I get it home, and her father and I will do that together."

"Well, whatever you feel is best for you," said Bethan. "If you have any more questions, I'm happy to answer them."

"I don't have any at the minute, but I'll be in touch if I do. I'm still trying to take in what you said about her backpack."

Bethan handed her a business card, and after once again offering condolences, left the room.

"Well," said Louise. "There's something very wrong here."

"The backpack," said Penny.

Louise looked startled. "You think so, too?"

"It's bothered me since I heard that it wasn't in her room. It is possible, I suppose, that she had it with her, and the tide took it, as Bethan suggested. The police have experts they can consult on such things."

"Here's the thing," said Louise. "She took that backpack everywhere, and if she'd had it with her, I'm sure it would have been found with her because she would most likely have been wearing it. She never carried it. She didn't like the way the straps dragged on the ground when she carried it by the handle."

Penny thought back to the moment she had first seen Jessica, and as her mother had just described, she had been wearing the backpack.

"I do have a lot of questions," said Louise, "and the backpack is just part of it. Everything that I've been told about the circumstances surrounding my daughter's death just seems like a dream that hasn't been pieced together right. What on earth would she be doing out there, on a cliff, alone, in an unfamiliar place, in the middle of the night?" She raised her hands in a small gesture of puzzled defeat. "And when she must have been exhausted?"

"It's possible that with the jet lag, she fell asleep, then woke up and couldn't get back to sleep and decided to go for a walk," Penny suggested. "The sun might have been coming up, and she could have decided to do a bit of exploring. Black Point is quite a long way from the hotel, but she wouldn't have known that. And then, exhausted and disoriented, she lost her balance and fell."

"That's possible, I suppose. She enjoyed the outdoors, and of course she was naturally curious, so she might have gone for a walk. But that doesn't explain how she fell off a cliff."

Seized by an idea, Penny asked, "Did she have any medical issues? Could she have had a bout of dizziness or vertigo and lost her balance?"

"I don't think so. She never mentioned anything like that to me, and if she'd been suffering from something like that, I'm sure she would have asked me to go to the doctor with her." Louise gave her head a little shake. "Oh, none of this makes any sense to me. I can't make head nor tail of it, and believe me, I've thought about nothing else since those police officers knocked on my door."

"Then tell me this, Louise, without overthinking it. What do you think happened to Jessica? What does your heart tell you?"

"I don't think this was an accident. I think she was taken to that place, and then something unspeakable happened, or else she was lured there to her death," Louise replied without hesitation.

*I agree with you,* thought Penny.

As if reading her thoughts, and with a flicker of something in her large hazel eyes that looked like fear, Louise asked, "What do you think? Do you think my Jessica was murdered?"

Not wanting her response to add to Louise's distress, Penny weighed her words before replying. "Although the police say there's nothing to show that Jessica's death was anything other than a tragic accident, yes, I believe it is possible that she was murdered."

Mrs. Graham's eyes hardened as her face clouded, and her lips pressed together in a determined line.

"Then something must be done. We must find out the truth, and I won't rest until I get justice for Jessica. If there's a murderer out there, that person must be found."

She reached out her hand to indicate she wanted the suitcase, and Penny brought it over to her. She rested her hand on the handle. "I wish the police hadn't touched this. I would have liked to be the first to put my hand where Jessica's was."

Penny stood silently for a moment, and then said, "Well, Louise, you've had a stressful morning. I'm sure you would like some time to yourself now, so I'm going to leave you to get some rest. You've got my number, so please just ring if you need me."

* * *

Victoria, who had dropped Penny and Louise off at Black Point, then spent the morning on a hotel site visit discussing arrangements for the capsule spa at the hotel with Sarah Spencer, joined Penny in the lounge just before lunch.

"How is she?" Victoria asked as she dropped into the chair opposite Penny's.

"She's resting now. Bethan delivered Jessica's suitcase, and that really seemed to knock the stuffing out of her."

"I'm sure it must have been so distressing," Victoria said, "seeing her daughter's belongings."

"She didn't actually open the suitcase when I was there. I'd say she's holding up pretty well, considering, but it's painful to see someone wrapped up in so much grief. I'll never forget that whimpering sound she made on the beach where her daughter's body was found. My heart is just breaking for her. And as if her grief weren't enough, she has a lot of questions about how

Jessica died. The police version doesn't make any sense to her, and I agree with her. It doesn't make a lot of sense to me, either. There are just so many gaps and unanswered questions."

"Well, I hope you're not encouraging her, Penny. That wouldn't be doing her any favours. The police investigated; they probably took measurements and checked tide tables or whatever it is they do, and their version of what happened is more than likely what did happen."

"But she's got all these doubts about what the police are telling her. She knows her daughter better than anyone, and what she's been told doesn't sound like something Jessica would do. People tend to behave in a certain way. They're predictable."

She blew out a long exhale. "And then there's the backpack."

"What backpack?"

"Jessica's."

"What about it?"

"What happened to it, that is the question."

"Does it really matter?"

"Of course it matters! Unless we find out what happened to the backpack, despite what the police think, I'm convinced that someone will get away with murder."

# Chapter
# Twenty-One

"Oh God," said Penny before Victoria could reply. "That's all we need."

"What? What is it?"

"Brace yourself. He's seen us and he's coming over."

Victoria turned around slowly to see Bill Ward, plaid shirt, fisherman's vest, green trousers and all, lumbering toward them.

"That's him? Mr. Let's Have Lunch and See Where It Leads?"

"I'm afraid so."

"'Oh God' is right." The corners of her mouth started to twitch, and Penny glared at her. "Don't. If you start, I'll . . ." But it was too late, and a loud burst of laughter erupted from both of them.

Penny managed to get her laughter under control just as Bill reached them, but the moment of merriment had left her face creased with a broad smile.

Interpreting that as delight at seeing him again, Ward returned the smile. "Hello, Penny. Back again, are you? Nice to see you."

"And you." She introduced him to Victoria, who met his eyes when she said hello, but avoided looking at Penny.

"And how is the art world treating you, Penny?" Ward asked.

"Oh, not too badly. Haven't had any time for painting since your weekend retreat, but I'm looking forward to putting what I learned into my next painting. I've got a few ideas for what I'd like to do next."

"She's been offered a spot to exhibit her paintings in a Christmas art show," Victoria chimed in.

"Oh, how exciting. Which gallery?"

"Oh, just a small gallery near us," said Penny before Victoria could reply. "Not a big one at all. Hardly even worth mentioning." Victoria shot her a questioning look, and when her lips parted as if she were about to say something, Penny frowned and gave a slight shake of her head.

Ward's eyes narrowed as he watched the exchange.

Finally, after a few minutes of stilted conversation, Ward checked his pretentiously large wristwatch, designed for tracking the kind of vigorous outdoor sporting activities he rarely, if ever, engaged in. "I was just thinking about lunch. If you two ladies don't have plans, I'd be happy if you would join me. My treat, of course."

"Oh, that would have been so nice, but unfortunately we were just saying it's time we left for home," said Penny, just a little too quickly.

"Yes, we have errands to do on the way, so . . ." added Victoria.

"Well, another time, perhaps," said Ward.

Victoria barked out a robust burst of laughter as soon as they were outside. "I can see why Bill Ward gives you the creeps. I almost lost it when he invited the two of us to lunch. I'm sure he was thinking, 'And let's see where this leads.'"

"What a thought."

"But what was all that about, when you didn't want him knowing about your paintings in the Christmas exhibit?" Victoria asked as they reached the car park.

"It's the gallery I didn't want him knowing about. I didn't have a chance to tell you, but his ex-wife, Cilla McKee, is the manager there, and I just thought it would be better if the gallery's name didn't come up. She's really bitter toward him, and God knows what he thinks of her."

"Oh, I see. Or at least, I think I do. It would have been awkward."

"Yes, and for some reason, I didn't want him to know that I know about his ex-wife," said Penny.

"Well, I don't know that it really matters." Victoria unlocked the car, and they opened their doors and climbed in.

"But your mentioning the art show reminds me I need to pick up the paintings from the framer," Penny said. "I can't wait to see what they look like. Good frames always make such a difference." As they pulled onto the main road that led to the bridge to the mainland, she added, as if to reassure herself, "I hope Louise is going to be all right. I'm worried about her, but she has my number if she needs me."

\* \* \*

A ringing or vibrating phone in the middle of the night is rarely a good thing. Penny groped for the mobile on her bedside table, not knowing what, or who, to expect. A vague thought flashed through her mind that it could be Colin ringing from Canada, where it was five or six hours behind the U.K., depending on what time zone he was in, but the number that glowed in the dark wasn't his. Her phone didn't recognize the number, and neither did she.

She was about to ignore the call, when her instinct told her to answer it.

"Hello?" After a pause came a torrent of slurred words.

*Oh, someone's had too much to drink and dialed the wrong number,* she thought, preparing to end the call. But just as she was about to take the phone away from her ear, she made out the word "help." Or she thought that's what she heard. She pressed the phone closer to her ear. "Hello?" she said again. "Do you need help? Who is this?"

"Laaweeese." The word was thick as if the speaker's tongue were swollen and heavy.

"Louise?" Penny, now wide awake, sat bolt upright. "Louise, is that you? What's wrong?"

When there was no response, Penny ended the call, called 999 and asked them to send police and ambulance to the Beaumaris Arms Hotel. She then called the hotel's night number and let the night porter know that an ambulance was on the way and to please take the first responders immediately to the room of Louise Graham and be prepared to unlock the door. And then, with nothing more she could do, she settled down to wait.

# Chapter
# Twenty-Two

Penny knew she'd have a difficult time getting back to sleep, and she did. But as the opening notes of the birds' dawn chorus filtered through her open window, she fell into an uneasy sleep and dreamt she was being chased through the corridors of a hotel, and when she reached the safety of her room, it was filled with the people who had been chasing her. She woke with a start, and remembering the middle of the night phone call, got up, dressed, and went downstairs. It was 6 A.M.

She put the kettle on, and just as she was about to pour the hot water into the cafetière, her phone rang. It was Bethan, who apologized for ringing so early but thought Penny might be up, and since she was, Bethan needed to speak to her in person. Penny added another scoop of coffee to the press, set out a second mug, and a few minutes later Bethan was in her sitting room, her hands wrapped around a welcome mug of coffee after a long night.

"How is Louise?" Penny asked. "Is she in hospital?"

Bethan nodded. "She's receiving the best possible care, and the doctor I spoke to expects her to make a full recovery."

Penny let out a sigh of relief. "Oh, that's good. I was so worried. As you can imagine, I had a sleepless night after that phone call. I could barely make out what she was saying. I thought it was a drunk with a wrong number. What on earth happened to her?"

"It appears she took an overdose of sleeping tablets."

"Oh no. And then she changed her mind and called me to ask for help?"

"Possibly."

"Wait a minute. You said 'it appears.' Either she did or she didn't. Did she?"

"Well, we found an empty bottle of sleeping tablets in the nightstand in her hotel room, and we checked with the prescribing physician in New Zealand. He said she asked for them just before her trip to the U.K., and he prescribed them. Said he could understand, what with the jet lag and the difficult circumstances surrounding her journey here, that she might need them. But he assured us he never would have given them to her if he thought there was the slightest chance she would use them to self-harm." She took a sip of coffee. "Only . . ."

"Only what?"

"She insists she didn't take one last night, let alone all of them. She said she was feeling so anxious and wound up the night she stayed with you that she took one then, and that was the only one she took."

"You hear sometimes of people taking a tablet, then when it doesn't work they take another, and they end up with an accidental overdose. Could it have been something like that? I'm sure with the terrible stress she's been under and the heightened grief of being so close to where her daughter died, and your giving her Jessica's suitcase filled with personal belongings, that it's understandable she could be a bit forgetful and anxious. But accidently taking a whole bottle doesn't seem possible."

"There weren't that many. This was just a short-term solution, and they were to be taken on an as-needed basis, to help her get through a difficult time. The doctor gave her only eight tablets, and she insisted the only one she took was the one on the night she stopped with you."

"So that would have left seven tablets."

"The doctor isn't sure that would be enough to kill her, but it could have. If she'd gone to sleep, that amount could have been enough to depress her breathing function. Fortunately, she hadn't had anything to drink, but if she had, the alcohol could have compounded the effect of the medication. So all in all, it's a good thing she was able to ring you and that you responded so quickly and appropriately."

Penny examined the contents of the mug resting on her knee while she considered her response.

"It looks to me as if someone's afraid that Jessica's mother is asking too many questions," she said. "And they panicked." She took a sip of coffee. "And what's more, I think if Louise Graham hadn't turned up, someone very likely would have got away with the murder of her daughter."

"I can't think of a plausible reason why someone would want to hurt her, or silence her," said Bethan. "But she wasn't in a fit state to be formally interviewed when I looked in on her earlier. Anyway, she's asking for you. You're the only person she knows in this country, and if you're available today, it would be good for her to have you there."

"Are you going back to Bangor to try to talk to her?"

"No. I'd give you a ride if I were, but I've been up most of the night on another case as well as this one, and I'm going home to get a couple of hours sleep."

\*   \*   \*

Three hours later, Penny pulled back the privacy curtain that had been drawn around Louise Graham's hospital bed. She was sitting up, eyes closed, the sheet drawn up to her chest, and her hands resting lightly by her side.

"Louise, it's me. Penny." The patient's eyes fluttered open, and her head turned toward Penny.

"Oh, thank goodness it's you." She stretched out her hand, and Penny grasped it as she lowered herself into the visitor's chair.

"How are you feeling?"

"Still a bit woozy, if I'm honest."

"Are you up to talking? I was very concerned by the state of you on the phone call. I barely knew it was you."

"Thank God you did. Who knows what might have happened if you hadn't?"

"That's what I'd like to know, Louise. Do you feel up to talking about it? Can you tell me what happened last evening?"

"I'm not sure I know what happened, but I'll try." She closed her eyes as she gathered her thoughts. "Let's see. Well, I didn't feel like having dinner in the hotel restaurant. Too fancy, and besides, I wasn't hungry. But I knew I should eat something, so I asked at the reception desk, and the receptionist said go out the front door, and there's a small supermarket that does sandwiches and the like, so I went there. Walked around for a bit, then back to the hotel."

"Did you eat your sandwich in your room?"

"No. I was going to, but there was an open place, like a square, with some benches across from the castle, so I ate it there and thought about Jessica."

Penny nodded, recognizing the description of the place where she and Colin had enjoyed their lunch of fish and chips. "And when you got back to your hotel room, did anything look disturbed?"

"No, everything was exactly the way I'd left it."

"Okay, so then what did you do?"

"I had a shower and watched a bit of the television. Then there was a knock at the door. For some reason, I thought maybe it might be you, so I opened it, but it was someone from the hotel with a tray. Hot chocolate and toast. I said I didn't order that, and he said it was compliments of the manager. So I thanked him and realized that hot chocolate was exactly what I wanted. And the toast was good, too."

"Comfort food."

"Exactly. The toast was covered with one of those round silver things with a hole in the middle that you lift off. He set the tray down on the desk and told me to leave everything in the hallway when I was finished with it, so that's what I did."

"And your sleeping tablets. Where did you keep them?"

"In my sponge bag with my toiletries. The bag was in the bathroom."

"And were the sleeping tablets in your sponge bag when you had your shower?"

Louise let out a small sigh. "Now that I can't say. Unless you're specifically looking for something, you don't really take any notice, do you?"

"The police say they found the empty sleeping tablets bottle in your bedside table."

"Well, I didn't put it there."

"And you're quite sure you didn't take a sleeping tablet last night?"

"I'm positive. The only time I took one was the night I stopped at yours. I told all this to the police." She closed her eyes and her breathing slowed.

"Are you all right, Louise?" Penny asked. "Should I leave you to rest now?"

Her eyes fluttered open. "Yes, I'm all right. The police were here earlier, but they didn't ask too many questions because I wasn't alert enough to talk. They might have said they'd be back later. I told them I didn't take the sleeping tablets, though."

"And when you were at the hotel, did you speak to anyone about Jessica? Did you ask questions about what she did or where she went?"

"Of course I did. That was the whole point of being there. I spoke to the fellow in the bar, and he told me he'd seen her talking to you on the Friday evening, which I already knew about. He seemed a fine young man. Polite. In fact, now that I think of it, he was the one who brought the hot chocolate to my room."

"The young man from the bar brought up your hot chocolate? That seems odd. You'd think someone from the coffee shop or kitchen would have done that. Oh, wait, was it after eight o'clock?"

"Just after, I think."

"Oh well, the coffee shop closes at eight, so it's possible they made your drink just before, and then, while the coffee shop person took care of closing up for the day, the bartender was asked to run it upstairs. It's a small hotel, and the staff probably just pitch in and do what's asked of them." Penny remembered that on the Friday night of the painting weekend, Sarah Spencer, the assistant manager, had worked at the bar on what was supposed to be her night off.

"And did you speak to anyone else about Jessica?"

"The woman at reception who checked me in said she'd been instructed to notify the duty manager when I arrived, and then asked me to wait for a minute, and then the duty manager came along and told me how sorry she was about Jessica."

"That would be Sarah Spencer."

"Yes, I think that was her name. She seemed a nice woman. Well spoken. And I asked her if she'd met Jessica, and she said, no she hadn't."

"Hmm. I suppose someone could have entered your room while you were out getting your sandwich, taken the sleeping pills, and then left the container in the drawer of the night-stand, to be discovered later, so it would look as if you'd taken them." She thought for a moment. "It was probably a safe bet that you wouldn't look in the drawer, but the police certainly would. Anyway, I'm glad to see you're feeling better. Did they give you any indication how long they expect to keep you in?"

"They said I might be able to go . . . I almost said 'I might be able to go home,' but that's not really the case. They said that I could be discharged later today or tomorrow morning."

Penny leaned forward. "Unless there's some reason why you want to go back to the hotel, it's probably best if you don't. Here's what I think we should do. I'll go to the hotel now, pack up everything in your hotel room, and let the front desk know you won't be returning. I'll take your suitcase home with me, and when you're discharged, you come straight to me in Llanelen. Unfortunately, if it's tomorrow, I can't come and pick you up because I've got to work, but the bus is easy, and I can tell you how to do that, or we can make other arrangements. And you can stay with me until you're ready to return home to New Zealand, or for as long as you like or need to."

"That's a very kind offer. But are you sure you can manage? It's not just my suitcase, remember. There's Jessica's as well."

"The bus stops right in front of the hotel, and if Victoria can pick me up in Llanelen and drive me home, I'll be just fine."

"I will never be able to repay you for all you've done for me," said Louise. "Unless, of course, one day you find yourself in New Zealand."

"There's no need to repay me," said Penny. "I got involved when I found Jessica, and I want to see this through. And I want to see that it's done right. For your sake and for hers." Louise relaxed into her pillow and closed her eyes.

"I can't thank you enough," she whispered.

"Now then, that's enough for now. All this talk has clearly exhausted you, so I'd better let you rest. Have you got the key card for your hotel room?"

"I'm not sure. I think it was on the dresser in the hotel room, but I don't really remember anything about when we left for the hospital. I have no recollection of any of that."

"The ambulance people probably grabbed your handbag," said Penny. "I'll just look in your locker for it, shall I?"

She opened the little door of the bedside cupboard, lifted out Louise's handbag, and placed it by Louise's side.

"Do you want to look in your bag for the key?"

Louise's eyes remained closed, and she murmured something that Penny didn't quite catch. When she didn't move, Penny opened the bag and scrabbled through the contents, unzipped inside and outside pockets, but didn't see a hotel key card. She replaced the bag in the patient's bedside locker, and then, after lifting Louise's hands under the bedclothes and tucking the light blanket around her shoulders, she took one last glance at the sleeping woman and crept out of the room.

# Chapter
# Twenty-Three

Penny walked up the stone stairs of the hotel's front entrance and made her way through the lobby to the front desk. She didn't recognize the receptionist on duty, but she introduced herself and explained that she was a friend of hotel guest Louise Graham, who had been taken to hospital the previous night.

"Oh yes," said the receptionist. "I heard about that when I came in this morning. How is she doing?"

"She's going to be all right, but she won't be returning to the hotel. I'm here to collect her belongings and let you know that she's checking out."

The receptionist pinched her lips together. "Did she give you her room key?"

"No, she didn't have it with her."

"Then I'm afraid I can't just let you into her room." She gave an apologetic little shrug. "I'm sorry. It's a security issue. Mrs. Graham is our guest, and without her authorization, as per hotel policy, I can't let you or anyone else into her room. I'm sure you understand."

"Yes, I can see that," said Penny, "but I'm sure if you check with your assistant manager, she'll give you her approval. She's familiar with the situation."

"She's not in today, unfortunately. It's her day off."

"This is rather important. Would you mind ringing her?"

"I'm afraid I couldn't do that. She doesn't like to be disturbed on her day off." She gave Penny a hospitality-industry smile. "Well, who does, really?"

"In that case, then, would it be possible for a member of the hotel staff to pack up all the personal effects in Louise Graham's room and bring them to me? I could wait down here."

"We don't know that you have Mrs. Graham's permission to take away her belongings, so I can't agree to that, either."

"Right. Thank you for your help. I'll be back."

With a determined spring in her step, Penny marched through the hotel, past the bar and coffee shop, and out the rear door. She walked along the promenade to the Georgian terrace, and up the pathway to the glossy black door.

From inside came the sound of hammering.

While she waited for the door to be opened, Penny faced the Menai Strait and drank in the peaceful beauty of the sparkling water.

At the sound of the door opening, she turned to find Sarah Spencer dressed in a pair of smart beige trousers, a dark brown jacket, and a hat with a broad black grosgrain band.

"Oh. It's you," she said. "Hello."

"Sorry to bother you. Looks as if you're just on your way out, but I need your help with a problem at the hotel."

"What's the matter?"

"There's an issue with Louise Graham."

Sarah crossed her arms and sighed. "You'd better come in, then."

Penny wasn't sure if Sarah knew that she'd viewed the house, but decided not to mention it. She admired the entrance hall as if she'd never seen it before, then followed Sarah into the sitting room. Sarah closed the door to block off the banging noise.

"Sorry about that racket. Getting a new kitchen fitted. Today's what they call demolition day. Taking out all the old cabinets and cupboards. That's why I'm going out. I can't take it anymore." *I pity the neighbours,* thought Penny. "Now what's the problem at the hotel that the staff can't sort out?"

"It's about Louise Graham. You heard what happened?"

"Yes, I was told that she took an overdose of sleeping tablets."

Convinced that Louise hadn't taken the overdose, but had been given it, Penny did not respond. "She's in hospital and won't be returning to the hotel. She asked me to let the hotel know and to pack up her belongings."

"And I'm guessing you're here because you don't have her key card."

"Exactly. And the receptionist on the front desk was unwilling to let me into her room."

"Good. That's what she was trained to do. We can't allow anybody into a guest's room without permission. I don't suppose Louise gave you something in writing?"

"No. I spoke to her for a few minutes at the hospital, but she's still poorly and went back to sleep."

"Sorry. I should have asked. How is she doing?"

"She's recovering and going to be all right, thank goodness."

"Well, we're not really supposed to allow anyone into a guest's room for security reasons. I'm really not comfortable with it."

"But if the police wanted in, you'd have to let them in? We could always go that route."

Sarah eyed her suspiciously. "That sounds a bit like a threat."

"Oh, not at all," said Penny smoothly. "Of course not. And it was very kind of you to provide Mrs. Graham with accommodation. She appreciates that. It's just she has no more need of the room, and she's going to come back to stop with me in Llanelen when she's released from hospital, so it would be better for everyone all round if I could take away her things today, and that would free up the room for the hotel. She really isn't in a fit state to collect her belongings herself. And you know that I helped arrange for her to stay here, so all I'm trying to do now is make it possible for her to leave as easily as she can. It's not as if I'm a stranger who appeared out of the blue asking you to hand over her belongings to me. You're familiar with the situation."

Sarah reflected on Penny's words, then reached for her phone. "All right. I'll call reception and let them know it's okay to let you into her room."

Penny stood up. "Thank you." A new round of hammering almost drowned out her words. "And I'm sure the kitchen will look wonderful when it's done. I love your apartment." And then she added, "Well, what I've seen of it. You look very smart, by the way. Going somewhere nice?"

"Not especially. Solicitor's office."

Sarah opened the front door, and just as Penny stepped onto the stone step, she asked, "How did you know I live here, by the way?"

Penny didn't turn around or answer.

\* \* \*

Penny retraced her steps to the hotel, but instead of going to the reception desk to ask for someone with a key to accompany her to Louise Graham's room, she made her way to the bar, where she found Llifon with his back to her as he wiped down an empty shelf. Bottles of wine were lined up neatly on the bar.

"Afternoon, Llifon."

He set down his cloth and turned to face her.

"Oh, hello. Sorry. Just doing a bit of cleaning. What can I get you?"

"Nothing right now, thanks. I won't keep you from your work. I just want to ask you a couple of questions."

He picked up a bottle and swiped at it with his cloth. "Fire away."

"You took a tray up to your guest Mrs. Louise Graham about eight o'clock last night."

"That's right."

"Hot chocolate and toast, was it?"

He nodded, turned his back to her for a moment while he replaced the bottle on the shelf, then turned to face her, and wiped down another bottle.

"And what did the toast come with? Jam? Butter?"

"No, there was a little pot of something. Brown, it was."

"Not jam." Penny mulled that over. "Do you know what it was?"

"I forget the name of it, but it might have been that spread that Australians like. I was just told to take the tray upstairs, so that's what I did. Why? What does it matter what was on the tray?" He gave the lined-up wine bottles a mournful look, and Penny couldn't tell if he was anxious to return to his task or hoped to put it off a few minutes longer.

"Bear with me, Llifon, for just a minute or two. I'm trying to find out what happened to Mrs. Graham. Can you tell me who told you to take the tray up to her?"

"The receptionist. She rang just after eight and said there was a note on Mrs. Graham's file that she was to have a bed-time tray at 8 P.M., and it would be ready to be picked up from the coffee shop and delivered. So that's what I did."

"And who covered for you in the bar while you were upstairs?"

"Mr. Hewitt. We weren't very busy at the time."

"Mr. Hewitt, the hotel manager?"

"That's right. Naturally I'm not supposed to leave the bar unattended, and he was coming out of his office, so I told him about the delivery, and he told me I'd better get on with it then and to be quick about it, and that he'd watch the bar until I got back."

"All right, Llifon. You've given me lots to think about. Thank you so much."

\* \* \*

"Funny you should ask," said Llifon twenty minutes later. "You're the second person to ask me about all that today."

Detective Inspector Bethan Morgan turned to Detective Constable Chris Jones. "Now I wonder who else would want to know what we want to know." And then, back to Llifon, "What did that person look like?" Before he could reply, she continued, "Let me guess. A smart-looking woman about this tall"—she held her hand a couple of inches above her own head—"with very nicely cut and styled red hair."

"Got it in one."

"And where is she now, do you know?"

At that moment Penny entered their line of vision as she crossed the hallway, two suitcases trundling along behind her, then disappeared from view as she continued on her way to the lobby and the front door.

# Chapter Twenty-Four

"Penny!"

At the sound of Bethan's voice, Penny stopped and turned in the direction of the voice.

"Oh, hello."

Bethan gestured at the suitcases. "Louise's?"

"That's right."

"Where are you taking them?"

"I'm taking them home with me. I've told Louise she can stay with me for as long she needs to—until all the legalities are wrapped up, and she can take Jessica's body home."

"She told me. And that's very good of you. Listen, I'm not happy with the way things are going. I've been doing a lot of thinking, and you might be right. This case has now taken a different turn, and I've asked the pathologist to take another look at Jessica's injuries, to see if anything was missed or misinterpreted in the postmortem."

"Oh, I thought you weren't one for speculation."

"I wouldn't call this speculation. I'd call it policewoman's instincts. When something doesn't feel right, chances are good it isn't. And now, I'm very curious in a way I wasn't before." She folded her arms. "Because somebody did a very stupid thing."

For the briefest of moments, Penny thought Bethan was referring to something she had done, and then realized what the policewoman meant. "They tried to make it look as if Louise took an overdose."

"That's right," Bethan replied. "But if you believe Louise's version of events, which, after just speaking to her again at the hospital I now do, someone decided to send her a powerful message to stop asking questions about her daughter's death, or perhaps even tried to silence her. So now everything I thought about Jessica's death is being called into question. We start over. If someone had left well enough alone, they might have got away with Jessica's murder."

"So someone's starting to panic," said Penny. "That's the significance of what happened with Louise."

"It looks that way. So at this point, you need to be careful. Stop asking questions. Leave it to us." She reached for one of the suitcases. "You'd better let me help with that. Louise is going to be discharged today. Like hospitals everywhere, they don't keep people in a minute longer than they need to. And they're satisfied that she's got someplace safe to go to for the next few days. And it's probably better for you, too, to have someone staying with you. It's lovely, your cottage, but a bit isolated. I do worry about you sometimes, you know."

"So you'll take the suitcases to Llanelen?"

"I will. I'll drive Louise there as well. Expect us this evening. Meanwhile, I'm going to take another look at the beach where Jessica's body was found."

"Do you want me to come with you?" An image of Louise Graham, on her knees, digging her hands in the rough sand and small pebbles that had briefly held her daughter's body, erupted in Penny's mind.

"No I do not, thanks all the same. I'm investigating Jessica's death from a different perspective now, and I want to get a feel for the place from that point of view. I need to be on my own."

*Well, at least we're on the same page now,* thought Penny. While she appreciated that modern policing methods required a measured, evidence-based approach, there were times when following your instincts could really speed things up.

"Would you like my thoughts?" Penny asked.

"Yes, I would."

"It has to be someone either from within the hotel or with a strong connection to it."

"That is now becoming obvious."

# Chapter
# Twenty-Five

"I thought I would have heard from him by now," Penny moaned at lunchtime the next day. She and Victoria were seated side by side, enjoying a picnic on what they considered "their" bench in the churchyard. One day at a time, the summer was drifting onward, and although it was too soon for the air to hold the first breath of autumn, that day was coming soon.

"How long has it been?"

"I heard from him when he got back to Canada, just before they set off on this expedition, and nothing since. He was meant to be gone for two weeks, and it's now closer to three weeks since I've heard from him."

"Didn't he tell you there wouldn't be any Wi-Fi or mobile service where he was going?"

"He said it would be unpredictable and spotty, at best, so I didn't expect to hear from him while he was away, but I thought I'd hear from him as soon as he got back."

"Well then, there's your answer. He's not back yet."

Penny raised her sandwich as if to take a bite, then lowered it to her lap, untouched. "Where did he go, again?" Victoria asked.

"He's with an international group of scientists in the Canadian Arctic, or at least the far North, photographing polar bear habitat. Or what's left of it." She took a sip of water from her refillable bottle. "It's for a magazine feature on the climate crisis, but Colin said he fears that what he's really doing is capturing the last days of so many species, and maybe even the planet itself, as we know it."

"That's a terrifying thought," Victoria said as her eyes swept over the River Conwy flowing past them. "Have you tried contacting him?'

"I sent him another text two days ago. And no response."

"Well, I'm sure there's nothing for you to worry about. They might have discovered something really interesting that took them in a different direction, or maybe the whole venture is just taking longer than they thought it would."

Penny made a throaty little noise. "That's really not what's been bothering me. It's not so much the logistics of the expedition that concern me, it's that I'm afraid that he . . ."

Victoria gave Penny time to finish the sentence, and when she didn't, Victoria prompted: "Go on. You're afraid that he what?"

"Well, that he's, you know, no longer interested in me. That he got back to Canada and thought all this"—she flapped her hand at the view before them in a light, encompassing motion—"was just a holiday romance. Or, more accurately, that I was."

Victoria's mouth opened in a little circle of surprise. "Oh no, Penny, you don't really think that, do you?" Her eyes widened. "I'm sure that you've got the wrong end of the stick here. I got the impression he was quite serious about you. How serious, I don't know, of course, but from what I could tell, he's very fond of you. You two really seemed to hit it off."

The door to the rectory opened, and Robbie, the much-loved cairn terrier who had been discovered by the rector's wife a few years earlier, shivering and abandoned in the churchyard, bounded out and raced toward them. He was followed by Bronwyn Evans herself, wearing a floral-patterned housedress and a navy-blue cardigan.

Keeping to the path that separated the church on one side from the graves on the other, she made her way to the bench in purposeful strides. "Oh, Penny," she said when she reached them, "I've just heard something on the noon news that might involve your friend."

"What friend?"

"Your Canadian photographer friend. Colin, isn't it?"

Penny's heart felt like a trapped bird beating against her ribs. "What about him? What's happened?"

"I'm so sorry. Of course, it might not involve him at all, but when I saw you out here, I thought I'd better come and speak to you."

"Please, Bronwyn," said Victoria, "for pity's sake, out with it."

"We just heard on the noon news that an international expedition of scientists studying the alarming rate of climate change in Canada's North is believed to be missing. Word for word, that's what they said. The BBC mentioned that two of the scientists are from Cambridge University. The newsreader didn't mention your friend by name, but that is the group he was working with, isn't it? So naturally I assumed he must be missing, too." She looked from one to the other, her eyes brimming with confused concern. "Of course, I could be completely wrong, and I hope I am. It might not involve him at all. But as Thomas said, how many scientific expeditions can there be at one time studying the climate in the Canadian North?"

Penny didn't answer, but pulled her phone out of her pocket. After thumbing frantically and jabbing at the small screen, and with an impatient exclamation, she put it away and jumped up, her untouched sandwich falling from her lap onto the ground in front of the bench. She raced through the churchyard, past the rectory, and disappeared down the narrow, cobbled street that led to the town square.

Seeing Robbie headed for the sandwich, Bronwyn snatched it up, tossed it in the wire litter bin, and took Penny's place on the bench beside Victoria.

"She was just telling me she hasn't heard from him," Victoria said as she picked up Penny's abandoned water bottle, made sure the lid was screwed on tightly, and placed it in her bag. "She's afraid he's lost interest in her."

"From what I observed at Mrs. Lloyd's party, I'd be very surprised if that were the case." Bronwyn kept a watchful eye on Robbie, who hadn't given up on the sandwich and was seated in front of the bin, alternately staring at the contents and giving Bronwyn a soulful, pleading look. "Where's she gone, do you suppose?"

"Back to the office to get on the Internet, probably. By the time I get there, she'll know if the group that's gone missing is the one he was with."

Bronwyn scooped up Robbie and put him on her lap. "In this day and age, with all the modern means of communication and GPS tracking and the like, you wonder how something like this could happen."

"Well, hopefully those modern means of communication will help find them."

# Chapter Twenty-Six

The look on Penny's face as she glanced up from her laptop when Victoria entered her office said it all.

"So it is his group," said Victoria. "I'm so sorry."

"I've read all the news stories and set up a Google Alert for when there's fresh information. The scientists and 'other members of the expedition,' as they're called, didn't return to their base camp when they were supposed to, so the authorities were notified, and everything is being done to locate them. Fortunately, they had a couple of Inuit researchers with them, who are familiar with the territory, and I'm sure the authorities will bring in experts who know what to do."

"You're taking this rather well, I must say."

"Of course I am. In this scenario, there's hope. In the one I was imagining, where he'd lost interest in me, there wasn't. It was over."

Before Victoria could reply, Louise Graham poked her head around the door. "I'm feeling so much better today that I thought I'd walk into town for a bit of exercise, and your receptionist said it would be all right for me to come back and see you." She looked from one to the other. "But maybe this isn't a good time. You seem involved in something, and it looks like I'm interrupting."

"No, it's all right," said Penny. "Come in. But you're right. It is something." She explained the situation about the missing scientists and her interest in the photographer who accompanied the group.

"Oh, I'm sorry to hear this. I hope they'll all be found soon. I'm sure they will be." She clasped her hands in front of her. "But the thing is, there's something I wanted to talk to you about. According to the policewoman, the case is now going in a different direction, and things could take a bit longer to clear up. Naturally, I'd like to stay on until we learn more, but I'm afraid that—well, my money's starting to run out. I wondered if you knew of any work going around here."

"I'm assuming you're here in the U.K. on a visitor's visa," said Victoria, "and unfortunately, that doesn't permit you to work. So I'm afraid we can't offer you anything, and I doubt any of the shops in town would, either. The authorities are very strict about that."

"You know that you can stay with me as long as you need to," said Penny, "but it might be better if you had something to do to keep busy. I'm sure it would be okay for you to do a bit of volunteering, if you feel up to it. There's the charity shops, and the dog rescue group always needs help. Oh, and Bronwyn's got her jumble sale coming up at the church, and she's always on the lookout for new recruits, if that would interest you."

"Yes, it would," said Louise. "I'm quite active in our church back home. And who knows? Maybe while I'm sorting out the jumble, I can pick up something new to wear."

"I'll ring her and see if—" But before Penny could finish the sentence, Bronwyn herself was standing in the doorway, with Robbie on his lead by her side.

"Oh, Bronwyn," said Penny. "Come in. We were just talking about you."

"Me?" Her eyes flickered over to Louise, standing beside Penny's desk.

After introducing the two women, Penny mentioned that Louise was interested in helping with the jumble sale.

"That's wonderful," said Bronwyn. "I'd be very glad of the help. But Penny, I just wanted to pop in and make sure you're all right. I was a bit concerned when you took off like that. And I wondered if you'd managed to find out anything more."

"There's very little information available," said Penny. "But it's getting a bit crowded in here, so why don't we all go to the quiet room, where we'll be more comfortable. And we might as well have some tea or coffee."

"Actually, I've got to get back to work," said Victoria. "Those invoices aren't going to pay themselves." She hesitated in the doorway. "But let me know the minute you hear anything."

"We should let you get back to work, too, Penny," said Bronwyn. "Louise, how about you and I walk over to the rectory, and we'll have a little chat there." And then, when a thought occurred to her, she added, "Have you had your lunch?"

"I was going to pick up something in town. I am feeling a bit peckish, now you mention it."

"Well, there's some leftover quiche, and then we'll have a nice cup of tea. I baked a *bara brith* yesterday and you might like to try a slice."

"What's that?" asked Louise.

"It's a quick bread with raisins. *Bara* means "bread" in Welsh, and *brith* means "speckled," so speckled bread. The raisins bring the speckle," she added helpfully. "You soak them in tea."

"Oh, that sounds delicious. Yes, I would definitely like to try that."

"I hope you don't mind dogs. Robbie here is still a bit annoyed with me because I wouldn't let him have Penny's sandwich. He won't be allowed any *bara brith*, either, because of the raisins, so his frostiness is likely to continue." They said goodbye to Penny, and after Louise had made a suitable fuss over Robbie, with Bronwyn leading the way, they slipped away into the hallway that would take them to the reception area and out the front door.

"I love dogs," said Louise. "I've got a rescue at home. We have no idea where she came from or what breed she is. There was a sign in the bank that said 'free to good home', so we brought her home, and she's been loved every day since."

"What's she called?" Bronwyn's voice was fading, and Penny could just make out Louise's reply.

"Dolly."

After that, she heard no more. *Those two are going to get on just fine,* she thought. *Nothing brings people together like a shared love of dogs.* And although Penny appreciated Bronwyn's thoughtfulness of inviting Louise home with her so she could get back to work, she doubted she'd get much work done that afternoon. She started looking through Canadian media websites, hoping that they would have more details because the event was unfolding on Canadian soil. And never mind the

Cambridge scientists. As far as she was concerned, there was only one person involved, and it was his fate she was worried about.

\* \* \*

"Bronwyn sent a few things with me for us to have for our supper," Louise said that evening. Penny looked up from her laptop. "I'll just go ahead and make dinner, shall I? It won't be anything fancy. Just a piece of fish and some vegetables."

"That would be lovely. Thanks." Penny returned her attention to the screen.

Half an hour later, Louise set their meals on the table, and Penny picked up her fork.

"This looks delicious." She set down her fork. "But I just don't have much of an appetite, I'm afraid."

"Neither do I," said Louise, "but it's probably best if we make an effort. Just eat what you can." Penny didn't move.

"I know you're terribly worried about your friend, but I get the feeling he's rather more to you than that. Would it help to talk about him?"

"His name's Colin Campbell, and he's a wildlife photographer."

"Yes, that much I do know," Louise said with a kind smile. "Bronwyn told me. Tell me what you like about him."

Penny's eyes sparkled. "I haven't known him that long, but I just enjoy being around him. There's a kindness to him, a gentleness, and he's smart, too. And I admire that he had the courage to pack in a life he wasn't enjoying, to try for one that was more suited to him—that he was willing to take that risk, even though it meant giving up a lot of money."

"So a bit like what you did, then?"

"Oh, I didn't give up anything. I had nothing to go back to in Canada, and there was no money involved. This—living here—was the best thing that ever happened to me. And I don't mean just the cottage, although I am so fortunate to have inherited it—I mean my whole life here in Wales. It's where I belong. So it was easy for me. I just found myself in the right place. Why would I leave?"

"Would you consider relocating back to Canada, then, if things move along in a good direction with Colin?"

Penny didn't hesitate. "No, I wouldn't. He'd have to move here. Otherwise, we don't have a future together."

"From your quick response, I gather you've thought about it."

A light pink infused Penny's cheeks. "Yes, it's crossed my mind. You know how it is. You picture yourself . . . you think of the possibilities . . ."

"You allow yourself to dream, don't you?"

"I hope I'm not being silly about this, that it is what I think it is, what I hope it is."

"What you want it to be. I hope so, too."

"And now, let's change the subject. Would you like to tell me more about Jessica? Was she ambitious, would you say?"

"All she ever wanted was to be a reporter, but she would never have been ruthless about it, and she had a really strict code about truth telling, which some journalists don't, as you probably know. She refused to lie her way into a story, as she described it. She was always up front with the people she interviewed.

"When she started out at the paper, they saw her as a young girl who could cover fluff stories, and she did that for a while, but then she wanted something more. She wanted harder news stories, to cover city hall. And when they gave her the chance, boy, did she run with it. She uncovered a story to do with a politician. There was a big paving contract up for tender, and when it was awarded to a bidder who didn't seem the best qualified, she decided to look into it. It set her antennae twitching, she said. And she was relentless. She just kept digging, and it turned out this politician had been taking bribes. There were meetings at the newspaper, and lawyers brought in, and the editors decided they would run the story. As a courtesy, Jessica called the elected member the night before the story would run, to prepare him, and he begged her not to run the story, ranting all about how it would ruin him, his family, and so on. But by then it was out of her hands, and the story ran."

"Could someone involved in all that have followed her here?" Penny asked. "The elected member, someone in his family, anyone from the paving company?"

"It's possible, I suppose. But I don't see why they'd go to all that trouble. And besides, all this happened last year." Her eyes brimmed with tears. "I just can't believe she's gone. It's shocking to me that her space in the world isn't there anymore."

"Oh, Louise, I'm so sorry." Penny reached for her water glass, then said, "There's wine. I'd like a glass. Would you care to join me?"

"It's probably nowhere near as good as our beautiful New Zealand wine, but I'm happy to give it a go."

"You probably won't like it. It's only that French muck."

Their plates of food remained untouched, but now, with a glass of wine, the conversation continued.

"The way you described Jessica just now," said Penny, "I'm struck by her tenaciousness. Now, I don't know if there's a connection here, but someone told me once that people often get killed because they heard something, or they saw something, or they've got something, and—this could be the important one—because they know something."

"But what could Jessica possibly have known?" cried Louise. "She'd only been in the country for five minutes."

"Well, maybe that's the thing," said Penny. "It's not what she knew. She was an investigative reporter. What if someone was afraid that she was going to discover something, and killed her before she could."

Louise reached across the table and rested her hand on Penny's arm. "My skin started to tingle when you said that."

"It wasn't what she knew," Penny repeated, as if to clarify it for herself. "It's what she was going to know. What she was going to find out. And whatever that information was, it was very dangerous and someone did not want her to find it out."

# Chapter
# Twenty-Seven

"She mentioned the stories she was planning to work on when we met her that Friday night in the bar," Penny said. "But I was a bit distracted, you see, because I'd just met Colin and was rather focused on him. But as I recall, Jessica mentioned she wanted to write some travel features, and something about a New Zealand man who disappeared while he was in England, and then of course there was Bill Ward. I wonder if he's got something shady in his past that wouldn't hold up to scrutiny in the cold light of day." She took a sip of wine. "And it seems reasonable to assume that the person who killed Jessica was the same person who tried to poison you with an overdose of your own sleeping tablets. And Bethan and I agree that whoever that person was, they have a close connection to the hotel. Now it could be someone who works there, but Bill Ward was a familiar face around the place. He holds his art weekends there, and he had a long-standing relationship with the assistant manager. I'm sure any hotel staff member who saw him wandering about the place wouldn't think twice about it. He could go wherever he pleases because he's practically one of them.

"And then," Penny continued, "There's the matter of Jessica's missing backpack. We all agree that could be important. It could factor somehow into her death. It may be that there was something in it the killer wanted."

"Her laptop?"

"Could be. She was a reporter. Did she use an old-fashioned notebook?"

"She used everything that a journalist needs to do her job. Notebook, tape recorder, smartphone, the Internet, social media . . . everything."

"And her phone?"

Louise shook her head. "It may be in the backpack, but it wasn't on her. Unless it's in her suitcase, which I still haven't opened. I don't have it." They sat in silence for a moment, and then Louise continued. "I'm still feeling unsettled—and anxious about everything, truth be told. Especially after what happened in the hotel."

"That's understandable."

"Yes, and while I'm very grateful to you for your hospitality, I'm a bit worried because your cottage is . . ."

"Isolated. Yes, I know it is."

"And I wasn't sure how to bring this up with you without sounding ungrateful, but when I mentioned this to Bronwyn, she suggested I might feel a little more secure if I stayed at the rectory with her and her husband. And as soon as she said it, it felt like the right thing for me to do. I feel I must listen to the little voice inside me telling me to go there. Please don't be offended. I appreciate everything you've done for me. I do hope you don't mind."

"Of course I don't mind. In fact, I think it's a good idea. You absolutely must do what you think is right for you to feel safe."

"And do you?" Louise asked. "Do you feel safe here?"

"Well, I always have, but then it wasn't me someone tried to hurt with those sleeping tablets. And will you leave in the morning?"

"We thought it best if they pick me up after supper this evening, after I'd had time to explain everything to you. And as I said, you've been very kind, and please don't think I'm ungrateful. It's just . . ."

Penny reached out her hand and touched Louise's. "Really, it's fine. I understand perfectly. I'd feel the same way, I'm sure."

"Good. That's settled then." Louise looked at their untouched plates. "What should we do about these? I'm starting to feel as if I might be able to eat something."

"Me, too," said Penny. "Let's heat them up and try again. I'm a waste not, want not kind of person."

"So am I. Maybe we had the same kind of upbringing, even though we were on opposite sides of the world."

"I was raised by my grandparents, and we didn't have much. It wasn't until I was an adult that I understood the sacrifices they had to make to look after me."

Each carrying a plate, the women trooped into the kitchen and waited in front of the microwave while their food heated. When each plate was piping hot, they returned to the table, and as they tucked in, Penny asked Louise about her life in New Zealand.

"Although we both come from Commonwealth countries, I don't know as much about your beautiful New Zealand as I should. But I believe both our countries have something in common: stunning scenery. Mountains and glaciers and lush forests and so on."

Louise's lips drew back at an attempt at a smile, but it somehow got caught on her teeth. She frowned and her head tilted to one side as she regarded Penny through thoughtful, slightly narrowed eyes.

"When you mentioned the scenery just then, it reminded me of something that happened recently in New Zealand that sounds an awful lot like what your Colin is going through. A group of inexperienced and completely unprepared hikers went missing in a dense forest. They were lost for three days, and in harsh conditions. The story was all over the media, and fears were expressed for their safety. But somehow they managed to find a spot where they could get mobile service, and they were able to contact the authorities to let them know the group members were alive, but the problem was they were completely lost. No idea where they were, so how could they tell the searchers where to find them?"

Penny groaned. "Oh no. What a terrible situation."

"Anyway, the police told one of the lost hikers to download this special app. Apparently, the whole world has been divided up into a grid, and three words are assigned to every square. So if someone in the missing group that you're worried about can get that app and then tell the authorities their three words, the searchers can pinpoint their location and rescue them."

"Would it work even in remote, heavily forested areas?"

"Yes, that's the beauty of it. It works everywhere. Every square metre of the planet."

"That's amazing! How have we not heard about this?"

Louise shrugged. "Do you know if the group lost in Canada has access to mobile service?"

"No," said Penny, as a feeling of excitement began to rise within her. "I don't know, but this is definitely worth a try. I'll ring Bethan, and she can contact the RCMP."

"The who?"

"The Royal Canadian Mounted Police. They're bound to be involved in the search at some level, and from one police force to another, I'm sure Bethan can get through quickly to the people in charge. Can you remember the name of the app?"

"I don't remember it exactly, but it's to do with three words. My Three Words or something like that."

A few minutes later, she ended the call. "She was stunned," Penny said. "She said considering how useful it is, it should be much better known than it is. Anyway, she's passing on the information, and we'll see what happens. Oh, and that app? It's called What3words."

She beamed at Louise. "Thank you so much for suggesting that. I feel better now. When something goes wrong, doing what you can to try to put it right helps lighten the feeling of helplessness."

"Yes, it does," Louise said softly.

"Oh, I'm sorry," said Penny. "That was thoughtless of me. I didn't think."

"No," Louise replied, "it wasn't thoughtless. It's quite all right. Our two situations are completely different. Jessica never went missing, and I never had an anxious wait, wondering where she was or if she would be found safe. And besides, we're going to do what we can to find out how and why Jessica died, and that's exactly what you meant, and it is helping me enormously. And not only that, if my suggestion helps you locate someone you love, then that makes me happy."

Penny was struck by the word Louise had chosen: "love." Did she love Colin? When is that moment that you realize you love someone? Or even become aware that you're falling in love? It had been so long since she had experienced these feelings, but it was all coming back to her, the giddy swirling of emotions and the lifting in her heart whenever she thought of him.

The two women finished their meal, and just as Penny was about to suggest coffee, a crunching of gravel outside Penny's front window signalled the arrival of Rev. Thomas Evans and Bronwyn.

"I don't think we'll stay for coffee, if that's all right," Bronwyn replied to Penny's invitation. "I've left Robbie at home, and I don't like being away from him for one minute longer than necessary. He gets up to mischief when he's on his own, and I never know what I'm going to come home to."

"Looks like we could get some rain tonight," Thomas remarked as he lifted Louise's suitcases into the car. After ensuring his two passengers were settled, he said goodbye to Penny, got into the driver's seat, and started the car. Penny waved Louise off in the care of the rector and his wife.

She took a deep breath of evening air, then stepped back inside her cottage, locked the front door, and set about tidying up the kitchen and laying out her breakfast things ready for the morning. She opened the back door to let out her cat, Harrison, and then sank into the sofa for one last browse of Canadian media websites. *Of course there's no news,* she scolded herself. *It's too soon.* But with a bit of luck, maybe by morning. She leaned her head against the back of sofa and let out a long sigh of exhaustion mixed with relief. As much as she liked

Louise—admired her even—she didn't feel up to having company tonight, so it had worked out for the best that Louise had gone to stay with the Evanses. Probably better for Louise, too. The Evanses were the kindest, gentlest people Penny knew, and they could be trusted to take good care of her.

Penny was surprised how emotionally and physically drained she felt, and in the gathering dusk, she was more than ready for an early night. Rather than switching on a lamp, she decided to just head upstairs, and after rechecking that the front door was locked on her way past, she climbed the stairs. She changed into her nightdress, and after giving her teeth the briefest of brushings and cleansing her face, she tumbled into bed and fell immediately into a deep, dreamless sleep.

* * *

She awoke to utter blackness and reached for her phone on the bedside table, to check the time. After groping for it and not finding it, she realized she must have left it downstairs. She switched on the bedside lamp and checked her bed. Harrison, who usually slept with her, wasn't there. She sank back in bed and recalled the evening's events. When she came to the part where she'd let Harrison out, she sat bolt upright. She couldn't remember making sure he was back in the house, with the back door locked behind him.

She swung her legs over the side of the bed, sat up, slid her feet into a pair of slippers, and walked to the top of the stairs. And then she sensed, rather than heard, a presence downstairs. She shrank back and stepped into the bathroom and stealthily closed the door. Yes. She could definitely hear soft footsteps, and with a pounding heart and her legs beginning to wobble, she heard the unmistakable creak of the bottom stair that could only have been caused by someone placing a foot on it. She lifted her bathrobe off the hook on the back of the door and slipped it on. As she cinched the tie around her waist, she felt marginally more in control.

She held out her hand and touched the key in the lock of the bathroom door, but as she wrapped her fingers around its silvery coolness, she hesitated. What if turning the key made just enough noise to alert the intruder that she was in the bathroom? She withdrew her hand. The shower stall was surrounded by clear glass; there was no curtain to conceal her. She considered positioning herself behind the door in the hope that if it were opened, she'd be hidden behind it. But that carried the risk that if the intruder discovered her, she'd be trapped. So she flattened herself against the wall on the other side of the door, and if the intruder opened it, her best hope was to bolt down the stairs and make a run for it out the front door.

She held her breath, afraid that the shallowest inhalation would signal her presence. She waited. And when a pinpoint of light pooled on the floor in front of her, and she heard the creak that came from the top step, she knew that whoever it was, they were here.

# Chapter
# Twenty-Eight

S he put her hand over her pounding heart, as if that would somehow slow it down. The beam of light showing under the bathroom door moved away as whoever was holding the torch advanced toward the bedroom where Louise would have been sleeping. *Thank God,* Penny thought, *that Louise listened to that little voice in her head and is now safe at the rectory with Thomas and Bronwyn Evans.*

The beam of light was back, this time moving slowly in the other direction, toward Penny's bedroom. The thought flitted through her mind that while the intruder was in there, she could try to escape. But that risked a direct confrontation, which might not end well for her. She remained frozen in place, and a few minutes later the light returned briefly, then disappeared, followed by the creak of the top step.

She let out a long, slow exhale of the breath she didn't realize she'd been holding, as the danger receded, and when her legs finally gave way, she sank slowly to the floor. And now, feeling it was safe to do so, she turned the key and locked herself in. She pulled the towels off the rail, spread them on the floor, and then lay on them, on her side, knees drawn up, and hands pressed between her knees. The towelling fabric felt both rough and comforting against her face as she gazed at the pipes under the sink.

She strained to hear the slightest sound, but everything was quiet. And then, from somewhere in the distance, came the sound of a car engine starting up.

She had no way of knowing what time it was or how long she'd spent in that position. Every minute was a struggle to stay in place, fighting the urge to run out of her cottage. But she told herself she had to wait until it was safe, until she was sure the intruder had left. She thought about Harrison. Was he inside the cottage, waiting for her downstairs? And then her churning thoughts turned to the intruder. What had he or she wanted? To silence Louise? To silence her? And an even more horrifying thought: *to silence both of us?* Or maybe it was just a burglar, here to take whatever valuables she had. Her laptop. Her phone. Her jewellery.

Finally, unable to bear it any longer, she eased herself to a sitting position, and then, stiff and sore, she grasped the towel bar and used it to haul herself to her feet. She turned the key, grimacing at the sound it made, and waited, and when no sound came from downstairs, she eased the door open and then stepped lightly into the hallway. Without looking in the bedrooms, she crept across the landing and placed her hand on the banister. Then, one stair at a time, pausing on each one, she made her way downstairs. When she reached the entryway at the front door, she glanced into her sitting room. She couldn't see it in the dark, but her phone, if it hadn't been stolen, should be on the table in front of the sofa. She inched her way across the floor until she felt the table against her knee, then lowered her hand and brushed it along the table, hoping to touch her phone.

It was there. With a huge sense of relief, she wrapped her fingers around it, then flew to the front door, unlocked it and bolted outside. As she raced down the road, she somehow controlled her trembling fingers enough to call Bethan's private number. When the policewoman answered in a sleepy voice, Penny blurted out what had happened and where she was.

Bethan, instantly awake, told her to wait by the side of the road and that she was on her way.

A light rain was falling and the night air was earthy, with a hint of grass and flowers, as Penny stood shivering in her sleeveless cotton nightdress with just the light bathrobe over it. She rubbed her upper arms, trying to generate some warmth, and hopped lightly from one foot to the other. Her feet, shod only in thin bedroom slippers, were now wet and cold.

After what seemed an eternity, two glowing headlights appeared in the distance, and then, as they got closer, Penny stepped out from the verge and planted herself in the middle of the road. When the police car stopped, she flung open the passenger door and threw herself inside.

"Oh, thank God!" she cried. "I've never been so glad to see anyone in my life."

"You look frozen," Bethan said, switching on the car's heater before continuing down the lane to Penny's cottage. She eased the car into the parking space, switched off the engine, and turned to face Penny.

"Stay where you are," she ordered. "I'm going to get the blanket out of the boot, but you mustn't go into your cottage."

A moment later she was back. She unwrapped an airplane-style blanket from its cellophane protector, and when she'd placed it over Penny, she asked, "Where's Louise? I thought she was staying with you. Why isn't she with you? Don't tell me she's still in the cottage . . ." Her words evaporated into silence.

"Oh no," said Penny, realizing Bethan feared the worst. "She's fine, as far as I know. She decided to stay with Thomas and Bronwyn because she didn't feel safe here. Turns out, she was right. They picked her up after dinner and took her to the rectory."

"Given what happened at the Beaumaris Arms Hotel, you should have informed me there'd been a change of plan."

She spoke a few words into her police radio. "No emergency call logged from the rectory tonight, but I've sent a car over there to check on them, just in case."

"Oh, you're not going to wake them up, are you?"

"An officer will assess the scene, and we'll take it from there. Now, tell me what happened here tonight."

"Someone got into in my house and came upstairs. It was terrifying. But the thing is, I'm really concerned about Harrison. Can you check and make sure he's okay?"

"I've called for backup. I can't enter your cottage until they arrive, so we'll have to just sit here for a few minutes. I promise you, I'll check on Harrison the first thing I'm inside. Now, tell me everything you can."

Penny recounted how she'd felt utterly exhausted after Louise left, that she'd let Harrison out, and then gone upstairs for an early night and fallen asleep almost immediately. "But I think I did something really stupid."

"Oh, please don't tell me you left your back door open when you let the cat out."

"I'm pretty sure I did. In fact, when I woke up and Harrison wasn't with me, that's the first thought that popped into my head. I was just about to go downstairs to look for him and check that I'd locked the door when I heard something. Or rather, I sensed that someone was down there, and then I heard a noise, so I hid in the bathroom."

"I'm glad you woke up when you did."

"I know. But please don't say anything about the door. Don't make me feel any worse."

"I'm not going to say it, Penny. People leave doors unlocked and windows open all the time, and nothing bad happens. You were just unlucky there, but in lots of other ways you were very lucky tonight. For one thing, you weren't hurt. Home invasions don't always end this well. And for another, Louise, who may have been the target, wasn't here. I don't suppose you know yet if anything's been taken."

"No, I just got the hell out of there."

"And quite right, too. You did the sensible thing, staying where you were and then waiting until you were sure the intruder was well and truly gone before making your escape."

"I was desperate to get out of there, but afraid to move in case there was still someone downstairs."

"We have a saying in the police that in a situation like that you must wait as long as you can, and then wait some more. Your sense of time is distorted. What seems like an eternity is probably only a few minutes. In most home invasions, the goal is robbery; the intruders are there to steal whatever they can get their hands on, and they don't want to run into anybody. Unless, of course, they need someone to tell them the combination to a safe or something like that, but usually they just want to get in, get their hands on whatever valuables are available, and get out, without bumping into anyone.

"And I say 'intruder,' but there could have been more than one, in which case your chance of getting out decreases substantially. But why did you wait so long to ring me? Why didn't you call from the bathroom? Were you afraid of being overheard?"

"I didn't have my phone with me. It was downstairs, on the coffee table. I grabbed it before I ran out the front door."

"Oh, I see. Well, that's interesting. If they left the phone, that means they probably weren't there to steal. So once your cottage is secure, I'm going to ask you to have a quick look around to see if you can tell if anything's missing. But don't touch anything. Do you have any good jewellery?"

Penny conducted a mental inventory of the modest contents of her jewellery box. "I have a pair of custom-made earrings that I think contain precious stones, and there's a diamond brooch in the shape of a snowflake. Both gifts from your old boss, Gareth Davies."

# Chapter Twenty-Nine

A second police are pulled up beside them, and two uniformed officers got out and approached Bethan's side of the vehicle. She turned to Penny as the officers opened her door, and said, "You're to wait here until I come back for you. No matter what happens, don't leave the car."

As the uniformed officers disappeared inside the cottage and Bethan hovered near the front door, Penny pulled the blanket tighter around her and sank down in the car seat. Lights came on in the sitting room, and a few minutes later, in the upstairs rooms. Watching the glow of warm, beckoning light spread throughout her home, knowing that police officers were moving from room to room, comforted and reassured her. And then the officers emerged from the cottage and spoke to Bethan. A few minutes later, she returned to the car and climbed in beside Penny.

"The back door was open, as you thought," Bethan said. "I'll bring you in now, and we'll go through the house together."

"Harrison?" Penny asked. "Did they see him?"

"Sorry, no. All this commotion could have frightened him, and he might be hiding outside. Does he often stay out all night?"

"Never. I let him out, he comes back, and then we go up to bed together. Only tonight—well, you know what happened tonight."

"He could have a found a safe spot somewhere in the house. Under the sofa, maybe, and he'll come out when he's ready and not a minute sooner. You know what cats are like. But don't worry; we'll find him."

When they reached the front door Bethan pulled on a pair of gloves. "Take a deep breath. You can do this in your own time, and in fact, if you'd rather not do it tonight, you don't have to. We can come back tomorrow."

"Tomorrow?"

"In situations like this, it's best to stay with someone else for the night, for two reasons. One, a home invasion is traumatic and you should not be alone; and two, because your cottage is now a crime scene, I've ordered a forensic sweep, and you need to be out of the way until the team has wrapped up. So you've got two choices. You can come home with me, or you can stay with Victoria."

"I'll stay with you," Penny replied immediately. "There's no point in disturbing Victoria at this time of night. Or morning, I guess it is." She took a deep breath and steadied her shoulders. "Let's get this over with. I'm okay to take a look around, and in fact I want to. We might find Harrison, and knowing he's safe would put my mind at ease."

"I'll be right beside you. Remember, don't touch anything."

They entered the cottage and walked through the downstairs rooms. After discovering that nothing looked disturbed, and searching everywhere a frightened cat might be hiding, Bethan indicated they should head upstairs.

In her bedroom, Penny glanced at her unmade bed, the top sheet and light bedspread arranged just as she'd left them. When Penny indicated her bureau, Bethan nudged out the top drawer, using the sides and bottom. She withdrew a red box and opened it. She tipped it toward Penny to show her that the diamond snowflake brooch was safe, and further inspection revealed that Penny's best earrings were there, too.

"Those are really the only pieces I've got that are of any value, and I presume anyone looking for something to steal would have known their worth."

"Okay. If you'd like to get dressed now and pack an over-night bag, I can either remain here with you or wait downstairs."

"Stay here with me, please. I'm starting to feel a bit shaky. I see now what you mean when you say it's a good idea to stop somewhere else with a friend for the rest of the night."

Penny slipped on a pair of comfortable trousers, a polo top, and a cozy jumper, then packed a few toiletries and a clean night dress in a carryall.

After instructing the police officers, who would remain on scene until morning, to keep an eye out for Harrison, Penny and Bethan departed.

"What do you make of it?" Penny asked as they drove along the darkened lane toward the sleeping town.

"Because your phone and jewellery were not taken, and because of the isolated location of your cottage, this isn't the work of opportunistic thieves who just happened to be prowling around the neighbourhood, noticed the back door was open, and decided to help themselves to whatever they could find."

"What do you think they were looking for?"

Bethan covered her mouth as she stifled a yawn. The sky had lightened to a deep lavender-grey, indicating that dawn was about an hour away.

"It's likely that they were after you or Louise, and given what happened at the hotel, my money's on Louise," said Bethan.

"Or what if this wasn't about Louise herself? What if it's about something she had that somebody wanted?"

Although her eyes remained on the road ahead, Bethan's shoulders turned slightly toward Penny. "What do you mean?"

"Jessica's suitcase. Louise has Jessica's suitcase."

"If it's the suitcase they were after, then that makes sense of the drugging at the hotel. Did anyone at the hotel know she was staying with you?"

"Yes. I told Sarah Spencer when I asked her to tell the hotel staff to allow me access to Louise's hotel room."

"And she would have been able to access the hotel reservation system to get your home address."

"That's right, she would have." Penny was silent for a moment and then added, "and Bill Ward has my address, too. It was on the form when I registered for his painting course."

The rain had started up again, and Bethan switched on the windscreen wipers. The only sound for the rest of the journey was the mechanical rhythm of their swishing back and forth.

# Chapter Thirty

Penny spent what remained of the night tossing and turning in the hard, narrow bed in Bethan's spare room, and when she got up, she discovered Bethan had already gone to work, leaving a house key with a note on the kitchen table, advising Penny to make herself at home and to please be sure to lock the door when she went out.

*Fair enough, after what happened last night,* thought Penny.

After a quick shower, she decided to seek breakfast elsewhere, and set off through the town for the rectory. As she passed the cricket ground, the morning mist skimming the trees was dissipating, and after the rain of the night before, the sodden ground gave off a rich, loamy smell of earth. Clouds were gathering over the hills, however, with the promise of more rain on the way.

She knocked on the bright blue door of the rectory. Bronwyn greeted her warmly, and after ushering Penny into the kitchen, cheerfully added another egg to the pan, popped two more slices of bread into the toaster, and poured another cup of coffee.

When Louise, Bronwyn, and the rector were all seated around the table, Penny described the events of the night before.

"Thank heavens Louise was here with us," the rector said when she'd finished. "The police rang us at eight o'clock this morning to ask if everything was all right, but they didn't give us any details, so I thought it was just a routine check, in light of what had happened to Louise earlier at the hotel in Beaumaris, and I was happy to report that all was well." He gave Louise a reassuring smile. "So Penny, if nothing was stolen from your cottage, and it wasn't a robbery, do the police have any idea what the intruders were after?"

Penny dropped a dollop of marmalade on her toast.

"Because my phone and the two pieces of jewellery I have that are of any value weren't taken, Bethan doesn't think these were opportunistic thieves who just happened to be passing."

"So in other words, your cottage was targeted," said the rector.

"Yes, but if that's the case, I don't think the intruder or intruders meant any harm to Louise or me."

Bronwyn leveled a steady gaze at her over the rim of her coffee cup.

"Why do you say that?"

"Because my bed was unmade. You know what a bed looks like when someone gets out of it in the night. The covers are thrown back in a careless way. So whoever the intruder was, they knew that my bed had recently been slept in. And if it was me they were after, they would have looked everywhere for me, including the bathroom.

"The bed in the spare room was made up, so they knew that room was unoccupied. And a spare room has a different look than a bedroom that's used every day. It's neater, more austere. No personal bits and pieces lying about. So they would have known Louise wasn't staying at the cottage. They checked the spare room first, and then they went into my room, so they must have been looking for something."

"So what were they after then?"

"I think they were after Jessica's suitcase. And what's more, I think that's what they wanted when Louise was drugged at the hotel, although it's possible that because she had been asking questions about Jessica, they may have wanted to silence her, too." When Louise protested that the police had said there was nothing in the suitcase but her daughter's clothes and other personal items and essentials, Penny replied, "Yes, but if that's what the intruder was after, they don't know that, do they? They don't know what's in the suitcase, but they want to find out."

Everyone mulled that over, and then Penny asked where the suitcase was now.

"It's upstairs in my room. What do you think we should do about it? Should I hand it back to the police for safekeeping?"

"No. We don't have to do anything about it. Bethan knows you have it, and she knows where you are, so if the police want it back for some reason, they'll ask for it."

Breakfast finished, Bronwyn left to parade Robbie through the town on his morning walk, and the rector retreated to his study, ostensibly to work on the Sunday sermon. Penny and Louise had insisted on being allowed to tidy up the kitchen, and as Louise stacked the cutlery and dishes in the dishwasher,

Penny gazed out the window to the path that ran parallel to the River Conwy. After a few moments, the rector drifted into view. He looked furtively up and down in both directions, and then withdrew a packet of cigarettes from his pocket and lit one. Penny gestured to Louise to join her at the window.

"What is it?" Louise asked. "What am I looking at?"

Penny pointed to the figure walking along the path. "It's the rector. He's been trying for years to quit smoking, but he just can't, and we're all in on the conspiracy. He pretends he doesn't enjoy the occasional cigarette, and the rest of us pretend we don't know he does it."

"What about his wife? Does she know he smokes?"

"Of course she does. Her only rule is that he can't smoke in front of Robbie."

Louise let out a fruity chuckle. "Is she afraid Robbie will learn from his bad example and take up smoking?"

"No. She just doesn't want her darling boy exposed to second-hand smoke."

"Quite right." Her face fell. "Jessica hated cigarette smoke." She dabbed at her eyes with the corner of the tea towel draped over her shoulder. "Everything reminds me of her. It flashed through my mind just then how she would have loved the story about the rector's secret smoking, and then in the next second I remembered that she isn't here and that we'll never again share a laugh over something silly like that." She let out a little sob, and Penny reached out and folded her into a comforting hug.

Just as she released her, Robbie raced into the kitchen, his toenails clacking on the slate floor. He ran to his food bowl, then turned expectantly to the doorway. After hanging up his lead and slipping out of her cardigan in the hallway, an out-of-breath Bronwyn followed him into the kitchen.

"You weren't gone very long," said Penny. "Didn't expect you back so soon."

"No," Bronwyn said. "We cut our walk short and hurried home. You'll be so relieved when you hear what I've got to tell you. We just bumped into Mrs. Lloyd, and she heard on the radio that the missing group has been found. They're safe! They were interviewed on the telly breakfast program, and Mrs. Lloyd even caught a glimpse of your Colin. She said he's got a beard; they all do." She burst out laughing. "Well, not the women, of course. Conditions weren't that bad. And they've all lost some weight."

"Oh, that's wonderful," exclaimed Penny. "That they've been found, not that they've lost weight." Her eyes widened and she let out a light puff of breath as she gripped the back of a chair and leaned on it. "Did the news report say what happened?"

"Apparently, the scientists and all their equipment were in several canoes, paddling their way to a remote site, and they got into some choppy water, and one of the boats capsized. A lot of their equipment was lost or damaged. They still had a mobile phone, but the problem was, they weren't sure where they were. They managed to find a signal and contact the police, and the rescuers eventually located them, and everyone is okay."

Penny and Louise exchanged a happy glance, and Penny remarked, "That's brilliant!"

"You must be so relieved," said Louise. "I'm so glad it ended well. For him and for you. For everybody."

"Me, too."

"I'm sure you'll hear from him soon."

Penny's phone pinged, indicating a text message. She glanced at the name of the sender, then with an "Excuse me," she stepped away and turned her back to the room. When she turned around, her eyes were shining, partly with excitement, partly with unshed tears, and mostly with the sense of joy that was flooding her body. "He's fine. He'll be here in a few days. He'll let me know when he's firmed up his flight."

Bronwyn clapped her hands together. "Well, there couldn't be better news, and all's well that ends well. Now, you'll have to excuse me. I must find Thomas to tell him the good news, and then I'm off to the church to make a start on sorting clothes for the jumble sale." She looked hopefully from one woman to the other. "Do I have any volunteers this morning? The infants and children's clothing are always such a mess and half of it needs washing. You'd be surprised at the state of some of it."

"I'd like to earn my keep," said Louise, "so I'm happy to help."

"I should drop into the police station to see where things stand with the break-in," said Penny, "and how long before they think it's safe for me to return home. And I'm desperate to know if Harrison turned up. I can't stop thinking about him."

"Of course," said Bronwyn. "You have more important things to see to."

"What if I call back after lunch? I thought I'd go to the Oriel Snowdonia in Betws this afternoon, and perhaps Louise would like to come with me? Give her an opportunity to see more of our beautiful countryside, and I always find an art gallery the perfect place to spend the afternoon when the weather's a bit dreary."

"Yes, I'd like that very much. If Bronwyn can spare me, that is."

"Of course I can."

"And if it's all right with you, Louise, I thought I'd ask my friend Alwynne Gwilt if she's free to join us. She was with me on the painting weekend, and while I don't think she met Jessica, and I'm not sure if she can tell you anything, I thought you might like to meet her, just because she was there."

"Oh yes, I'd like that very much."

*　*　*

"The police have wrapped up their forensics examination of my cottage," Penny said as she, Louise, and Alwynne walked to the bus stop under an overcast sky. The wind was picking up, and the darkening sky threatened to bring an afternoon full of rain. "Bethan's confident that the intruder won't be back, so I can go home today, if I want to."

"And do you want to?" asked Alwynne.

"Yes, I do. I'd like to make sure everything's all right, and be there when Harrison turns up."

"I mean, are you feeling apprehensive or uneasy about it?"

"A little, maybe. I felt uneasy last night when we checked to see if anything was missing, but with this weather closing in, it's my dear little cat I'm worried about. I hope he's all right. We don't know where he is or what happened to him. But I don't feel comfortable going home on my own, so Victoria's going to drive me home later and come in with me. Bethan said sometimes the full impact of what happened doesn't hit people until they return home."

"I can understand that. The very thought of a stranger roaming about your home, touching your things, is appalling. Makes your skin crawl."

"Yes, it does. But the police offered victim support services, and I've got good friends seeing me through this, so in that, I'm very fortunate."

The bus dropped them at the gallery, and after a short walk up a tree-lined lane, they reached the front door. "When we've finished looking at the artwork," said Penny, "they've got a rather nice café where we can have some tea and cake, if we want it."

"Let's see what happens," said Louise. "If the rain sets in, we may want to wait it out, but if it's still on its way, we may want to try to get home in time to beat it."

They entered the first gallery and circled the room, admiring the work of an emerging artist whose paintings captured the spirit and feel of rural communities. As they were about to cross the main entranceway to explore galleries on the other side of the building, Cilla McKee emerged from the hallway that led to her office.

She and Penny greeted each other, and Penny introduced her to Alwynne, as a member of her painting group, and to Louise, without mentioning her relationship to Jessica, simply explaining that she was a visitor from New Zealand.

"Oh, please be sure to sign our guest book," said Cilla. "We get the occasional visitor from Australia, but New Zealanders are rare birds in these parts."

"Rare kiwi birds," said Louise.

"Exactly." Cilla gave her a professional smile and then focused her attention on Penny. "Now, if I could just have a quick word. I was going to ring you, but since you're here, if you wouldn't mind, I have something to ask you."

"No, of course I don't mind. How can I help?"

"It's just that we want the gallery to do more community involvement activities that we feel could create good publicity for us and hopefully be of benefit to local artists, too. I know about your artist's group in Llanelen, and I wondered if you'd be interested in being part of our new initiative. Would you ask your group if any of the artists would consider donating a painting for an auction next winter to raise money for a good cause? It's a creative arts group for children that encourages and supports youthful involvement in music, art, dance, writing—all those lovely things that don't get the same attention as sport does."

"It's certainly a good cause," said Penny. "We'd be happy to share this with our Stretch and Sketch Club, wouldn't we, Alwynne."

"Good," said Cilla when Alwynne agreed. "I'm preparing a letter now with all the details, and I'll make sure you get a copy. I'll send it you, shall I, Penny? I have your address on file. Right, well, I won't take up any more of your time." She acknowledged Alwynne, then held out her hand to Louise. "It was nice to meet you. I hope you enjoy the rest of your stay. How much longer will you be here?"

"I'm not sure. Depends what happens. Maybe another week?"

"Well, I'll let you get on with your visit to the gallery, and I'll leave word in the café that coffee and cake for all three of you this afternoon will be complimentary."

"Oh, thank you. That's very kind," said Louise. Cilla pursed her lips and seemed about to say something, but hesitated. Reading the situation, Alwynne touched Louise lightly on the arm.

"I think Cilla wants a word with Penny about the upcoming Christmas exhibit. I'm curious to see what's upstairs. Shall we?"

As the two women disappeared up the stairs, Cilla said, "That was perceptive of your friend. I did want a word alone with you, but not about the exhibit. It's something I wouldn't have felt comfortable saying in front of your friends."

"What is it?"

"Well, it's just that now that I think about it, Sarah Spencer's husband, the one who conveniently moved away, leaving her free to move in with Bill Ward— he was from New Zealand. Although, it actually happened the other way round. The two of them moved in together, and then the husband moved away."

"It's been a long time," said Penny, "but I don't suppose you happen to remember his name?"

"Yes, it has been a long time, but when your husband leaves for you another woman, believe me, you remember every detail. Mark Currie, his name was."

"And you don't know where he moved to?"

"No, he and Sarah split up about the same time as Bill and I did. Mark and I met for coffee a couple of times. We thought talking it over might help us come to terms with what had happened."

"How did he take it?"

"Even worse than I did. He was shocked. I suspected Bill was cheating on me, but Mark had no idea his marriage was in deep trouble. Anyway, Bill and Sarah moved in together, and poor Mark was determined to win Sarah back, but not long after I last spoke to him, I guess he saw it was hopeless, and then he obligingly made himself scarce. Everyone assumed he'd returned home to New Zealand, and eventually my husband and that woman moved to Anglesey. End of story."

"And were they ever divorced?"

"Not as far as I know."

Seized by an idea, Penny got out her phone and thumbed through the camera roll until she came to the photo Colin had taken in the dining room of the Georgian house in Beaumaris where Sarah Spencer was living.

She showed Cilla the image of the couple standing in front of what she and Colin thought could be a country hotel. "Is that Mark Currie?"

Cilla held the phone, expanded the image and stared at it. "It's been a long time, but yeah, I'm pretty sure that's him." She handed back the phone. "And that's her, of course. Where on earth did you get this?"

"It's a copy of a photo in Sarah Spencer's dining room."

"Huh. Interesting she'd have that out for all to see." Her body twisted slightly as she turned away. "Well, I'd better get back to work. And do let me know if your group is interested in donating to my auction. It could be good exposure for them."

Cilla returned to her office, and Penny raced upstairs in search of Louise and Alwynne. "How would you feel about having that complimentary coffee now?" she asked when she found them examining a series of seascapes.

"What about seeing the rest of the exhibits? We've only just got started in here," said Alwynne.

"I'm sure there'll be plenty of time for that after. There's something I need to discuss with Louise."

"Oh dear, has something happened?"

"Let's go downstairs and have a chat. I've just heard something that might help us find out what happened to Jessica."

Louise spun on her heel and led the way to the café.

When they were seated with their coffee at a table with an open view of the surrounding green fields and forest, with low clouds seeming to hang in the tops of the trees, Penny rested her arms on the table as she wrapped her hands around her mug. "When I was talking to Cilla just then, something that might be important came back to me."

Louise ripped open a packet of sugar and tipped it into her coffee. "Sorry, I don't understand. What came back to you?"

"Something Jessica mentioned when we spoke to her in the bar on the Friday night. She said she was here in the U.K. to find out what happened to a man from New Zealand who disappeared several years ago, but she didn't mention his name. Or at least, if she did, I don't remember it. Now this is a long shot, but I need your help."

"Anything. What do you want me to do?"

"I'd like you to email Jessica's editor at the newspaper— Dave, I think she called him—and ask him to give you all her assignment details. Everything she was meant to be working on while she was in this country. Will you do that?"

"I could ring him if that would be faster, although I'm not sure about the time difference."

Penny tapped a few times on her phone, and then replied, "New Zealand is twelve hours ahead of us, so it's the middle of the night there. Email is better, so he'll see it when he wakes up or gets into the office. And besides, it would be better if we had his response in writing."

"You sound very serious. Is this important?"

Penny gave a slight shrug. "I don't know, but it could be. I'm getting that tingly feeling I get when I'm on to something. One tiny detail, one piece of missing information, sets off a cascade, and then everything comes together."

"Yes, but why is this name important?"

"I'd rather wait to discuss it until I know for sure. If you can get the man's name from Jessica's editor, we'll take it from there. But I will say this. Sometimes a fresh approach to an event that happened in the past can shed light on something that happened in the present." She smiled at the two women. "Let's leave it at that for now, and wait and see what happens." She picked up her fork. "Tell me about the paintings you were looking at upstairs. Anything interesting?"

"Well, yes," said Alwynne. "Louise and I were just looking at a rather nice painting of the South Stack Lighthouse at Holyhead, and I was explaining to her that it welcomes travellers home to Wales from Ireland, when you caught up with us."

"Jessica was enthralled with lighthouses," said Louise. "She would certainly have been eager to see the one at Beaumaris."

"Oh, Penny," said Alwynne. "That reminds me. You know that question we had about why lighthouses are round? I looked it up. It's to do with the displacement of wind and waves. Apparently, the round shape disperses the energy better than a square or rectangular shape."

Penny's eyes flickered away from the table and settled on the slopes of the ancient hills that would soon be drenched with nourishing rain.

* * *

Penny inserted the key in the lock of her front door and turned it. She hesitated for a moment and glanced at Victoria, who gave her an encouraging nod, and then entered. After pausing in the small entryway, she moved into the sitting room, and when Victoria turned to close the door behind her, Penny spoke.

"Leave it open for a few minutes. It feels as if all the air has been sucked out of the place. Do you feel it? Not just the air. The life. It feels stale and lifeless." She ran a finger over the coffee table, where a light dusting of fingerprint powder remained.

"We'll send Gwennie over tomorrow to clean up," said Victoria. "If I'd thought of it, she could have come today so everything was a bit better for you." She carried a bag of groceries through to the kitchen and unpacked the contents, placing some items in the fridge and leaving a few on the worktop.

Penny walked through the kitchen, unlocked the back door, and called out, "Harrison! Come home, Harrison." Leaving the door open, she said, "I'm so worried about him. He should have been back by now."

"He's probably hiding nearby," Victoria said. "I expect all the coming and going scared him off, and then the door was locked so he couldn't get back in." She reached out to Penny and hugged her. "This has been a major disruption in his life, but he'll be back—you'll see." She released her, then gestured at the food on the work top. "Shall we make a start on supper? What would you like?"

"Just something light."

"How about your old favourite, scrambled eggs on toast?"

"Sounds good. Have we got a bit of cheese we can add in?"

"We do."

Dinner over, and arrangements made for Gwennie, who kept the Spa clean and tidy, to come in the next morning, Penny and Victoria relaxed in the sitting room over cups of decaffeinated coffee.

"You must be really looking forward to seeing Colin again," said Victoria. "Have you heard when he'll be here?"

"He's got a few loose ends to tie up in Toronto and a meeting in New York, and he'll be here when all that's sorted. Early next week, he thinks. And yes, I can't wait to see him." Penny drained the last of her coffee and stood up. "I'm absolutely knackered. I think I'll have a bath and then get into bed. Thank you so much for stopping with me tonight. It means a lot to me that you're here."

"I'm glad to be here. There's no way you should be on your own, and besides, I know you'd do the same for me."

"Of course I would."

Victoria stood up. "I'll come up with you. Tell me where I can find a set of clean sheets, and while you're in the bath, I'll make up your bed."

Penny started to pick up her coffee cup, but Victoria stopped her. "Leave that. Go have your bath. After I've made your bed, I'll tidy up down here, and then I'm going to watch a bit of telly."

"I need to make sure that the back door's locked." While Victoria waited, Penny checked the door, and then, as they passed the front door on their way to the stairs, she checked that door, too.

* * *

Warmed and refreshed after her bath, Penny slipped into her clean, fresh bed and pulled the sheets up under her chin. She ran her hand over the coverlet where Harrison should be, sighed, and then, unable to stay awake, turned on her side and immediately fell into a dark and dreamless sleep.

A creak on the step awoke her. Heart pounding, she sat up in bed, paralyzed with fear. And then the steps came closer and outside her door, stopped. A moment later, came the sound of the lever handle of her bedroom door being pushed down, and slowly the door opened, letting in a muted light from the hall. A shadowy figure in the doorway entered the room and approached the bed.

"Penny?" whispered Victoria. "Sorry, did I wake you?"

"Yes," Penny croaked.

Victoria bent over the bed and set down a small furry bundle. "I've got somebody here who missed you."

Penny scooped up Harrison into her arms, eager to hold him, and buried her face in his fur.

"How did you find him?"

"He found me, really. I opened the back door to check on him one last time before coming up to bed, and there he was. I must say he made his entrance in a very lord of the manor kind of way, strolling in like nothing had happened. So I fed him, changed his water, and then brought him upstairs."

Harrison wriggled to be released and then curled up beside Penny, and in a moment the sound of his purring filled the room and her heart.

"And you locked the door after he came in?" Penny asked as she leaned back against her pillows.

"Yes, I did," said Victoria. "Everything's locked up, and Bethan texted me to say a police car will drive by a couple of times during the night to check up on us. If we need assistance, we're to leave an upstairs light on."

After a whispered goodnight, Victoria closed the door, and a few minutes later the hall light was switched off. With Harrison beside her, Penny slept peacefully through the night until she was awakened by the ping of an incoming text.

# Chapter
# Thirty-One

The text was from Louise. *See email,* it read. Now fully awake, Penny raised herself up in bed, opened her email, and clicked on the message Louise had forwarded.

*Dear Mrs. Graham,*

*In reply to your question about the stories Jessica had been assigned to work on during her stay in the United Kingdom, her main reason for being there was to write a news story (or stories) in response to the resurgence in interest surrounding the disappearance of an Auckland man, Mark Currie, whose family has not heard from him for coming up seven years.*

*She was also to research several travel stories, which we left open to her discovery—she was free to explore and write about whatever caught her attention that she thought would interest our readers, and while she would research these while she was in the U.K., we expected she would complete them on her return. And finally, the* Jubilee Terrace *actor Bill Ward had agreed to an interview with her.*

*May I say once again, on behalf of all of us at the newspaper, how very sorry we are for your loss. The newsroom isn't the same without Jessica, and we all miss her terribly. If I may provide any further information, please be in touch.*

*Dave*

Penny checked the time. Almost seven thirty. She gave Harrison a good-morning stroke, threw back the bedclothes, got dressed, and headed downstairs, with Harrison padding after her. She unlocked the back door and opened it for him. Then she put the kettle on, pulled a couple of croissants from the freezer, and switched on her laptop. "Mark Currie," she Googled, and then started devouring everything she could read about him.

Half an hour later, Victoria arrived downstairs, and after a brief greeting, said, "Checking for the latest on Colin, are you?"

Penny raised her head, and her eyes left the screen a few seconds later. "Oh, Colin. No, he's fine. It's Mark Currie I'm interested in, actually."

"Who's he when he's at home?"

"If I'm right, and I think I am, he's the key to all this."

Victoria poured a cup of coffee and then helped herself to a warm croissant, pulled it apart, and slathered on some raspberry jam.

"The key to all what?"

"He could be the key to Jessica's murder, and I'm trying to work out how and why. Jessica was here to do a story on him, and Cilla told me yesterday he's the husband—or perhaps former husband—of Sarah Spencer, so that gives us a strong link to the hotel.

"Here's the thing. He disappeared about seven years ago. Now the seven years is significant for two reasons. One, it was around the time Sarah Spencer's affair with Bill Ward was getting serious, and two—and here comes the big one—it says here," she continued, gesturing at her laptop, "Mark Currie comes from a very wealthy family. His family makes millions in the farming and exportation of lamb. Every sheep in New Zealand is somehow connected to a Currie business. "

Victoria groaned. "I'm sure they've heard every possible joke about lamb Currie."

"I'm sure they have. Now then. Because he's been missing for seven years, the family has applied to have him declared legally dead so they can settle up financial matters like wills, investments, trusts and inheritances, and all the rest of it."

"Fancy and complicated money matters that ordinary people don't have to worry about."

"Exactly. Issues that only people who are well off have to worry about. This is what happened when Lord Lucan disappeared. His family had to have him declared legally dead so his son could inherit the title.

"And although neither Jessica nor her editor mentioned this, I'd be willing to bet that the seven-year anniversary of Mark Currie's disappearance is the reason she was working on this story now. Journalists often use dates as the hook for a story, and the timing here is important."

"So, that means because it's been seven years since Mark Currie disappeared, if he is declared legally dead and Sarah is legally declared his widow, she could stand to inherit a lot of money?" asked Victoria.

"She could," said Penny. "Depending on what's in Mark Currie's will."

"But if this Mark Currie had all that money, why would he be working in a hotel?"

"Good question. But we don't know that he was working in a hotel. He could have been doing anything when he was married to Sarah. Anyway, from what I read here"—she motioned to her laptop screen—"it seems the Currie family business was started by one of those old-fashioned rags-to-riches type of man who was determined that his children and grandchildren would have to work for a living like he did, not just have access to a lot of easy money. But it would definitely be worth knowing the terms of Mark Currie's inheritance."

"And if he had a will and, if so, what was in it."

"Oh, I'm betting there was a will leaving everything to his wife, Sarah. In fact, I overheard Bill Ward saying something about Sarah coming into some money soon. And I'm thinking of that old saying, 'Where there's money, there's motive.'"

"Motive for what?"

"Murder, of course."

# Chapter Thirty-Two

"Mark Currie is dead." Inspector Bethan Morgan folded her arms and sat back in her chair in her orderly office in the Llanelen police station.

"Are you sure?" Penny asked.

"We can't be one hundred per cent sure because his body was never found, but the police in Manchester, where he was living when he disappeared, investigated his case thoroughly, and they had no reason to believe he's alive and living under a new identity somewhere."

She rested her forearms on her desk and clasped her hands together. "You see, in cases like that, the person has to have a compelling reason to want to escape his old life. He's fleeing something. Maybe he committed a crime or is burdened by overwhelming debt. But police found nothing in Currie's life to indicate he had a reason to disappear."

Bethan raised a hand. "And before you ask, yes, his wife was interviewed at the time of her husband's disappearance, and although a couple of officers had their doubts about her, they couldn't find any evidence or proof of foul play."

"And of course not having a body complicates matters if there is suspicion of wrongdoing," Penny said.

"It sure does, and believe me, killers count on that. It means that occasionally a missing persons case remains just that, when it should be classified as homicide."

"So in this case, a man goes missing, is presumed dead and possibly about to be declared legally dead, and a young woman has died. And the strongest connection between the two is a woman who works at the Beaumaris Arms Hotel," Penny reasoned.

"Well, Sarah Spencer certainly had a strong connection to the man who went missing, but a somewhat tenuous connection to the dead girl, I'd say."

"And there's also Bill Ward," Penny said. "He would have known that Mark Currie was Sarah Spencer's husband, and he had a connection to Jessica Graham as well. *Jubilee Terrace* is hugely popular in New Zealand, so she had arranged to interview him for a feature story. She was even given a name badge for the painting weekend. She called it 'press accreditation' and seemed rather proud of it.

"But there's something about Currie that would be really useful to know," Penny continued. "Can you find out if Mark Currie had a will and what the contents were? I'm sure that would be in the police report from the investigation into his disappearance."

"You're thinking this is relevant because his family is applying now to have him declared legally dead after seven years?"

"Yes." Penny checked her watch and stood up. "Well, I'll leave it with you. My lunch hour's almost over, and I've got a couple of appointments this afternoon, and then I've got to get ready for Colin's arrival."

"And he arrives when?"

A broad smile spread across Penny's face, and a light of excitement glowed in her green eyes. "Tomorrow."

\* \* \*

The train pulled into the station, slowed to a stop, and the doors slid open.

As passengers began to make their way along the platform toward the exit, Penny scanned them anxiously. And then, there he was. He raised a hand to show he'd spotted her, and the next moment he'd set down his bags and she was in his arms.

They clung to each other for a long, delicious moment and then walked out of the station together, into the waiting taxi. Victoria had offered to accompany Penny to the railway station, but she had declined, saying she wanted to meet Colin's train on her own.

By an unspoken agreement, Penny and Colin spoke little on the journey along the twisting country lanes to Llanelen, content to just hold hands in the back seat, glancing occasionally out the windows, on opposite sides of the vehicle, at the magnificent landscape of hills and valleys, and then turning back to each other and exchanging secret smiles.

The taxi dropped them off at the local garage, where they unloaded Colin's bags, and a few minutes later, the car hire paperwork and payment complete, they placed his bags in the hire car and set off.

"I can't believe you're really here," said Penny. "I want to hear all about what happened to you. We've got so much to talk about."

"Yes, we do," said Colin as they pulled up in front of Penny's cottage. Penny unlocked the door, they entered, and Colin set the bags down. They both eyed them. "Let's get these out of the way so we don't trip over them," Colin said. "I'll take them upstairs."

"Would you like something to eat or drink?" Penny asked. "I'm sure you're exhausted. That overnight transatlantic flight is a killer."

"I am tired, but I always try to fit in with local time, so let's just sit for a moment. Then maybe a shower, and after that we'll work out what to do next."

When they were seated on the sofa in the sitting room, Colin's eyes met Penny's for a moment, and then he took her hand. "I'm not very good at this. In fact, I've never done it before, but I haven't stopped thinking about you. I don't know how you feel, but I hope . . ."

He reached into his pocket and pulled out a small blue box with the name "Birks" embossed on the top in gold letters. Sensing what was coming, Penny's heart began to race.

"When we were stranded in the wilderness," Colin said, "there was a time when we didn't know if we were going to make it out, and all I could think about was you. I held on to the very idea of you, and I told myself if I did make it out, I would ask you to marry me. I know we haven't known each other very long, and we still have lots to learn about each other, and it's a huge risk for both of us, really, but I just know that we were meant to be together. We belong together." Emotion threatened the evenness of his voice. As he placed his hand on the edge of the sofa cushion, turned his body toward her, and started to slide off the sofa, Penny grabbed his arm and stopped him. "Colin, please no. Don't do that."

His eyes clouded and his mouth drooped.

"Oh, I'm so sorry. I know it's probably too soon to ask you, but I just . . ." He covered his eyes with one hand and let out a little exclamation of embarrassed dismay.

"No," said Penny. "It's not that. I meant you don't have to do the get-down-on-one-knee thing. Just keep talking to me." He slid back onto the sofa beside her.

"I'm new at this. I've never asked anyone to marry me before, and I thought that's what women expected."

"Most women might, but not this one. This is all so unreal. I wasn't sure how I'd react in the moment if you did actually get down on one knee, but I'd rather we just talk about it."

"That's fine. I was feeling a bit silly, to be honest." They both burst out laughing. "Talk about ruining the moment."

"No," said Penny. "Nothing's ruined. It's even more special. This is us, and we'll do it our way."

Colin grinned. "Well, there is a tradition that I really hope you'll like." He opened the box to reveal a ring consisting of three clear centre stones flanked by pavé diamonds set in platinum. "I didn't think you'd want anything over the top, but these are conflict-free diamonds from Canada. I thought you'd want that, and I hope you like it." He removed the ring from the box and held it out to her.

"It's beautiful. I love it."

"So, you'll marry me?"

"Oh, Colin, yes. Yes."

Penny held out her left hand, and he slipped the ring on her finger. She gazed at the depths of its icy beauty, then massaged the ring and its precious stones gently between the thumb and two fingers of her right hand, as if to assure herself they were real.

"The design is perfect. And so are the centre diamonds—not too ostentatious, and"—she gave him a mischievous grin—"not too small, either. Just right. And I love the setting. Modern, but classic."

"That's what I thought. Like you, really." He leaned forward and kissed her.

"Of course we don't have to be in any rush to get married," he said. "We can take our time. In fact, we should take our time because we've got a lot of details to work out. Where we're going to live, and so on."

"Yes, we've got a lot to talk about."

# Chapter
# Thirty-Three

The clinking of glass bottles under her window early the next morning woke Penny. She slipped out of bed and pulled back the curtain in time to see the milk float gliding away down the narrow road. After seeing the milk delivery in Beaumaris, she'd contacted the local dairy and asked for a pint to be left on her doorstep twice a week. Except to add to her tea and pour over her morning bowl of oatmeal, she didn't consume that much milk, but she liked the idea of having the milk she did use delivered in old-fashioned glass bottles.

Colin stirred and reached out for her as she slipped back into bed beside him.

"What is it?" he murmured sleepily.

"The milkman's just dropped off a pint."

"Oh." And after a moment he asked, "What time is it?"

"Just before six."

"I didn't know you had the milk delivery."

"I ordered it after that time we spent in Beaumaris."

"Right." He fell silent, and Penny thought he'd fallen back to sleep, when he murmured, "The things he must see at this time of the morning, when the world belongs to him." Colin wrapped his arms around her and pulled her closer to him, and then his breathing slowed, and a few minutes later he was asleep.

Penny was just drifting back to sleep, when her eyes opened and she was instantly alert.

* * *

"So what would you like to do today?" Colin asked as they prepared their first breakfast together in Penny's small kitchen. "It looks like it's going to be a beautiful day. Anywhere special you'd like to go?"

"Beaumaris," Penny replied. "I'd like to go back to Beaumaris and stay overnight at the hotel. There's someone I want to talk to."

"Oh, okay. That's easy enough to arrange. Is it Sarah Spencer you want to talk to?" He pulled two mugs out of the cupboard and set them on the table, then opened the fridge door.

"I do. If she's free later today, the plans for the new hotel spa are ready for her to look at. The spa, which was your clever idea, by the way. But there's someone else I'd like to talk to, and he's not at the hotel. We'll have to be up early to catch him."

"Oh, who's that, then?

"You said it yourself: 'The things he must see when the world belongs to him.' It's a long shot, I know, but let's hope the milkman just happened to be in the right place at the right time to see something on the morning Jessica Graham was killed."

"So is this how it works, then, your amateur sleuthing? You go around asking the questions yourself?"

"That's what I do," said Penny as she poured hot water over the coffee in the French press, "and so far, it's worked out quite well, though I say so myself."

Colin stepped out of her way as she carried the coffeepot to the table.

"And what about our engagement? Are you going to tell anyone today, or would you rather wait?"

A slow smile spread across Penny's face as she handed him a loaf of bread. "I'm going to start by telling Victoria the moment I see her this morning. I can't wait to tell everybody!"

He placed two pieces of bread in the toaster, pressed the lever, and held out his arms to her.

"Well, let me drive you to work, and then I've got a lot of paperwork to catch up on and calls to make, and then I'll pick you up whenever you say, and we'll head to Beaumaris. I'll make the hotel reservation for tonight, shall I? Should we arrive in time for dinner?" he said to the top of her head, resting against his chest.

"That would be wonderful." Neither moved until the toast popped up. And from that moment on, the smell of toast always triggered feelings of warmth, love, and comfort in her.

\* \* \*

"Morning, Penny." Rhian looked up from her desk and then tilted her head to one side. "I must say, you're looking cheerful this morning."

"Oh, I am. I don't think I've ever been happier. Is Victoria down yet?"

"No, I haven't seen her."

"Okay, I'll just run up to the flat and catch her before she comes down."

Penny sent a quick text, and a few minutes later tore up the steps to the first floor. The door to Victoria's flat was open, and her voice floated down the hallway. "Just finishing up. I'll be out in a minute."

As Penny always did, she made for the sitting room window that overlooked the River Conwy, and peered out. Then, she retraced her steps and waited for Victoria in the kitchen, leaning against the worktop, her hands behind her back.

"Is everything all right?" Victoria asked as she entered the kitchen. "Something's up if you need to see me so urgently that you can't wait until I get into the office. What is it?"

Penny withdrew her left hand from behind her back and held it out, showing off her ring.

"Oh, Penny," Victoria exclaimed. "I'm so happy for you," she said, holding out her arms and folding Penny into a warm hug. "Happy, but not really surprised. I had a feeling from the moment you told me about Colin in the coffee shop in Bangor, when I picked you up after your painting weekend, that this relationship was something really special."

"Of course you did." The two women laughed. "Colin and I have so much to talk about, so many plans to make. For example, we don't know yet where we're going to live, so I have no idea what this is going to mean for me here at the Spa."

"I have some thoughts on that," said Victoria. "I mean I've been thinking about it, and what you might want to do. I suspect you'll be spending less time here because you'll probably want to travel with Colin to those far flung places he's always off to." She checked her watch. "We'd better get downstairs. We can talk about all this later."

"You know that I'll want you for my bridesmaid, or whatever that role is called now," said Penny as they descended the stairs. And when they reached the last step and entered the hallway through the private door just outside the nail studio, she added, "Of course you were the first person I told."

"I heard that!" came a cheery voice from the manicure room. Mrs. Lloyd, who had just settled herself into the client's chair, turned her face eagerly toward Penny and Victoria in the hallway. "What did you tell Victoria, Penny? Is there news? Come in and let me be the second person you tell." Penny and Victoria exchanged amused looks, and Victoria gave a little "see you later" wave and continued on to her office. Penny greeted Eirlys, who was standing by ready to begin Mrs. Lloyd's manicure, and then spoke to Mrs. Lloyd.

"Yes," she said. "I do have news."

Mrs. Lloyd tilted her head and scanned Penny's face, taking in her bright eyes and the little smile that played at the corners of her lips. "Good news, by the look of you. So come on, don't keep us waiting. Tell us."

As she had done just a few minutes earlier, Penny held out her hand. "Colin asked me to marry him, and I said yes."

"Oh, my dear, that's wonderful news! I knew this would happen! I said as much to Florence when we were tidying up after our little drinks party. And when will the wedding take place?"

"We have all those details still to sort out," said Penny. "But I promise that you'll be among the first to know once everything's decided."

"So there's nothing more you can tell me now?"

"Not really. It just happened last night. I'm still getting used to the idea myself."

Mrs. Lloyd stood up. "Do you know, I don't think I'll stop for a manicure this morning, after all. I'll check back later, and if you've got a spot open this afternoon, I'll pop back. Otherwise, I'll see you when I see you." She picked up her handbag and looped the handle over her arm. "I'll see myself out." And with that, she was gone.

Penny and Eirlys burst out laughing as Penny slid into the chair Mrs. Lloyd had just vacated. "Well, Eirlys, since I'm going to be showing off my ring today, I can't think of a better reason to get a manicure, can you? And isn't it convenient that a spot just opened up."

Rhian appeared in the doorway. "Oh, Penny, Mrs. Lloyd just told me your exciting news. Congratulations!"

"She'll have almost reached the town square by now," said Eirlys, "so give it another twenty minutes and the whole town will know."

"Still," said Rhian, "it's wonderful that she's spreading such good news. Honestly, Penny, everyone is going to be so happy for you."

"I can hardly believe it myself," said Penny. "On one hand, it all seems to have happened so quickly, and on the other, it seems as if he and I've known each other forever."

# Chapter Thirty-Four

P enny and Colin walked hand in hand along the Beaumaris promenade. One by one, the days of summer had drifted into early autumn.

"I've been thinking," said Penny. "About my cottage. It won't do for the two of us to live there. We're going to need a bigger place."

"Yes, we are," said Colin. "Have you thought about where you want to live?" He gestured to the intoxicating view of the Snowdonia mountain range across the Menai Strait. "What I mean is, could you see yourself living here?"

"Here? Do you mean here in Beaumaris?" Penny mulled that over. "Yes, I think I could. You?" He nodded.

They had reached the Georgian terrace, and Penny pointed at the FOR SALE sign that now featured an "Under Offer" banner in bright red letters splashed across it.

"Looks like our apartment's been sold," she said as they stood in front of it. "Lucky people."

"Our apartment?"

"Well, you know. The apartment we looked at together."

Colin smiled. "What if it were our apartment? Could you see yourself living there?"

"Living there? But how could we? It's . . ." Colin raised his eyebrows, turned his head slightly, and gave her a conspiratorial smile. "You!" Penny exclaimed. "You made the offer! Am I right? Did you? Did you make an offer? Was it you?"

"Well, I'm in talks, as they say. Pending approval. Your approval, that is. Nothing's been signed off yet, of course. The minute you agreed to marry me, I made some phone calls. I know how much you love this property, and I thought it would be the perfect base for us if you were willing to move from Llanelen. True, it needs a lot of work, but it's got great bones, and we could do it up together."

"I'm utterly speechless. I can't take it all in. You did that for me? For us? Oh, I don't know what to say."

"Say yes? After all, we have to live somewhere. Why not here?"

"To say I'm gobsmacked is putting it mildly. It's really incredible you would do this."

"I just got the ball rolling, that's all. If you hadn't wanted to live here, in that beautiful Georgian terrace, then it wouldn't have gone any further. But what do you say? Shall we take the next step?"

"I feel as if I'm in a dream, but yes!"

"Good. Oh, and just to be clear, it's my money, but it's not me buying the apartment. It's you and me. It'll be in both our names."

He kissed her lightly, then wrapped his arms around her. After a moment, she looked up at him and took a step back.

"I've got a meeting in a few minutes to go over the plans for the capsule spa with Sarah, but after what's just happened"—she gestured toward the terrace—"it's going to be awfully difficult to think about anything else. But it's probably best I don't mention anything about us buying the apartment. Let's keep that between ourselves for now."

"No problem."

"I really want to ask her about her husband and his disappearance, but I'm not sure what to say."

"You shouldn't say anything. Don't even think about it. We don't know who broke into your cottage, and it could have been one or both of them. Her and Bill Ward. I don't trust him." He touched her on the arm. "Promise me." She nodded. "I'll wait for you in the hotel bar when you've finished. And if you're gone longer than—what? Half an hour?" Penny nodded. "Let's say thirty minutes. If you're not in the bar in thirty minutes, I'll come looking for you. Agreed?"

Penny nodded again.

\* \* \*

Penny unrolled the plans Victoria had drawn up as she and Sarah entered the ground-floor space off the lobby where the new spa would be located.

"What used to be here?" Penny asked.

"Oh, it's been lots of things over the years. At one time the gift shop was located here, but with so many gift shops scattered all over town now, it was decided the space could be better used. Most recently the catering office operated out of here, but this is more space than they need, and they don't need to be front of house, so we're really pleased that you're going to be operating a spa in here. The space can make money for all of us."

"Besides the clients we already discussed, it'll be really popular with hotel guests going to weddings," Penny said. "And couples staying here on romantic breaks. I'm sure you get lots of those." *And you know a thing or two about hotel romantic breaks, don't you?*, Penny added to herself, thinking back to what Cilla McKee had told her about how Sarah and Bill Ward had met.

The two women did a walk-through of the room, discussing what service would be offered in which area as they referred to the plans that Penny had spread out on an empty table.

"So reception desk here, just as you enter," Penny pointed out. "Manicure station under the window, hair over there, and massage and facials back there, behind screens."

"And the wall colour?" asked Sarah. "What did you decide about that?"

Penny held out a strip of sample paint colours. "We thought a watery colour, to suggest the sea. It will be a soft blue-green. Soothing and relaxing."

Sarah nodded. "Fine. I've sent the legal documents over to Victoria, so as soon as your solicitor approves them and everything's signed off, we'll get started. Once construction is underway, I expect you or Victoria will be on site often to make sure it all goes to plan. We need to sort out an opening date and think about the publicity."

"It's going to be a busy autumn," Penny said. She thought about the December show at the Snowdonia art gallery but decided that, with the connection to Cilla McKee, it would be another topic she'd be smart to avoid. Anyway, it had nothing to do with Sarah. But perhaps a little mention of Bill Ward wouldn't do any harm? "I haven't seen Bill Ward around today. Is he in town, do you know?"

Sarah shrugged. "Possibly. I don't keep track of his comings and goings."

"Someone told me you two used to be an item." Sarah gave her a look like thunder. "I prefer not to discuss my personal life when I'm at work, if you don't mind. Let's keep this professional, shall we?"

Penny decided to chance it, to see what kind of reaction she'd get. "Well, I just wondered if he was around, because someone broke into my cottage, looking for something. Do you think it could have been him?"

Sarah's eyes narrowed as she gave Penny an icy look. "Look, Bill and I have our differences, but breaking into your cottage doesn't sound like something he'd do. What could he possibly have wanted? To steal your paintings?" She let out a little snicker. "Right, now. Let's just keep our attention on the plans here, shall we?"

"Of course. But I wonder, if you don't mind me asking, what brought you to Anglesey?"

"I thought the sea air would be good for my health."

# Chapter
# Thirty-Five

Penny propped the rolled-up construction plans against the wall as she slid into the chair beside Colin in the hotel bar.

"From the look on your face, I'm guessing it didn't go well," he said. He gestured at the glass of white wine on the table in front of Penny. "Hope that helps." He waited until she had taken a sip, and then continued. "Do you want to tell me what happened?"

They were seated about halfway down the length of the room, midway between the entrance and the bar. About half the tables were occupied, some with quiet solitary drinkers checking their phones, others with couples ignoring each other as they checked their phones.

"I didn't get very far with her." Penny retrieved the rolled-up plans for the capsule spa and stood up. She pointed with them, indicating another table, and said, "Since we're here, let's sit where we were on that Friday night when we were talking to Jessica. I'd like to go back over that. Do you mind bringing the drinks?"

Colin followed her to a table near the entranceway. "I think this was our table," Penny said. "Do you think it was our table?" She gestured at the table beside it. "Or was it that one?"

He glanced at the doorway, then gave a little shrug and sat down. "I think this was the one, but I didn't take too much notice, to be honest. I was totally taken up with meeting you. Have a seat and try it out from a sitting perspective."

Penny picked up a chair from a neighbouring table and set it beside their new table. "Let's think back to that evening and remember everything we can. No detail's too small. Everything's important until we know that it isn't." She gestured at the empty chair. "Right. Jessica's sitting there. Her backpack's leaning against the wall, and she's telling us about the stories she's planning to work on while she's here."

While they mulled that over, two couples seated across from them drained the last of their drinks and made a show of gathering up their belongings. When they had left the room, Llifon came out from behind the bar, carrying a tray.

As he piled the empty glasses on the tray, with his back to them, Penny said, "And then she made that comment that startled us. 'I'm here to investigate a murder,' she said. Remember?"

"How could I forget?"

"And now we know that the person she was referring to was Mark Currie."

After piling the glasses on the tray, Llifon wiped the table with a white bar cloth. He then left the tray on the now-clean table and approached Penny and Colin.

"Sorry," he said, "but I couldn't help overhearing what you said just now. About Mark Currie." He glanced up and down the room, and then added, "Did you know Mark Currie was Sarah Spencer's husband?" He said this almost in a whisper. "The police have been around asking a lot of questions."

At that moment, Martin Hewitt the hotel manager, appeared in the doorway. Catching sight of him, Llifon scampered back to the nearby table, picked up his tray, and trotted off to the bar with it.

And that, Penny realized, is how it happened. Sarah Spencer's routine act of collecting used glasses from bar tables set in motion the train of events that led to Jessica Graham's death.

# Chapter Thirty-Six

"Do we have to?" moaned Colin. "It's still dark. I don't want to get up. It's so nice and cozy here with you. Just a few more minutes?"

"Sorry," said Penny. "But this is what we came for, and I'm going now. I'd really like you to come with me, but of course you don't have to if you don't want to."

Colin threw back the covers and sat up. "And let you do all the sleuthing by yourself? I don't think so."

They got dressed, hurried out of the hotel, and with sunrise still over an hour away, made their way along the dark, empty street. They waited in the silent shadows across from the Georgian terrace until they heard the quiet, humming swoosh of the electric milk float approaching. It slowed to a stop, as they knew it would, and the milkman got out and picked up his tray with half a dozen full bottles loaded between the metal slots.

"Excuse me," said Penny, as she approached him, and then, after introducing herself and Colin, she continued. "May I ask you something? Won't take a minute. It's just that you're out and about really early, and I'm sure you see lots of things."

The man looked from one to the other and let out a soft laugh. "Yeah, I do see things, right enough. People leaving buildings where maybe they shouldn't have spent the night." He looked from one to the other. "Say, are you two private detectives or something like that?" Assured that they weren't, he continued. "I haven't got long, mind. Got a schedule to keep to. How can I help?"

Penny held out her phone and showed him a photo of Jessica Graham that Louise had sent her. "Did you happen to see this young woman when you were making your rounds on the morning of Saturday, August the first?"

He peered at the screen. "May I?" Penny handed over her phone, and he held it closer to his eyes. "Yeah. I think I did see her one morning, but I can't remember if it was that morning."

"It would have had to be that morning because that was the only morning she was in Beaumaris. She arrived the afternoon before, and she was found dead at Black Point later that morning."

"Oh no, that's terrible." He looked at the photo again. "And that's her? The young woman who died?"

"Where do you think you might have seen her?"

"She was leaving the hotel. She walked a little way and then stopped."

"In what direction?"

He pointed back the way Penny and Colin had come. "She was walking away from the hotel, headed in this direction."

"And you were able to get a good look at her?"

"I did. I took notice of her because of what I said earlier. Usually it's men I see walking at this hour. I always think they've spent the night away from home, if you know what I mean, although some are bound to be on their way to work. So I did notice her because I don't often see women out by themselves at that time of the morning. You might see that in a big city, but here?" He gave a dismissive little shrug. "Nah."

"And you're sure this is the woman you saw?"

"I can't be absolutely sure, but yeah. I noticed she was young and pretty, and I wondered what she was up to. She wasn't alone, though. A car stopped and she got in. In fact, I got the impression that she'd been waiting for him."

Penny's heart began to beat faster. "Do you know whose car?"

"Oh, yeah. It was Bill Ward's. Everybody around here knows his Land Rover. Drives like he owns the road."

"This is such important, critical information. Can I ask why you haven't contacted the police?"

The mildly sheepish look that crossed his face was quickly replaced with a defensive set to his jaw. "Well, I probably would have done under normal conditions, but that Saturday morning was my last shift before the wife and I went away on holiday. We left that afternoon, and we didn't hear about the girl's death until we got back.

"We were out in Spain, and whilst we were there, the tour company we were with went broke, and we had a hell of a time getting home, I can tell you. I was that worried about how I'd pay for our extra airfare, if it came to that, and I was worried about my job as well because I was a few days late getting back. So what with everything that was going on, it slipped my mind. I suppose I should contact them now."

"Yes, you definitely should," Penny said. "Believe me, the police will be very interested in what you can tell them. Well, look, I mustn't keep you any longer. Sorry for taking up so much of your time."

The milkman shifted slightly, preparing to walk away, and then said, "If you don't mind me asking, what's your interest in all this? You said you weren't a private detective, but you're asking a lot of questions."

"I'm the one who found Jessica Graham's body, and her mother asked me to look into the circumstances of her death. She wasn't satisfied that it was an accident, as the authorities seemed to think."

"Oh, right. That makes sense, I guess, although isn't that what the police are for? Anyway, look, I've got to get on."

Penny and Colin remained where they were as the milkman, glass bottles rattling cheerfully in their carrier, set off across the road.

"Well, what would you like to do now?" Colin asked. Penny mulled that over.

"Let's go back to the hotel and see if the kitchen's open. And if it is, let's ask them to prepare us a breakfast picnic, and then I'd like to take you up on that offer you made a few weeks ago to take me to Black Point. We can watch the sun come up over the Irish Sea."

# Chapter Thirty-Seven

The blackness of night had lightened to grey as they spread the green plaid picnic rug the hotel had included with their breakfast on the cliff at Black Point. They lowered themselves onto the blanket and sat close to each other, Penny nestled into Colin's side, with his arm around her. The air was fresh and cool, with a strong hint of the autumn to come, but they were wrapped up well in their jackets and their love for each other. Every five seconds a flash from the lighthouse lit up the rocky coastline, and every thirty seconds the fog bell tolled a mournful warning.

The first hints of red and orange streaked across the sky, signalling the coming dawn. Penny reached for the flask of coffee, poured them each a cup, and then dipped into the basket the hotel had provided and handed Colin a still-warm breakfast sandwich.

"So what do you think?" he asked as he unwrapped it.

"I've been wondering why Bill Ward and Sarah Spencer moved to Anglesey from Manchester."

"Because it's beautiful here for Bill's painting?" He took a bite of his sandwich. "Sarah was offered a job at the Beaumaris Arms?"

"Possibly. But I think there's more to it than that. Here's the thing. Cilla McKee, Ward's ex-wife, told me that they—that is, Bill and Sarah—moved to Anglesey, specifically Beaumaris. But although people do move for work, as you mentioned, they usually move to a place they're familiar with, that they know and like."

"That's true. That's exactly what they do. People often discover a small town or a resort area on holiday, and they like it so much they end up moving or retiring there," Colin said. "Places where they were happy."

"So let's talk this through. As a police detective, Bethan doesn't allow herself to have theories or to speculate, but we can, so let's just suppose for a minute that Sarah and Bill Ward start an affair and decide they want to be together. But Sarah's husband, Mark Currie, proves troublesome, and he lets her know he isn't going to go quietly. He's from a wealthy family, and she's named as the principal beneficiary in his will, and perhaps he reminds her that she won't see a penny of that if they divorce, hoping that will convince her not to leave him, but instead it has a much more sinister effect."

"They decide to kill him," said Colin. "Or she decides to kill him, and Bill Ward gets roped in to help."

"Yes," said Penny. "Either way, let's assume they are in it together. They decide to kill him, but they don't want the body found because if it looks to the authorities as if Currie's gone off somewhere, they just have to wait seven years until he can be declared legally dead, and she stands to inherit a lot of his family's money."

"Some people might think seven years is an awfully long time to wait."

"Yes, indeed, they might think that, and they'd be right. It is a long time. And it seems to me that anyone capable of playing such a long and complicated murder game has to be some kind of sociopath. But for Sarah Spencer, her life would go on as usual, knowing that at the end of the seven years, just when she might want to think about early retirement, Mark Currie could be declared legally dead, and she'd inherit millions while she was still young enough to enjoy them. Her choice was divorce now and get nothing, or wait seven years and inherit a fortune. So, she was prepared to wait."

"Makes sense. From my perspective as an investment banker, I've seen people wait longer than that for their investments to pay off. But it does take a special kind of patience, though."

"That's a great way to look at this. As Sarah Spencer's investment in her future. An almost-guaranteed retirement fund, if you like. She could have her cake and eat it, too. If Mark went missing before he had time to change his will, all she had to do was sit tight and she'd inherit his estate. Everything. Of course, that would mean she was still legally married to Currie for the whole seven years, and she couldn't marry Bill Ward, but what did that matter? They could still live together, and from what his ex-wife told me, Bill Ward wouldn't have married her, anyway.

"Of course Currie's disappearance was investigated at the time," Penny continued, "but even though the police suspected something wasn't right, they couldn't turn up any evidence of foul play. And although the Currie family hired private detectives to investigate his disappearance, they came up empty.

"And then," she continued, "young Jessica turned up, ready to dig into the story of her missing countryman, Mark Currie. She would have done as much background research as possible into the story before she got here, so she would have known that Mark's wife was called Sarah. But Jessica couldn't have known that Sarah Spencer was Mark Currie's wife. If she'd seen photos of her, taken around the time Sarah was with Mark, her hair was a different colour, and of course she was younger and looked different."

"And Sarah had gone back to using her maiden name, so Jessica wouldn't have made the connection that Sarah Spencer is the former Sarah Currie," said Colin.

"Right. She wouldn't have known any of that—yet." Penny sipped at her coffee. It was now lukewarm, but she barely noticed. "I'm sure that she would have worked it all out, though, just as we did, and probably quicker, too.

"And then," Penny continued the narrative, "do you remember what happened in the bar yesterday? You and I were having a drink while Llifon was wiping the table across the way from us, and he couldn't help but overhear what we were saying."

Colin's eyes narrowed. "Yes, I do remember that."

"Well, when that happened, I remembered that Sarah was wiping down tables across from us in the bar on that Friday night when we were talking to Jessica. It's something you don't take any notice of because it happens all the time in a restaurant or café or bar. Someone on the waitstaff comes along and clears tables and wipes them down for the next customers. But Sarah must have overheard Jessica telling us that she was here to investigate a murder, and from Jessica's accent, Sarah assumed she was talking about Mark Currie. Sarah would have recognized a New Zealand accent because she'd been married to a New Zealander, and we always relate things personally to ourselves, don't we? So she told Ward and they just couldn't take the risk that Jessica, eager and keen as she was, might discover what happened to Mark Currie. Which, as we now believe, she would have done.

"So Sarah got her room number, went up there personally, and told Jessica that she'd been asked to pass on a message that Jessica would have to be ready to meet up with Bill for the interview really early in the morning because he'd be tied up all weekend with the painting retreat.

"Or I imagine it happened something like that, although I must admit that even to me that sounds like a pretty lame reason."

"She went to Jessica's room in person so there'd be no record of a phone call from her," Colin said.

"Exactly." In the silence that followed, the lighthouse bell tolled. Penny stiffened, and then sat up. "Of course!" She let out a little cry. "The answer's been right in front of us the whole time. They offered to show her the lighthouse by moonlight, and how could she refuse? Louise said Jessica would have wanted to see the lighthouse, and that's what brought her here. That's what brings everybody here." She sank back into the warm reassurance of Colin's body. "So they arrange to meet, and he picks her up in the Land Rover."

"Did he pick her up, though? The milkman said it was his vehicle, but we don't know for sure that he was driving."

Penny acknowledged this. "It must have been both of them. Jessica would never get in a car with just Bill Ward, but if there was a woman with him, that would have seemed safer. But in fact, it was just the opposite. It was a deadly combination."

Colin groaned. "Oh, I hate to think of that. Poor Jessica."

"But they got something wrong," said Penny. "Either they left the body too far up on the beach, or they got the time of the tides wrong. Because surely Bill Ward would have expected that one or more people from the painting group would choose the lighthouse that morning. I said at the time to Alwynne that I was surprised it was just the two of us. I thought more painters would have opted for the lighthouse. So Sarah and Ward must have figured that the body would be gone by the time the painters arrived, or they never would have left it there to be discovered. The tide was doing its work, but just not fast enough."

"So you were right," said Colin. "Sarah and Ward were afraid of what Jessica was going to find out. What she was going to know."

"The milkman as an eye witness seeing Jessica get into Bill Ward's car is a good start, but we need more. I'm convinced now that Sarah Spencer and Bill Ward killed Jessica, but we need to find proof that they did.

"And we also have to find a way to connect Jessica's murder to that of Mark Currie, seven years ago. Now, if a body were to be swept out to sea from here, I wonder where it would end up."

Colin thought for a moment. "I have no idea, but I know someone who might."

"Oh, really? Who?"

"A scientist buddy who works for an oceanography institute. He knows just about everything there is to know about currents and tides, and if there's something he doesn't know, he's got every resource at his disposal to find out." He reached for his phone. "I'll text him. What should I say this place is called?"

"Tell him it's Penmon Point, on the extreme southeast end of the island of Anglesey. In fact we can use What3words to pinpoint the location."

"Do you know What3words?" Colin exclaimed. "That was the program the police told us to use when we were lost in Canada, and because of it, the searchers were able to locate us. I was amazed I'd never heard of it."

Penny smiled as she typed "Penmon Point, Anglesey" into the What3words app on her phone and seconds later she read out, "Scoop.overheard.starter." Tell him to enter those three words on the What3words app, and he'll know exactly where the beach we're interested in is located."

By now, the entire sky was rose-petal pink, shot through with brushstrokes of gold. Colin sent the text, then stifled a yawn.

"What do you say we go back to the hotel?" he said as he placed his empty coffee cup in the basket. "We've got a few hours before our appointment to view the apartment again, and we could try to get some more sleep."

"Hmm. I'm not sure what 'try to get some more sleep' means, but I like the sound of it."

# Chapter Thirty-Eight

Dylan Rees, the same estate agent who had shown them over the apartment on their previous visit, greeted them as they walked up the path that led to the front door of the Georgian terrace property.

"I knew the minute I saw you that you two would be the perfect buyers for this lovely flat," he said, "and I can't tell you how pleased I was to receive your offer. Let's hope today's visit will seal the deal."

He unlocked the front door and followed them inside.

The airy, spacious entrance hall with its magnificent staircase looked even grander than Penny remembered it, and as they toured the rooms, empty now of furniture, the charm and beauty of the period details—marble chimneypieces, plaster cornices, and ornate ceilings—were revealed.

The last room on their tour was the kitchen, which gave off the distinctive renovation odour of fresh paint and new building materials.

"Only the finest quality paints and appliances were used in this renovation," said the estate agent. "And I can assure you the work was done by skilled builders."

The cream-coloured Aga range that Penny had admired on her first visit remained as the centrepiece of the room, enclosed in its own alcove and flanked on both sides by glass-fronted cupboards painted a muted blue-grey.

"That's a lovely colour," said Penny. "Do you happen to know what it's called?"

The estate agent referred to his notes. "That's Farrow and Ball Pigeon."

"Farrow and Ball," Penny repeated. "Yes, that's quality, all right."

She ran her hand along the granite worktop, admired the hardware on a cupboard door, and then pulled on it. The door opened and closed smoothly.

She opened a door beneath the sink and discovered a soft-close drawer with compartments for recycling and rubbish.

"Nice attention to detail here," she said.

The door of the tall cupboard at the end of the worktop unit was open slightly.

"I guess this is the broom cupboard," she said, opening the door completely and peering into the empty space. She closed the door, and took a few steps away from it, then stopped and returned to the cupboard.

She stretched her arm into the cupboard to get a sense of its depth, then did the same on the outside.

"There's something not right with this cupboard." Frowning, she asked the estate agent if he had a measuring tape.

"Yes, in my bag. I left it in the hall. I'll be right back."

"What is it?" asked Colin when the man had stepped out of the room.

"I'm pretty sure this cupboard has a false back. It's not as deep inside as the outside indicates it should be. I wonder why?"

She took out her mobile, turned the torch on, and leaned into the empty cupboard, shining the bright white light from her phone into the corners. "Yes, there's something different here. It's not finished to the same standard as the rest of the kitchen. The back of this cupboard is just cheap, unpainted particle board."

She stood back and folded her arms. "I want to know why that false back is there. There must be a reason."

A moment later the estate agent returned and handed Penny the tape measure, and she reached into the cupboard and measured its depth. Then she measured the adjoining worktop from the backsplash to the edge. "With the false back, the cupboard depth is about fifteen inches too short," she said.

"Maybe it's a hiding place for a trove of Georgian silver," said the estate agent with a nervous attempt at a little humour. "But really, I don't think it matters, when you consider how harmonious and functional the kitchen is now, and how beautifully appointed it is, updated with all the latest appliances, as you can see."

"Hiding place!" exclaimed Penny. "I'm sure that's exactly what it is. I think I know what's in there, but let's find out." She looked around the kitchen. "Are there any tools? A hammer? Anything like that?"

"No, of course not," said the estate agent. "The kitchen installation is complete. Workmen always take their tools with them. They don't leave them lying around."

"Well, then I'm just going to have to . . ." Penny positioned herself as close as she could to the rear of cupboard, and then kicked at the back. Her shoe landed with a soft thud, but did not break through. She tried again, and this time the noise was a little louder. She stepped away, and opened and closed lower cupboard doors, glancing inside, as she moved methodically down the kitchen. All the cupboards were empty.

"There has to be something I can use," she muttered. And then she spotted the brushed steel kitchen pedal bin, picked it up and carried it back to the cupboard. Before Colin or the estate agent could stop her, holding the bin with both hands, she smashed the back panel of the broom cupboard. Again and again she threw her weight behind the raised rubbish bin, battering the particle board.

Alarmed, the estate agent jabbed buttons on his mobile, and a moment later when someone answered, he shouted, "You'd better get over here right now. I'm showing this property of yours to what I thought were a couple of qualified buyers, and the woman's going berserk. She's demolishing your kitchen."

The sound of splintering wood filled the room as the bin Penny was brandishing broke through the wooden panel at the rear of the cupboard.

"There!" said the estate agent. "Did you hear that?" He listened for a moment. "She's bashing away at the broom cupboard. I've never seen anything like this. She's . . ." he paused, and then when he realized the person he was speaking to was no longer there, he pressed the button to end the call and turned his attention back to Penny.

"Please, Mrs.— er, I really must insist that you stop," he said. But Penny kept going.

"Penny!" exclaimed Colin. "What the hell are you doing? You can't do that. This isn't our kitchen. We haven't bought the place yet." Colin turned to the estate agent. "Look, I'm really sorry. I don't know what's got into her, but I'm good for the damage. I'll pay for everything."

"Too bloody right you'll pay for all the damage she's caused. I expect the owner is on his way over, and he's not going to be best pleased, I can tell you."

Bits of splintered wood fell to the floor of the cupboard as Penny continued attacking the panel with her bare hands.

"I know what happened now," she cried. "It's in here. I know it is."

"Penny," said Colin, as he placed a hand on her shoulder, "stop for a minute." She paused for breath, and when she backed away from the cupboard, he took her raw, reddened hands in his. "Stand back. You're going to hurt yourself. Let me finish this for you." He calmly removed the last of the shattered, splintered panel, shone the light from his mobile phone into the cupboard and then turned to Penny. "It's here. What you were looking for. What you needed to find." When she didn't move, he beckoned to her. "It's all right. Come here. You need to see this."

As she took a step toward him, Colin reached out, pulled her close to him, and put a supporting arm around her waist. She rested her head on his shoulder, and he shone the torch on his mobile into the cupboard.

And there it was. A black backpack with a cabin baggage tag hanging from the straps, and printed on the tag, the distinctive Maori koru logo of Air New Zealand.

Penny turned to the estate agent. "You saw that, didn't you? When we pulled the false panel out of the cupboard, the backpack was hidden behind it. It was in the cupboard."

The estate agent nodded. "Yes, I saw that. The backpack was in the cupboard. In fact," he held up his phone, "it's all here. As soon as my phone call ended, I started recording." He stepped toward the cupboard with his hand outstretched. "I don't understand why it's so important, though."

"Don't touch it," said Penny. "I'm calling the police. You can look if you want to, but don't touch it.

As she finished the call, Bill Ward burst into the kitchen, with a red-faced and out-of-breath Sarah Spencer on his heels. Before he could say anything, Penny pointed to the cupboard.

"We found Jessica Graham's backpack hidden in the cupboard of the newly renovated kitchen in a property that you own, Bill. That paints a different picture of what happened to her, doesn't it?"

"The whole thing was her idea!" Ward shouted, pointing at Sarah.

"Shut up, you fool," hissed Sarah, her eyes darting with alarm from Penny to Colin. "Don't say anything."

As Ward advanced toward the cupboard, Colin positioned himself in front of it and folded his arms. "No," was all he said, and Ward stopped in his tracks and threw a "what now?" look, infused with fear and hatred, in Sarah's direction.

"You bloody idiot!" she shouted at him. She hesitated for a fraction of a second, as if about to say something else, and then spun around and attempted to step into the hallway just as Detective Inspector Bethan Morgan filled the doorframe.

"Ah, Sarah Spencer. The very person I need to speak to." Bethan's words, spoken in an even, non-confrontational tone that could even be described as pleasant, filled the kitchen. "I was just at the hotel looking for you when I got Penny's call." She gestured to PC Chris Jones and two other uniformed officers behind her, who entered the kitchen. "And you, Bill Ward, let's be having you as well."

She pointed to the cupboard and tipped her head at one of the other officers. "And we're going to need an evidence bag for that backpack. And then ask Mrs. Graham to identify it. Good thing it was found today because she's planning to return home in a few days."

"I don't quite know what to say," said the estate agent when the police had left with Sarah Spencer and Bill Ward. "But I do know I will never experience another showing like that one. And now, if you don't mind, I'd best lock up. I don't suppose you'll be interested in the property now, and who knows what's going to happen to it with the owner in such a predicament?"

Penny and Colin exchanged a quick glance, and when Penny nodded, Colin said, "Oh, we're definitely still interested, but we've just knocked a few thousand pounds off what we're prepared to offer."

"Well, if you're sure, call into the office as soon as you can, and we'll complete the paperwork."

The estate agent locked the door behind them, and just as Penny and Colin set off down the path, his phone pinged with a new text. He glanced at it and then said to Penny, "It's that scientist friend I asked about the tides. He says although the tides can be quirky, it's most likely a body washed out to sea from here would end up on the east coast of Ireland. But a lot of factors come into play, so it's unpredictable."

"Still," said Penny, "we'd better let Bethan know, just in case that's what happened to Mark Currie. She'll want to follow up."

# Chapter
# Thirty-Nine

"Sometimes," Detective Inspector Bethan Morgan began, "old mysteries beget new murders."

The evenings were drawing in as autumn got its wet grip on the land, and a week later, the curtains in Penny's sitting room were closed against a rainy night as Louise Graham, Victoria, Colin, Alwynne Gwilt, and Thomas and Bronwyn Evans gathered at her cottage so Bethan could informally bring them up to date on the Jessica Graham case. Louise was desperate to know what happened to her daughter, and although Bethan had offered to brief her in private, Louise decided she preferred to hear everything surrounded by her caring new friends. It had been agreed that if the details became too overwhelmingly painful, Thomas and Bronwyn would take her home to the rectory.

"The truth can remain hidden for years," Bethan continued, "and then something happens that leads to a fresh murder being committed to cover up an older one. Sadly, this was one of those times.

"Seven years ago, Sarah Spencer and Bill Ward killed Sarah's husband, Mark Currie, so she could inherit his money,

Yes, we checked the terms of his will, and he disappeared before he had a chance to change it. And then, just when the seven years were almost up, and Currie could be declared legally dead, along came Jessica, a curious and smart reporter, here to reopen the story. Naturally, they were afraid she would discover what happened to Currie."

"This is what upset Sarah during the meeting on the Thursday before the murder," chimed in Penny. "The meeting that Llifon told me about. During that meeting, the hotel manager advised her that a reporter from New Zealand would be staying at the hotel, and on the Friday night, when she overheard Jessica telling Colin and me that she was here to investigate a murder, well . . .'"

"Poor Jessica's fate was sealed," Bethan finished the sentence. "And Bill found a way to use all this to his advantage. Although the two of them had killed Mark Currie, Sarah was the one who insisted Jessica had to die. And since he'd been having problems getting Sarah to move out of his house when they broke up, now, in return for his helping her with Jessica, she agreed to go."

Bethan nodded at Penny. "You're the one who put all the pieces together, so why don't you take over from here, Penny? Start with the events in the hotel bar on the Friday night."

Penny and Bethan switched places. As Bethan lowered herself into a wing chair, Penny, holding her wine glass in both hands, stood and faced the rapt, expectant faces of her friends.

"While Sarah was collecting the used glasses in the bar, she overheard Jessica telling Colin and me that she, Jessica that is, was here to investigate a murder. Sarah realized she had to do something to stop her, and for that, she needed Bill's help. The two of them were seen and heard arguing in the bar, and later, around midnight, after the bar had closed and Sarah was in the coffee shop, Bill shouted at her from the parking lot. This was the confrontation I overheard from my room. Bill had been drinking that night and should not have been driving, and this is what they were arguing about. Drunk, he was practically useless to her. She'd have to drive but she would have had to go along in the Land Rover anyway, because Jessica would never have got into the car with Bill Ward. We saw for ourselves how he creeps women out. But it was reasonable on Jessica's part to think she could trust them. One was a well-known actor and the other, a woman who worked in the hotel, so they weren't exactly strangers."

"But why on earth did she get in the car with them?" Alwynne asked.

"I wondered about that, too," said Penny. "It made no sense that she would conduct an interview with Bill Ward at the edge of a cliff in the dark, so it couldn't have been for the feature story. And then Louise said something that made me realize what it was. What was there that Jessica would have wanted to see?"

Louise raised her hand to cover her mouth.

"The lighthouse."

"Exactly," replied Penny. "They offered to show her the lighthouse by moonlight. They would have explained it was too far to walk. How lovely it must have seemed. The crashing waves, the flashing light, the strange, mournful tolling of the bell.

"And we come now to the difficult part, so Louise, if you want to step out now . . ."

"Nothing you can tell me could possibly be worse than what I've already imagined," said Louise. "I want to know the truth. All of it." Bronwyn reached over and took Louise's hand.

"It would have happened quickly, and Jessica wouldn't have suffered," said Penny.

"They pushed her," said Louise. Penny looked to Bethan, who nodded. "She wouldn't have suspected anything." Louise buried her face in her hands, but then indicated she wanted Penny to continue.

"And then, because Bill was in no fit state, Sarah scrambled down to the beach, probably on the easier path, and although she tried to move Jessica's body closer to the water, she couldn't," said Penny.

"If the body had been moved any distance, we would have found forensic evidence of that," said Bethan. "There would have been sand and pebbles in the clothes, and so on."

"So because the body was too far up on the beach, the tide took longer to get to it," said Penny. "And this time, it didn't have enough time to claim the body, as it had done seven years ago with Mark Currie."

"And Jessica's backpack?" asked Victoria.

"She left it in the car, and Ward and Sarah didn't discover it until they were back in Beaumaris. Of course it contained Jessica's research notes into Mark Currie's disappearance, so Sarah told Ward to get rid of it, and he thought since the kitchen was being renovated, that would be the perfect place to hide it, so he stuffed it in the cupboard and fitted a false back panel. Job done, or so he thought."

"Why would he do that, though?" asked Rev. Thomas. "Surely it would have been better to—oh I don't know—toss it out with the hotel rubbish or chuck it in the sea."

"Actually, blocking it off in the kitchen cupboard was a reasonably smart thing to do," said Bethan. "If they'd tossed it in with the hotel rubbish, there's a good chance someone would have found it because scavengers go through those bins all the time. And if someone found it, realized its significance, and handed it in to the police, that could spell trouble for them.

"And the same thing goes with tossing it in the sea or the strait. It might have washed ashore, or someone fishing could have snagged it and managed to retrieve it.

"And besides"—her face softened with the slightest hint of a smile—"they were acting under a lot of pressure and had to make critical decisions quickly. Criminals get sloppy and make mistakes because they're not thinking clearly, and it's lucky for us that they do.

"A colleague of mine in England recently had a case where the mother of a lad who committed murder hid his blood-stained clothes in the chimney, and the police discovered them when they were searching the house on a warrant related to another offense. You'd think she would have found a better way to dispose of the clothes, but the truth is, people in desperate situations panic."

"Ward and Sarah definitely panicked," said Penny. "And that's why they went after Jessica's suitcase, drugging Louise to try to get it."

"How exactly did they do that?" Louise asked.

"Sarah took your sleeping tablets while you were out, crushed them up, and mixed them into a little pot of Marmite that was on the tray she had sent up to your room that evening. She was quite certain, from having being married to a New Zealander, that you'd be partial to it,"

"Ah. Well, that's true. But we love our New Zealand kind. The British version is different, and she probably counted on the difference in the two to disguise the taste of the sleeping tablets," said Louise.

"But they had access to Jessica's suitcase in the hotel when they got back from Black Point," said Colin. "Why didn't they go through it then?"

Bethan took a sip of wine. "Because they didn't think of that until it was too late. They'd got the backpack, been through it, and thought they were safe. And then later, the 'what if' questions started to creep in. What if there's something incriminating in the suitcase? What if, for example, she'd made backup copies of her research documents and put the second set in her suitcase, as insurance in the event that something happened to the backpack?"

"The suitcase was in the custody of the police until Louise arrived at the hotel," said Penny, "and they decided to drug her to get it. But when they saw it, with the police seal on it, they realized they couldn't go through it in the hotel. Nevertheless, they were determined to have it, and the act of trying to steal it from my cottage shows how desperate they were by then."

"So which one of them entered Penny's cottage?" Bronwyn asked.

Bethan hesitated, then said, "Bill Ward has admitted that he entered your cottage looking for Jessica's suitcase, so we've added that to his list of charges."

"And Mark Currie?" asked Rev. Thomas. "What happened to him?"

"Colin's scientist friend was right. We've received confirmation from the Irish garda that an unidentified male body recovered from the sea almost seven years ago is that of Mark Currie. So now he can be returned to his family for a proper burial."

Louise's eyes filled with tears. "And Jessica, too," she said. "I can bring her home now. I'm so grateful to all of you for everything you've done for her and for me. But I will never stop thinking about all her unlived years. The stories she never got to write, the man she never met, the love she never found, and the children she never had."

# Chapter Forty

"How are the wedding plans coming along?" Victoria asked the next day as she, Penny, and Colin enjoyed a picnic lunch on the favourite bench in the churchyard.

"We're still working on details," said Penny. "If only you could be in two places at once. I want you to be my bridesmaid, but it would be lovely if you could play the harp at the service."

"And have you decided where the service will take place?" asked Victoria.

"We're thinking about Anglesey. That's where we met and where we'll be living, so . . ."

"So many details to sort out," said Colin. "But I'm leaving all the wedding planning up to Penny. Whatever she wants, whatever she decides is just fine with me. Everyone has been wonderful and even though there are a lot of logistics, everything seems to be falling nicely into place. We weren't sure what to do about Penny's cottage, but you came up with the perfect solution for that."

A composer friend of Victoria's who'd been looking for a quiet place to work had leapt at the chance to rent the cottage.

Penny thought about Emma Teasdale, her dear friend who had bequeathed the cottage to her. Emma had loved music and she would be delighted that her cottage would now be home to a Welsh composer, creating within its walls the kind of music that Emma had loved so much.

*　*　*

"Brace yourself, Penny," said a grinning Rhian two days later. "There's a delegation here to see you. I've left them cooling their heels in the quiet room. But be warned, they're on a mission."

"Mrs. Lloyd?" Penny asked.

"Oh yes. And she's brought reinforcements."

"Hello," Penny said as she entered the room. Mrs. Lloyd hovered near the doorway, hands clasped in front of her. Florence, her companion, was seated on one of the chairs facing Bronwyn Evans, the rector's wife, with Robbie, her cairn terrier, seated on her lap.

Three solemn faces turned to her, each tinged with a touch of annoyance and something else, although the frowning scowl on Mrs. Lloyd's face revealed her as being the most displeased. Florence seemed more dismayed, and Bronwyn seemed anxious and upset. Even Robbie looked annoyed.

"Don't you 'Hello,' me!" exclaimed Mrs. Lloyd. "We've heard a rumour that you intend to be married on Anglesey, and I hope that's all it is—a rumour. But if it's true, we're here to tell you that we're not having it."

"Really, Mrs. Lloyd," said Bronwyn. "That's coming on a bit strong. Of course Penny can marry wherever she chooses, but we did just think we'd pop along this morning and ask if it's true, that you are planning to marry on Anglesey, and if it is, we're here to ask you to please reconsider. You must know how shattered Thomas would be if he couldn't officiate at your wedding, so we hope you'll choose to marry in Llanelen."

"I was hoping you'd ask me to make your wedding cake," said Florence eagerly. "I've never had the chance to make one, and I'd be utterly thrilled. Please let me do that for you."

"Well, we haven't really decided anything yet," said Penny. "We talked about Anglesey, of course, because that's where met and where we'll be living, but nothing's been decided."

Bronwyn placed Robbie on the floor and stood up.

"Penny, you've lived here with us for so many years. We've all been through so much together—good times and bad. We're your family. We love you, and we want to make your wedding special for you. Please let us do that. Please let us be part of it. It would mean so much to all of us to be able to share your happy day with you."

Mrs. Lloyd handed Penny an envelope. "It's from Emyr. Go ahead. Open it and read it out loud. We all want to know what it says."

Penny was deeply fond of Emyr Gruffydd, the local land-owner. Over the years, she had worked with him on several special events at his home, the beautiful Ty Brith Hall. Emyr had given Penny her beloved Harrison, rescued as a kitten with his mother from a fire. And when Emyr's fiancé went missing on the morning of their wedding, all those years ago, it was Penny who had solved the mystery in her first case.

Penny opened the envelope, unfolded the paper it contained, and did as Mrs. Lloyd asked.

"*Dear Penny,*" she read. "*I've just heard your brilliant news, and I wondered if you'd like to be married from the Hall. It would breathe so much life and happiness into the old place, and bring us all so much pleasure, if you would agree.*

"*I thought you and Victoria could spend the night before the wedding here, and I would be honoured to escort you to the church and walk you down the aisle, if you have no one else in mind. After the wedding, we would all return to the Hall for the reception.*"

She raised her head to meet her friends' eagerly hopeful faces. "And then it's signed 'Emyr.'" She folded the letter and tucked it in its envelope.

Penny was deeply touched by Emyr's offer. She could not think of a more beautiful place than Ty Brith Hall, a grand house situated on one of the hills surrounding the town, with magnificent views over the valley.

"Well, Robbie, what do you think about that?" He gave a little bark and everyone laughed as the tension evaporated. "Everything sounds absolutely lovely. How could I say no?"

# Chapter
# Forty-One

And so, bathed in the splendid sunshine of a bright morning in early June, Penny stepped into the Rolls-Royce under the portico of Ty Brith Hall. With Emyr by her side and Victoria riding in front, they set off down the drive, flanked by beech trees, that would take them to the main road and then the short distance into Llanelen.

"All right?" Emyr asked as Victoria turned around in the front seat to offer a smile of encouragement.

"I'm just fine," said Penny.

"You've been remarkably calm this morning," said Victoria. "And you look absolutely beautiful."

A light, summery haze under a brilliant blue sky graced the tops of the hills as the vehicle drove slowly on, giving Penny time to take in the tapestry of open green fields. An occasional stone cottage, with a stream running alongside it, gave way again to open countryside with retreating ranges of distant green, wooded hills. Everything seemed rich, vibrant, and sharply in focus. *I must remember every moment of this day,* she told herself, just as the car entered the town and then arrived at the gated entranceway to the church property.

Bronwyn Evans, wearing a pale blue summer dress with a matching hat, waited on the rectory steps to greet them. When everyone was out of the car, they all fell into step as they walked together through the churchyard, with the River Conwy flowing smoothly alongside. Penny paused for a moment to gaze at the bench where she and Victoria had enjoyed so many picnic lunches. The double doors of the solid grey stone church stood open, and the sound of pastoral organ music, played by Haydn Williams as the wedding prelude, filled the air.

"Everybody's in their places," Bronwyn assured them. "When you're quite ready, I'll enter the church, take my seat, and that will be the signal to Thomas that you've arrived, and he'll take over from there. He'll let Colin know you're here, and then Haydn. When you hear the tempo of the music change, you can start your procession down the aisle."

"And Colin?" said Penny. "How's he doing?"

"He's doing very well, if maybe a little nervous. But bridegrooms always are." She gave Victoria and Emyr a once-over glance. "Ready?" When they nodded, she touched Penny lightly on the shoulder and kissed her cheek. "I know you're going to be a very happy woman." She stepped back and her eyes swept over Penny. "You look absolutely beautiful. I've never seen you look so lovely."

Penny had insisted she wouldn't wear anything traditionally white or bride-like. No long gown, no poufy dress, and no veil. She had selected a knee-length dress with a matching coat in the palest shade of green, with a pill box hat in a similar shade, decorated with flowers and netting, set at just the right angle on her red hair. And then, after one last reassuring squeeze of Penny's hand, Bronwyn disappeared into the cool dimness of the church.

Penny took a deep, cleansing breath and then tucked her hand through Emyr's right arm and accepted her bouquet from Victoria. The local florist had made her a simple but elegant arrangement of roses in various shades of pink, tied together with red and white ribbons that fluttered slightly as she moved.

The tempo of the music changed, and the three took their positions at the entrance of the church. After pausing for a moment to allow their eyes to adjust to the contrasting dimness of the interior, they stepped forward, and all heads turned toward them. After assuring herself Colin was waiting for her in front of the altar, Penny turned her attention to the people she passed who had meant so much to her over the years.

Seated at the rear, ready to be the first to leave for Ty Brith Hall where they'd look after the catering, were Gwennie and Florence.

Penny nodded hello to Dorothy Martin and her husband, Alan Nisbett, who had come from Shrewsbury, and at Bethan and Mrs. Lloyd, and then the faces became a blur until she was standing beside Colin, and the ceremony was underway.

"Dearly beloved," began Rev. Thomas Evans. And then, just as it began, it was over, and Penny and Colin led the way out of the church. As everyone gathered around the doors, offering good wishes and congratulations to the newly married couple, Penny held her new husband's arm.

As they led the way out of the churchyard to the waiting cars that would take them to Ty Brith Hall for the reception, Penny paused beside a simple gravestone.

Emma Teasdale
1934—2009

She let go of Colin's arm as she gracefully bent her knees and placed her bouquet on the grave, then stepped back and bowed her head for a moment in silent tribute.

She placed a hand on the brooch she wore on her left shoulder, a replica of the Queen's leaf brooch that had been a 1953 Christmas gift from the women of Auckland. Hers had been sent to her by Louise Graham, with a request that she wear it today in memory of Jessica.

And then she slipped her hand through her new husband's arm, and with a backward glance at the friends who had loved and supported her over the years, she took her first confident steps into her married life.

# Acknowledgments

E very book starts with a germ of an idea. Gilbert Roberts, a former sailor, described the wind over tide phenomenon, and that got me thinking about what might happen to a body on a beach under those conditions. I first visited Penmon Point, on the easterly tip of the island of Anglesey, many years ago with him. This rocky promontory, at the north entrance to the Menai Strait, turned out to be the perfect setting for *On Deadly Tides.*

Thank you to Sylvia and Peter Jones for a memorable day in early December 2019, as we walked along the pebbly beach, absorbing the sights and sounds of the beautiful Trwyn Du Lighthouse.

For plot purposes, I took some liberty with local geography, making Penmon Point and the lighthouse seem closer to the town of Beaumaris than they actually are.

Throughout the writing of the Penny Brannigan mystery series I have drawn inspiration from the town and people of Llanrwst. In this outing, Ffin y Park Gallery serves as the model for the Oriel Snowdonia; several enjoyable plotting

# Acknowledgments

sessions with Eirlys Owen took place here over lunch or coffee and cake.

For their help with the manuscript, I'm grateful to Eve Dowd, Sheila Fletcher and Elaine Spicer. Retired Toronto Police detective Des Ryan provided details regarding police procedures. Any errors, however, are mine.

What3words is a real app, and has saved lives. I hope you'll download it today, because you never know.

Thank you to my agent, Dominick Abel for his guidance and insight, and at Crooked Lane Books, I'm grateful to Chelsey Emmelhainz, Matt Martz, and Melissa Rechter for their professionalism and support.

And finally, heartfelt thanks to my son Lucas Walker, for his love and companionship on our many trips to Wales, and especially during the time of Covid-19.